TO TAME A FAE

WINTER'S THORN, BOOK 2

MILA YOUNG

CONTENTS

DEDICATION

I have an amazing team who work with me on polishing and editing my stories, so I'm dedicating this book to Dara, Nic, Sara, Meghan, Amy, Andrea, Christine and Graeme!

You guys rock and I'm super lucky to have you on my team.

Mila
XOX

To Seduce A Fae
To Tame A Fae
To Claim A Fae

TO TAME A FAE

The spell that bound her fate to their realm has unleashed its crippling curse. She's the only thing standing between them and total destruction...

I can't control my powers or the brooding princes who won't let me out of their sight. And I can't keep my secrets safe for long. Which scares me as much as the dark pasts haunting my warrior princes.

I shouldn't want them by my side, but I do. I need them, especially here among the fae court, a dangerous place with even more enemies hiding in plain sight...and among them, I fear my own parents stand waiting to end my life.

Not that any of that will matter if I can't get my powers under control.

They've already cost me so much and put us all in

great danger. With time running out to save one of my own from becoming a cursed creature, I'll have to rely on my erratic powers and my bond with the princes to let us live to fight another day.

But with every win, another shadow befalls us. Our odds of coming out of this alive grow less by the day. And less with each step we take toward learning the truth behind this insidious curse and what fate awaits me when it's finally over...

Scorching sequel in the 'WINTER'S THORN' saga.

FAE LEGENDS

There's a legend that says when fated souls meet, the Universe will move the stars themselves to ensure their love endures.

CHAPTER 1

DEIMOS

My lips whisper over the tender curve of Guendolyn's neck, and I kiss down to her collarbone. She pushes my head down to her full breasts. Her nipples easily respond, pressing erect against the fabric of her blue dress. I cup one in my mouth with the cloth between us.

Her breaths rush as she moans, and her arms wrap around my shoulders, fingers digging into flesh. I have her pinned to the wall, those delicious legs around my hips, and her blue dress pushed up to her waist. My fingers stroke those beautifully swollen lips between her thighs. She's so fucking wet. So stunning and exactly where I want her to be.

I lift my head and capture her lips again. Her scent paralyzes me, the taste of her mouth rousing an intense raw hunger within me. She kisses me with a brutal desire, and I dart my tongue inside. My cock punches in my pants as I return the chaotic kiss. My finger swirls around her bud, then flicks her clit.

I need so much more of her. I need it all, over and over.

She hisses out a breath against my mouth. At the same time, her hand dips down between us, and she strokes my erection through my pants, moving up and down. The friction drives me absolutely insane. I push my cock against her hand, letting her feel how hard I am, how fucking much I want her right here, right now.

I press one finger into her, then two. She tilts her head back as whimpers fall from her lips. She makes me feel filthy with desire. I'm so horny, I can barely hold myself back.

"Gods, you feel incredible," I growl.

She belongs to me, and I belong to her.

This is how it should always be.

Me and her.

Kissing.

Fucking.

Every-fucking-where.

My heart hammers in my chest at how drawn I am to her. The sensation snaps through me. Truly snaps at the realization that she affects me so strongly.

My balls pull up so tight, they ache for release. It's a fucking beautiful ache that robs me of all reason. I lick her neck, and memories of finding her on Earth come to mind. This lost girl who needs to be reminded of who she is. Our times together never leave me and heighten with each lick. Us escaping through the Wandering Realm woods, barely escaping the Blood-cursed to enter the kingdom. Her still not remembering her last visit to our kingdom. My brother, Luther, insisting that she's his. Thoughts fly through my mind of how close we came to losing Guendolyn. My brain won't shut the hell up.

"Deimos." She purrs my name and I lift my head. She looks at me with those intoxicating ocean blue eyes. Her white-blonde hair sits messily and is still slightly damp from her earlier bath. But those eyes stay with me... They were the first things I noticed about her when I met her two years ago on her first visit to the Wandering Realm. Back then, she had no idea who she was dealing with when she met us or the trouble she had been brought into. That craving I felt for her back then never dissipated. It waited for the moment we reunited. For when I made it through the portal to collect her from the human world and brought her back to the Wandering Realm, where she belongs. She may not accept it yet, but she will soon see this is her home.

She softens under me. This is how I've pictured her. Spread and wet and calling for me. I nibble on her lower lip, gently tugging on it with my teeth. I finger her harder and faster.

Her eyes glaze over, her body trembling with pleasure. I could get used to having her by my side every day.

An ache builds deep within me to the point that it almost hurts. I don't know where it's coming from, but I push it aside along with the thoughts. What I want is right before me. I desperately need her.

Pleasure consumes me as energy flares down my arms. All I feel is the sensation drumming through me, the arousal curling around me.

Guendolyn's body shudders as I continue fingering her. She groans louder, and my world spins. I'm drowning in her presence, in the lust tightening my cock. The entire room seems to be shaking, though I'm certain it's all in my head.

She is so ready for me.

I'm on the verge of losing control and being a savage animal with her. Of ripping off her dress and going all wild with her. I want to hear her scream as I fuck her raw.

My skin ripples with a sudden energy that races down my arms like tiny bites. Energy that feels like mine except I haven't called to my power. Before I can pull back and make sense of it, a huge, metal bell peals in the distance. The sound rolls through the whole kingdom like thunder, signaling a breach in our kingdom.

God damn the Seven Hells of the Wandering Realm.

The bells keep ringing.

FUCK! I pause and take a deep breath. Anxiety suddenly rips through my chest at the idea of things going to shit at the worst possible time.

Guendolyn freezes against me.

I jackhammer my head up abruptly, and with one fluid movement, pull my fingers out of her sweet core. Gathering her into my arms, I lower her to her feet.

The ringing continues, hammering in my head. Each dong vibrates through me. Someone has broken into the kingdom. It has to be the Bloodcursed.

"Shit!" I hiss between clenched teeth and storm over to the door. My heart is pounding a mile a minute.

"What's happening?"

I hear the fear in her soft voice as she follows me. I bite back the need to take her into my arms, to tell her all will be right. We just arrived at the mansion today, and we told Guendolyn we ought to keep her a secret from the king until we work out how she can use her power to eradicate the curse placed on our kingdom. Except that plan's a fucking waste if the kingdom falls in the next few hours. Tension flares between my shoulder blades.

"The kingdom's under attack," I explain. "Those bells you hear signal a breach." I abruptly open the door as I talk.

Maids are running down the hallway in a panic. My mind activates survival mode, adrenaline pulsing through my veins. The last time those bells rang was two years ago when Guendolyn unknowingly unleashed the curse on our kingdom. When she was ripped from our world and thrown back onto the planet she'd been raised on. When those blood-sucking Bloodcursed poured into our home. We spent weeks eradicating them and lost so many lives. This can't be happening again. Not with Guendolyn here as well and in danger.

"Is it the Bloodcursed?" she asks.

I face her. "Stay here. I'll go find out what's going on and come back."

"Maybe I can—"

"No, you're staying here." I kiss her quickly on the mouth, then whip outside the room, shutting the door behind me.

I don't have time to argue with her, and I can't put her in harm's way.

Heavy footfalls accompanied by voices echo down the hall, and I sprint toward them. My gaze skims over every shadow for any sign of chaos.

Around the corner, Mael, Ahren's advisor, is standing tall with his back to me. He bellows at the helpers, "Everyone, listen up! Leave everything behind and go to the underground cells now." He turns to his right and sighs at a maid who seems shell-shocked. "Dana, are you listening?" He snaps his fingers as she gathers her long skirt in her hands and darts through the door that leads to the stairs.

There are underground cells for everyone to hide in during emergencies, and Mael is right about everyone getting to safety fast.

As if sensing my presence, he pivots around. His brown eyes are wild with terror, his face blanched. His short, white hair appears messy, as though he's run his hand through it half a dozen times.

"It's the Bloodcursed," he says between panting breaths. "There are so many of them."

"Where did they enter from?" I demand to know.

"The throne room."

His response has my mouth dropping open. "What?"

"Your Highness, you need to evacuate before it's too late," he pleads.

My insides freeze. Luther and Ahren were in the throne room with our stepfather. But how did the Bloodcursed breach the throne room? It's located in the most central spot in the palace. Someone would have noticed them if they broke through a wall or our magical barriers. The notion horrifies me.

Mael watches me, waiting.

"Go with the rest," I command. "Keep them safe."

"But what—"

"I'm fine," I reply when soft footfalls approach from behind. I know it's her before I turn around. She doesn't listen to me, so it doesn't surprise me that she refuses to stay in the room. Did she leave the room the instant I did?

I turn to Guendolyn. She's staring at the door the staff left through moments earlier, but her eyes widen as soon as she realizes I've noticed her.

"Gue-Gainy, good timing," I chide.

She arches a brow in reply. She hates the fake name I gave her, but now isn't the time to have Mael ask questions. Everyone knows the name Guendolyn in this kingdom, and I have no time for questions.

"Mael will take you to safety until I come to collect you."

The captivating blue of her eyes belies her fiery demeanor. Her lips twitch, and her nose wrinkles, drawing my attention to the light fanning of freckles over her pale nose. "I need to come with you to the throne room."

How long was she listening to our conversation?

Her stubbornness infuriates me. I glare at her as she stands before me with her hands behind her back like she's testing me. We don't have time to argue.

"Your Highness?" Mael asks me.

"This isn't negotiable." I raise my voice at Guendolyn, looming over her. My heart would shatter if anything happened to her. Doesn't she see this? I don't take my gaze off her, saying over my shoulder to Mael, "Take her with you—by force, if needed."

"Deimos, please, no. You don't understand," she insists.

"I do understand. You are safer underground until I get a handle on the situation." I grimace.

"No, you don't," she snaps back as she rushes past me, her shoulder knocking into my arm on purpose. She stops near the wall behind a marble statue of an eagle, so I'm guessing she wants to talk to me in private.

I march up to her. "What's going on? We don't have—"

She places her hands out in front of me, out of sight of Mael. Blue threads of energy dance around them.

My breathing steadies as I study her hands. "Your magic—" I whisper, but she cuts me off.

"It's the same feeling I had each time I opened up the portal between our worlds." Her words send a shiver down my spine at the realization of what she's saying.

I tilt my head forward and whisper, "Your magic caused the breach?"

She shrugs, that paleness returning to her cheeks. "I think so." She chews on her lower lip nervously.

Hell! Guendolyn's magic has been all over the place, so it's very likely she opened a portal from outside the kingdom to the throne room. The blood drains from my face.

"And the energy isn't going away like last time." She glances down at her hands. "I think the portal is still open." She holds her arms across her stomach to hide the magic lingering on her hands.

Nerves in my temple twitch like a tiny heartbeat. I rub my jawline, the roughness of growth grating against my touch. If what she says is true, she'll be the only person capable of closing the portal.

"Have you tried closing it?"

"Yes. That was the first thing I did, but something's wrong. Usually, it closes itself, but why is the magic still on my hands? I think I need to be near the portal to see if that makes a difference."

I sift through my thoughts.

My decision made, I turn to face Mael. "Change of plans. She's with me. You make sure everyone else gets to safety."

Mael studies me, languishing there like he's about to protest. He has always been a kind fae, and he moved to this kingdom with us when Mother married the king of the Shadow Court. He's always looked out for us. Mael is close to fifty in fae years and more of a father to us than our real father, so I trust he won't speak of this if he saw or overheard anything.

He doesn't argue. He simply bows his head and rushes through the open door to safety.

I snatch Guendolyn's hand, a prickling sensation flaring up my arms from her magic, and drag her into a run with me down the long corridor. We bound down the stairs before I realize I'm not carrying any weapons on me. "Fuck, fuck, fuck."

The dark stone hallway we pass through is silent. We employ a skeleton staff to keep the drama and gossip of the kingdom out of our lives as much as possible, but now I feel the bareness of the place.

We pass statues of bears and wolves, and I hate those damn things. Our stepfather insists on them to ensure our mansion shows some semblance of royalty. How the hell statues represent royalty is beyond me.

I swing left down a long hallway and stop outside my chamber. "Give me a moment." Pushing open the oversized black door, I'm greeted by bright sunlight pouring into the room. I loathe curtains that steal the natural light, so I had them ripped off my windows long ago. I march across the room toward a long, wooden box that sits a few feet away from the stone fireplace. Rapidly, I pull it open and reach down to collect a sword. The leather feels soft and perfectly fitted to my grip.

Guendolyn stands in the doorway studying my room, her gaze lingering on the enormous bed. What's my little kitten thinking? What it will be like to sleep in my bed while in my arms? I intend to bring her back sometime and introduce her properly to where I plan to have her spend time with me. But now, we need to hurry. I march toward her and take her hand.

"We need to run," I say.

She doesn't protest, and an expression of determination crosses her exquisitely beautiful face. Together, we take off down the hall and follow the main vein of the mansion, which takes us to the grand bridge that crosses between our mansion and the palace.

"What if the king sees me?" Guendolyn asks, her words breathy.

I meet her gaze. "Right now, that's the least of our worries. If we don't stop the Bloodcursed, there'll be no kingdom left."

Looking back, part of me knew that being intimate with Guendolyn might activate her power. Or maybe I hoped it wouldn't happen. I should have known better.

CHAPTER 2

GUENDOLYN

My heart lurches in my throat.

The sight in front of us crashes through me like a tidal wave. It hits me over and over and still my brain refuses to accept the chaos spreading before us. Bloodcursed fill a spectacular hallway made of marble with gold trimmings along the crown molding, and guards are battling them in a vicious fight.

The soldiers wear metal helmets and armored chest plates. They brandish swords and slice at the infected fae. These creatures have lost their souls and now crave blood and flesh to feed. One bite is all it takes to become one. Their skin is pale and blotchy with blood. Clothes hang off their lithe frames, but they move fast—terrifyingly so—and the sure-fire way to stop them is to cut off their head.

Savagery pours from the monsters' gazes, while my hands prick with the magic that released them. The same magic I inhale. It smells like a dying fire, but underlying the magic is the stench of blood choking the air.

"Where's the throne room?" I ask Deimos in the corridor we're hiding in, my voice barely a whisper to avoid drawing any of these things' attention to us. My gaze sweeps over the battle, the hairs on my arms lifting.

"It's just beyond this hallway," he responds.

Sounds of metal hitting bone flood the room. In the distance, a Bloodcursed overcomes a guard. He falls, his sword clanking to the marble floor, then two fellow guards jump to his rescue.

Deimos charges forward from our hiding place at a creature rushing in our direction. I flinch at how quick the Bloodcursed moves, how I never saw it coming at us.

Sword pulled back over his shoulder, Deimos swings the blade out, cutting through the air ferociously. The sharp edge bites right into the Bloodcursed's neck, slicing all the way through. The slurping sound of a blade cutting through flesh leaves me grimacing. The creature's knees buckle, and it drops down, landing feet from Deimos with a dull thunk.

My heart is racing, and all I can think about is how incredible Deimos looks fighting without fear. All those muscles. Long, white hair swinging across his back with each movement. His broad shoulders and chest.

Another scrambling fiend rushes for Deimos.

He pivots and kicks a deadly blow to the creature's gut. It stumbles back, slamming into the wall, but Deimos doesn't waste a second. He leaps after it and drives his sword through the monster's head, then back out with a disgusting wet sound.

I scan the room for the other princes and find Ahren, the eldest, at the rear of the room in combat. He's powerful and swings his sword with tremendous strength. He's captivating to watch, but I don't have time to stare at him and get lost in the things I want to do with him.

Closer to my left, two Bloodcursed charge a soldier. They jump on his back, and he flails, crying out in terror. The sight leaves me shuddering.

Deimos' brother Luther emerges with speed from behind a marble column like a knight, wielding short swords, one in each hand. Two swipes, and the creatures' heads roll off their shoulders. Their bodies follow seconds later, dropping to the floor like sacks.

The whole scene horrifies me. Bloodcursed outnumber the soldiers.

Luther tucks one weapon into the sheath on his belt. He reaches down with his free hand and fists the back of the fallen guard's jacket before dragging him to his feet. Fright startles the man's face, which is splattered with blood, but he doesn't seem bitten. Luther pats his shoulder and swings back toward the fight, just as he catches me peering out from behind the corner. He does a double take, and his eyes widen with shock. They glint with the color of flames.

Then he mouths my name, his brow furrowing. But I can't hear his voice over the commotion and thuds of battle. Dark hair sits messily around his face and flutters over his shoulders as he flies across the room toward me. He's still wearing his military-style jacket with silver buttons running down the middle and a high-collar top underneath.

"What are you doing here?" he growls as his hand closes around my arm and pushes me backward.

"Don't." I knock his hand aside and lift my palms to show him the thin threads of magic lingering over them. "I think I accidentally opened a portal in the castle, and that's how the Bloodcursed came in." My words rush out in one breath. "I don't know how as it's never happened like this before."

I tilt my head back, taking in his strong jawline, his full lips turned downward, his sharp cheekbones. And those intense eyes that seem to pierce right through my soul. Luther is a fae who leaves me weak, and his presence squeezes my heart. I used to wake up with fragments of dreams about him and his name on my lips. Even if our past remains hidden from me, I feel the ache in my chest that he means so much more to me than I remember. But now, he looks at me with a terrifying realization as my words sink in. I don't want to be someone he loathes or fears. The thought is a blade to my heart.

"What did you do, little wolf?"

My breath catches in my throat. "I'm sorry." The words slip past my mouth. "I didn't mean for it to happen. But I can fix this." I pray I can. I have to, because I can't destroy their kingdom on my first day in the palace.

My hands prick with lingering magic while my heart beats frantically as I wait for Luther's fury to pour out. I can't blame him, because I caused this. I should have been more cautious, should have remembered that last time I kissed Deimos, we teleported from Earth to this realm.

"Then we need to get you to the throne room," he instructs, believing me instantly, while doubt curls in my chest. What if I can't get rid of the portal? What if… I suck in a shuddering breath and shake myself. I can't overthink this. It has to work.

"Deimos," he calls out over his shoulder impatiently. Tension and fear cloud Luther's eyes when he glances to address me. "We get you into the throne room, you do your magic, and I'll take you back to the mansion. If the gods are blessing us, our stepfather won't find out about you. I don't want to deal with his shit on top of everything else."

I don't want to face the king, either. Please let this work smoothly. I don't ask for much, Universe, but just this once, back me up.

My entire body goes rigid as I keep thinking about wanting to tell Luther what's on my mind. How I'm scared that I won't be able to close the portal. I want to have him tell me I'm being foolish and embrace me.

Except this isn't the time for weakness. Everyone is standing tall and fighting for all our lives, so weakness has no place here. I can't lose my shit, so instead, I find my bravery and throttle it.

Deimos darts toward us, heaving for breath. He holds his blade by his side, the steel coated in red. Splatters of blood dot his shirt and a few blotches mark his neck. He stands next to his brother. Both are similar in size, but they're like night and day. Deimos has pale skin and white hair, while Luther has fiery pupils and hair the color of ravens feathers.

In the short time I've known Deimos, he's captured my heart, and I feel closer to him. Even if my heart aches for Luther, there's so much I still don't understand about our past...which isn't helped by my vanishing memories ever since I unknowingly unleashed a curse on the Wandering Realm. A curse that makes Shadow Court the target for every Bloodcursed in the entire damn realm. And now, I've brought these monsters into the castle...into the throne room, of all places.

God, if the king finds out, he'll have me killed.

"I'll carve a path while you stay behind her and keep her safe," Luther orders Deimos. "With so many soldiers here, we may be able to avoid an ambush by these fucking Bloodcursed."

Deimos' free hand settles on my lower back. "I'll keep you safe the whole while. Don't stop following Luther. Hopefully, we can do this fast."

"I'm ready," I admit, even if uncertainty clings to my ribs.

We swing toward the main hall, and the Bloodcursed are close. Guards fight as more creatures keep pouring in. How long before the monsters overpower the army and win?

"Now!" Luther snaps as he surges forward into the grand hallway, swinging his sword at a fiend's head. He's carving a path for us through the mass battle and makes it look effortless as he destroys the enemy.

I breathe hard and rush out after him, sensing Deimos at my back.

Creatures are too close for my liking as the tangle of battles rage around us. I step over a decapitated head and rush to keep up with Luther. My feet slide out from under me across the blood. Deimos catches my fall, his strong hands on my back, then pushes me back upright. My insides clench, but I won't stop because I have to end this.

A Bloodcursed springs toward me. I raise my fists.

Luther sidesteps toward it, driving an elbow into its face. One swift turn followed by Luther's extending arm, and his blade bites into the tenderness of the fiend's neck.

I look away at once to avoid the spray of blood.

Don't scream. Just keep running. Keep running.

The deafening clink of armor and growls flood the hall. Nothing about this place is normal, and I'm starting to suspect I'll never experience normality again.

I push back the terror clawing at my flesh, and somehow, manage to race forward and remain coherent through all of this. Everything about this attack screams at me to run and hide, but I don't dare. I can't.

Devastation surrounds us, but I never stop following Luther.

A hand snatches my arm, icy cold fingers digging into my skin.

I flinch and spin around, coming face to face with a monster. Sunken eyes, the life stolen from them, worn lips thinning over rotten teeth.

Deimos hauls me against him and away from the

Bloodcursed. I slam into Deimos' body behind me, and he's like a wall of strength and protection. With one hand clasped over my chest, the other drives his sword through the predator's gut, sliding in as easy as knife in butter.

Luther is already on his heels, bringing his sword to the fiend's neck.

My stomach plunges at the sight, but there's no time to dwell on it. We're already racing forward, shoving past others.

To stop means death.

We know this too well.

Another creature grabs my arm and yanks me toward it. A scream strangles my throat before Luther swings around and drives a fist into its face, then kicks the thing into a mass of Bloodcursed bodies.

When we reach the other side of the enormous hall, we don't pause. We follow Luther as he races down a corridor, and we stop in front of a grand room. Double doors as dark as night stand wide open, one hanging off its hinges.

The war continues around us, but inside the throne room, it's so much worse.

It's a ruined mess. Golden statues of women with wings are pushed over and broken near the side walls. Bloodcursed bodies layer the floor, and there's too much gore and body parts to assemble the pieces. A few soldiers are lying among them, and my heart bleeds. Others are fighting.

Seeing the chaos makes me sick, and bile hits the back of my throat.

The room is enormous, and toward the back is a set of platform steps. Two black thrones stand on top. Behind them is an oversized round window, light pouring over the massacre.

More Bloodcursed are stumbling out of the portal that sits in front of the thrones. There's a large black hole, the edges sparking with blue energy. The same power that curls around my hands.

"It's too dangerous to go in there," Luther says as he twists around. "You need to close the portal from here."

"Deep breath," Deimos murmurs in my ear. "You can do this."

I suck in several harsh breaths and try to ground myself. In my mind, I reach out to the magic.

Energy dances along my skin as the power intensifies. It thrashes through me, lashing out like a whip, and spears outward. It ripples the air, barely seen, but I recognize the energy. My chest is burning with fury at myself at the sight of the injured guards, at the destruction I've caused. Scorching energy erupts in violent sparks from my body.

But nothing is happening. It's like I have the key in my hand, but it's not fitting into the lock.

Panic flares over my mind.

"What are you waiting for?" Luther growls. "It needs to close now."

Before I respond, he's thrown himself at the assault surging in our direction.

I try my hardest to think this through, to figure out how to close that portal. Everything always comes back to the same thing.

I glance over to Deimos. "You need to kiss me like I mean the world to you."

His eyebrow arches. "I always kiss you like that."

Snatching the fabric of his shirt across his chest, I draw him toward me as I push myself onto my toes. Our mouths clash like they're engaging in a great war of their own, lips crushing, tongues tangling. Except I don't feel the surge of energy. We break apart, both exchanging glances, our breaths shaky.

"I don't know what's going on," I insist.

He sweeps his gaze over the hallways and throne room, where dozens of guards are slowly losing to the onslaught of Bloodcursed. "We don't have much time. You have to close it now."

Rippling power is everywhere. I feel it in the air, clawing at us, seeping into my very essence. Why the hell can't I summon my power to shut that fucking portal?

CHAPTER 3

GUENDOLYN

I feel the whole room closing in around me. I choke on the stench of blood and death while everything starts to blur together.

Soldiers battling Bloodcursed. More creatures pouring in from the open portal. My princes fighting. But I can't get a handle on my power. Goddamnit, I only just discovered I carried such an ability, so I don't have any clue how to wield it. But I have no choice now.

People are dying because of me.

Panic curls in my chest with each raspy breath I suck in. I have to calm myself if I intend to figure this out. But how the hell am I meant to uncover anything about the power in my veins at this moment?

Sighing deeply, I realize I need to rethink this.

"Guendolyn, hurry," Deimos urges me from behind, his back against mine as I face the open doors leading into the throne room. He uses his body to shield me from the creatures, and I adore every single inch of him.

I search my thoughts, going over every incident where my power flared up.

Kissing Deimos.

Battling the Bloodcursed back on Earth.

All moments of high stress. High anxiety. Intense emotion.

Death surrounds me, so I don't think it can get crazier than this. Except there's a small difference. Back then, my focus was wholly on the attack and the kiss, while now my brain is scattered with the battle, the fear of not controlling my magic, the fear of letting the king see me. My thoughts fray at the edges.

Deimos tenses against me.

I swallow a shudder and dig my heels in, ready to make this work.

Concentrate.

I shut my eyes, and the portal in the throne room flutters in my mind. I grasp on to the thread, and there's a sudden shift in the air that ripples down my arms. The thin blue lines snap wildly around my fingers like a live wire flickering and whipping about. It's responding to the change in the atmosphere, just like the threads of magic I've seen around the fairies' wings. They crackled and popped as those little critters swarmed me outside the kingdom's entrance. Did they carry a similar power?

Deimos bumps into me. My eyes flutter open, and I slam into the open door. I jerk around, my pulse racing.

Two Bloodcursed attack him, and he jumps at them in response, his sword swinging.

I grasp onto the entrance to the throne room and

stare at the black portal, at the creatures coming through.

That's all I imagine now, and I picture it closed, calling the power to me, drawing it into me. I shove all other thoughts aside.

A surge of energy sweeps through me, bitterly cold. It punches me in the gut, biting into my skin, leaving a bitter, metallic taste in my mouth. I look down, and the blue lines are dancing over my body. My heart soars with the possibility that I can do this, my adrenaline racing.

Fae howl and roar with rage around me.

The hairs on my head shift, and the air around me once again seems to change. It carries a chill.

I imagine it coming from me, rushing across the throne room and crashing into the portal, lacerating the connection, shutting out the creatures.

Pain lashes my chest, the moment drawn out as I stare at the portal, wishing it out of existence.

Sweat drips down my spine, and a nerve pulses in my neck. Energy suddenly snaps outward from my body, leaving me stumbling on my feet.

In the blink of an eye, the portal pops out of existence. Just like that, it's gone. No more Bloodcursed coming through.

"Deimos!" I cry out. "I did it!"

The rush of power surges through me once again, stronger than before, as if retaliating against me. It shakes me to the core as terror cleaves through me.

In the middle of the throne room a darkness descends, shaping into a solid form. A long oval shape...

just like… My stomach drops through me as I watch another portal coming to life before my eyes.

I want to scream and cry as the earlier spark of hope inside me shatters like glass.

A heart-wrenching screech snatches my attention. I spin on my heels and look out into the hallway behind me, where everyone fights. Where no one knows how close I came to stopping this. Sorrow clings to my ribs, swallowing me.

Until my gaze sweeps over to Deimos.

A Bloodcursed savagely bites into his shoulder, and he collapses to his knees.

I scream and stumble forward. My world dies as I watch him fighting the beast that overpowers him. My movements seem to decelerate, my every step agonizingly sluggish, like I'll never reach him.

He looks at me, his green eyes meeting mine, burning with terror.

Blood pours from the wound, then another creature lunges for him.

Blinding rage bursts inside me, dark and violent. "Get away from him!" I scream. I want to die right this moment.

I charge through the masses, pushing past them with unimaginable strength. A terrifying ache splinters my heart in half.

With fury, I grasp the back of one of the monster's torn coat, fisting the fabric, and haul him off Deimos with all my strength. I'm shaking uncontrollably, and all I can picture is ripping his head off with my bare hands.

"Sonofabitch!" I bellow as Ahren spears the second

Bloodcursed in the head with his sword. I lift my gaze toward him. But the first creature turns on me in an instant. It snatches my neck, bony fingers digging into my skin with a vise-like grip. It sneers, blood dripping from its mouth...Deimos' blood.

My hands fly at the creature's face instinctively, pushing my palms against its forehead to keep the gaping mouth as far from me as possible.

I can't breathe, and I swing wildly at him with my free hand as I stumble backward.

My back slams into a wall in the hallway. Then it all happens too fast.

The creature suddenly pushes past my hand and bites my forearm. The momentum sends me flinching backward, and my head cracks into the wall. My vision reels from the blow, throwing the room into a spin.

Sharp teeth sink deeper into my arm, tearing. I feel every lick of its tongue, every rip of skin. Tears rush from my eyes.

Unbearable pain shoots up my arm, feeling like blades ripping over my skin.

I'm choking but don't stop slamming my fist into its head, over and over. The fuckwit is still latched to my arm, making slurping sounds that sicken me. The edges of my vision feather with darkness. I picture my death, being left in this realm to wander as aimlessly as one of them. A Bloodcursed.

I don't want to die.

I hit the monster with the last of my strength, then something buzzes past my ear. Seconds later, a small bird flutters above the Bloodcursed.

No... not a bird, but a fairy. The same type I'd encountered outside the kingdom's entrance.

A tiny face, big black eyes, and a wide mouth filled with serrated, pointy teeth. Translucent wings reflecting a rainbow of colors rapidly beating. Greenish scales covering a humanoid body. She's small, maybe the size of my outstretched hand.

She watches me. Then something brushes past my arm, and dozens of fairies rise up around me. They dive at the Bloodcursed, ripping at its flesh. Vicious little things, they leave nothing untouched.

Wings slap me in the face, and I pull sideways, fighting to rip my arm free.

They wrench the fiend backward, away from me. I stumble and use the wall to catch myself when I break free. I desperately gasp for air again, filling my lungs.

A cloud of fairies bombards the Bloodcursed, who bats its arms at them, but it's too late. It vanishes behind a wall of whipping wings, unleashing a screeching sound.

My heart is hammering frantically. I clasp my bloody arm and cradle it against my stomach. It stings so badly, I want to collapse and just bawl my eyes out. I stare at my injury, and all I see is blood and deep red flesh.

How long before Deimos and I become one of them?

The room around me morphs into pandemonium.

Energy jolts through me, rattling me as though the earlier power has again awakened inside me. All I feel is the devastating ache from the bite.

Fairies swoosh through the palace, attacking every single Bloodcursed.

Madly, I push myself off the wall in the hallway and whip around to look into the throne room. Fairies are flying out of the second portal, not Bloodcursed. Somehow, I've called them, opening a doorway to these little beings who saved my life once before. I welcome them to do what I can't.

They ravage the Bloodcursed, not touching any other fae. They make fast work of the creatures, ripping into and devouring them. All that remains are bones, hair, and clothes.

"Deimos," I cry, my cheeks drenched as I try to peer through the chaos in the hall behind me to find him.

Those green eyes are all that remain in my mind… The devastation in his eyes when he knew it was too late for him.

I hiccup a cry, hurrying forward as half a dozen fairies zip around me.

Translucent wings flap wildly. They congregate over my wound, and I feel their tiny tongues licking me, tasting me. No teeth. They don't intend to harm me, I know it… They're feeding on me, and I can only assume it's my payment for their help. Just as they did down in the woods when they saved my ass the first time.

They saved me, so I have no intention of pushing them away.

I shove forward through the chaos regardless.

"Deimos!" I yell out. "Ahren!" All I see is the flutter of fairies flying all over the place and Bloodcursed falling everywhere.

A tiny squeal that pierces my ears has me cringing.

I twist my head in the direction of the sound to see a soldier grasping a fairy by a vibrant blue wing. The other wing is bent backward, broken. The fae raises his blade with his other hand.

Instinct takes over, and I rush to him, screaming, "Stop!" I remember Deimos calling them "blood-sucking vermin." Except to me, they're my saviors.

The soldier doesn't hear me, and I practically bowl him over. He teeters on his feet, his eyes wide with shock, and drops the injured fairy. I hastily snatch her out of the air. I have no idea of the gender, but she seems like a female to me. They all do.

"What the fuck?" he growls.

"They're saving us," I bark back. "Look around you. Do you want them all to turn on you?"

He blinks hard and looks around as if seeing the reality of the situation for the first time.

I gather the little fairy closer and hold her with one hand to my chest, her good wing tucked against her body, the other sticking out at a strange angle.

"Sorry, little one. I'll help you. I promise," I coo, but first I must reach Deimos before we both turn into monsters. I want to tell him how sorry I am. The thought leaves me dizzy, but I swallow down past the fear.

The tiny fairy glances up and shakes her head before pressing her cheek to my chest. I hear the soft whimpers of her pain.

I whirl around to find Deimos leaning against Ahren, who has an arm around his brother, holding him up. Deimos clutches the side of his bloody shoulder, moaning.

Color has drained from his face, and he looks sick. Gravely sick. The infection is moving fast through his body, yet I feel none of the infection in my body yet.

He meets my gaze through the bloodbath surrounding us and gives me a half-grin. Despite every-thing, he still smiles. This is why I fell for him so fast, why my heart bleeds at seeing him hurt.

"Deimos." I shudder and rush up to him, stepping over bodies as the flutter of fairies starts to slowly dissi-pate. I look behind me and into the throne room, where many are flying back through the portal. They've left only dead Bloodcursed in their wake.

"Guendolyn, what did you do?" Ahren growls, his gaze lowering to the fairy in my hand when I face him.

My bitten arm dangles by my side, the pain excruci-ating, but no one seems to notice.

"I'm fine," Deimos lies terribly, drawing my attention to the terror that swims in his eyes. I hear the fear in his voice.

"Deimos, stop pretending." My voice breaks.

"I've never been a good actor." He half-snorts into a laugh.

"No, you haven't," Ahren snaps. "And you sure as fuck aren't going to die today."

Blood oozes from between Deimos' fingers, drip-ping onto his dark shirt, seeping into the fabric.

Ahren maneuvers them through the masses. The Bloodcursed are all dead, and fairies are zipping out of the room quickly.

"Guendolyn, stay close," Ahren orders. He's barely looking at me, his eyes all over the room. "We need to get him to the healers."

I move alongside them, sidestepping the dead. The soldiers stand around bewildered. But I glance back at the fairy portal, needing to close it.

The fairy in my hand chirps like a small bird. I look down, and she raises her hand and puts it to her mouth, then dips the fingers forward. She blows a breath, and out comes a blue fog, similar in color to the magic threads.

She chirps again and points to the throne room.

I don't waste a moment and turn around, facing the open doorway to the throne room, staring at the gaping black portal. The last few fairies vanish inside. With my good hand, I tuck the fairy inside the top of my dress, then place a palm to my mouth.

Lowering my fingers forward, I focus on the image of the portal shutting. Then I blow out a breath.

A surge of energy rises through my stomach, up to my throat, and rushes out. A pale blue fog spears from my mouth and rushes through the air, darting around bodies, over heads, until it reaches the portal. It smothers the opening, and the black passage dissolves, crumbling into thin air.

Several guards explode into cheers.

I look down to my new friend. "Thank you." She's exactly what I need...someone to help me understand my power. And I need to work out how my ability is related to these fairies.

"Hurry up," Ahren growls. He doesn't say my name, but I know he's talking to me.

With a hand clasped over the fairy, I twist around and hurry after the princes.

Deimos' face is a gray color now. "Hold on," I say, my shattered heart breaking into even more pieces.

He blinks before looking up at the ceiling. A tear pools at the corner of his eye.

"Deimos, fuck." I'm trembling. "I need you. You can't…"

Two soldiers push past me and shove me aside. I stumble on my feet, holding on to the fairy so as to not lose her.

"Don't fall behind," Ahren calls out. "I need you to stay with me to heal him."

My head still spins, and his words jumble in my mind. How can I heal him when I've been bitten too?

I move to catch up to Ahren and Deimos, who've vanished down a corridor, the shadows stealing them from view.

My throat tightens, and I choke on my breaths. Agony tears at my insides as all kinds of images of our time together slam into my head. Ones that make me feel like the worst person in the world, because I caused this. I hurt him. Deimos was bitten by a Bloodcursed. For those few moments, I struggle to move. Maybe I deserved to be bitten… It's payment for what I unleashed here today.

I search the room for Luther.

Slipping past a group of guards, I glance over my

shoulder instinctively, as if sensing someone watching me. I suspect it's Luther.

My gaze collides with a well-rounded man who stands tall, his chin raised, eyes narrowing on me. He's dressed in a black coat buttoned to his chest and has a short, white beard. My sights land on the golden crown sitting on his head.

All the blood drains from my body.

Fuck!

CHAPTER 4

LUTHER

My muscles feel heavy and sore from fighting.

Sucking in a sharp breath, I lift my gaze to the hallway littered with Bloodcursed. The soldiers are aiding injured fae, and their voices blend together into a humming sound in my ears, just like the buzzing of the fairies who came to our rescue.

For the life of me, I can't work out how fairies got into the palace as well.

One moment we're battling for our life, and the next, those little vermin are rushing in and attacking the Bloodcursed. I guess I can't exactly hate them now, seeing as they assisted us. But so much doesn't make sense. How did they get in here? Why did they only target the Bloodcursed? Don't get me wrong, I'm not complaining, but things aren't adding up. There's a reason for everything.

Tucking my swords into the sheaths on my belt, I

groan from the ache in my arms as I walk through the aftermath. Cutting off heads is fucking hard work.

Everyone is running all over the place to provide help and start the cleanup. I catch sight of two of our mages walking into the throne room, scanning the massacre. Their black robe-skirts drag over the dead bodies as they step over them, the metal chains they wear around their waists rattling with each movement. A tiny fairy skull the size of my fist hangs from their necks and sits halfway down their bare chests. Their white hair is kept short and is woven with feathers, their cheeks imprinted with various magical symbols—markings inked on their faces on their first day as mages. Not many of their kind are born. They carry the power of multiple abilities, stronger than most fae, and most end up working under the king's command for life.

Which begs the question: Did they open the second portal and bring in the fairies? It was a risky move that paid off, if that is the case. Except I've never known them to have such a power.

My stepfather marches into the throne room toward the mages, and I turn away before he sets his sights on me. The king is the kind of fae who believes a busy man is a happy man. In truth, he uses that line to order people around to do his shit. And considering the mess in his throne room right now, he'll be a raging bull.

I have no doubt he'll come and interrogate us about what we saw. He'll turn this kingdom upside down to uncover how the Bloodcursed entered.

There is no way I can let him get his hands on Guendolyn. He's already promised to kill the girl who cursed Shadow Court. Coupled with that, if he finds out she accidentally let those fucking bloodsuckers in, she'll stand no chance.

What I need is to uncover how the hell she did it and ensure it never happens again.

Soldiers grunt around me as they start to haul Bloodcursed outside for burning. I sidestep a guard and end up stepping right into Guendolyn's path.

Her eyes widen with a beaming smile. "Luther!" She blows her hair out of her eyes and stares up at me as if she's been lost.

My attention zeroes in on the fairy half-sticking out of her top in her cleavage.

"What the hell—?"

"Don't. Not here." She quickly glances behind her at the throne room, then hurries toward the corridor where I found her earlier. I track after her and ensure no one follows us.

Once we reach the shadows and are clearly out of earshot of the others, I grab her arm and force her to stop and talk to me. She winces and flinches from my touch.

I look down at her arm. There's blood everywhere. The flesh on her forearm is torn and dripping with blood.

I can't think straight for those few moments, but reality punches me in the chest. "Fuck, Guendolyn. Don't tell me that's a Bloodcursed bite."

"Luther," she begins, her voice trembling.

So much pain crowds behind her eyes. I should have

done more to keep her protected. I believed each Blood-cursed I slaughtered made her safer, but I was wrong.

I let her down just as I did my real father, who reminded me daily I was worthless in his eyes. In the years since he left my mother, I've wondered how things might have been different if I'd been the son he wanted.

I didn't get a chance to fix that shitshow, but with Guendolyn, maybe all hope isn't lost.

"Fuck!" I roar as my heart jolts in my chest. I pace back and forth in the corridor and run a hand over my face. Ice rushes down my spine and penetrates my bones.

"Don't freak out," she pleads.

"How else am I meant to react?" I snap. The girl I found years ago on Earth, a lost fae from our world, who I believe can save our realm and who stole my heart, is now going to die from a fucking Bloodcursed. I want to drive my fist through the wall over and over.

I pause in front of her. "I can't lose you." I taste the words in my mouth as they roll past my lips.

"Luther," she whispers while I'm breaking apart on the inside.

I cup her face with my hands and draw her mouth to mine, kissing her desperately, memorizing everything about her as she kisses me back. I want nothing more than to claim her, to conquer her until she is mine forever. I want to really taste her, to finally sink between her gorgeous thighs, to release every piece of built-up emotion that has slowly driven me crazy over the past two years.

She pulls away from me, staring into my eyes as if she might remember more about our past. I grasp on to that hope, but when she doesn't say anything, I know it's just my tortured mind craving her.

"How did you open the portal, little wolf?" I ask to break the silence. "And why the hell are you holding a fairy? They're vicious." I look down at the critter, who watches me with its huge black eyes, its lips peeling back off the row of sharp teeth. It knows I'm talking about it.

The thing hisses at me while Guendolyn steps back and shifts her hand to hold it closer to her chest. It looks up at her with admiration swirling in those dark eyes. How in the Seven Hells did she tame such a creature?

"Dammit, Luther, listen to me," she scolds. Her anger seems to outweigh her distress. "I was bitten, but I'm not feeling any symptoms yet. The real problem is Deimos was bitten too, and he's slipping fast. I don't know where Ahren took him, but I need to see him." Her words dance with shakiness as heartbreak slides over her face and fresh tears track down her cheeks. I'm not blind to the fact she has strong feelings for Deimos, and I swallow past the hurt. Right now, that's not as important as my brother's impending transformation, the news a punch to my chest.

"Deimos got bitten as well?" An invisible hand seems to wrench into my gut and rip out my insides. I choke on air, struggling to get it into my lungs.

How did they both get bitten? We just arrived back

at the kingdom today, and all hell's broken loose already.

"I don't know where Ahren took him," she cries. "Where would he go?"

In my periphery, soldiers linger at the end of the corridor, collecting bodies. With my stepfather and the mages nearby, we need to get a move on. There's so much at stake.

"This way," I command, wanting to take her hand, but I realize with her holding that fairy and her other arm mangled, it's not going to happen.

"Do you have a cure for a Bloodcursed's infection?" she implores as we storm down the corridors of the palace as far from the throne room as possible. She gives me a ghost of a smile, filled with hope.

"No, but we have healers who might be able to help," I lie, the words sour on my tongue. Many fae have turned into Bloodcursed from bites in the last two years, and our healers have been helpless to save them. But I can't terrify Guendolyn any more than she already is. I let out a hard breath and let the lie linger between us in a silent moment.

We rush past marble walls that are elaborately decorated with gold trimmings. Tapestries. Paintings. Vases. Candle chandeliers. Midnight blue rugs run the length of every hallway in this place. No soldiers or guards anywhere, which is a good thing right now.

Instead of worrying about losing Guendolyn and my brother to this curse, I focus on moving as fast as possible and ensuring no one sees her leaving the palace.

When we reach the rear exit, I push open the metal-studded door that connects the palace to our mansion. The wind is ferocious outside, the sun blinding.

I shove my shoulder into the door and hold it open for Guendolyn. She spills outside onto the stone bridge that spans the one-hundred-foot distance.

She's clutching on to her fairy and glances around at the enormous castle we just emerged from. Our mansion in the distance is made of steadfast stone walls that glint in the sunlight. On either side of us is a slope from the hill the castle is built upon. Hundreds of homes flood the landscape within the kingdom walls.

Black and red roofs gleam beneath the sun with trims of varied colors around the windows. Down there, the rest of the fae live in cottages. The homes built higher up on the mountain and closer to the palace belong to the more affluent families.

I turn to Guendolyn, who looks so lost, her cheeks scarlet. Her blonde hair flutters over her face, but she just doesn't seem to care. Her irresistible blue eyes seem cold today.

Panicked voices from the fae down below tell me word has spread about the Bloodcursed breaching the palace.

Guendolyn whirls on her heels and runs onward toward our mansion, and I run after her.

I try to tell myself she and my brother will be fine, except I've seen the effects a bite has. Terror crawls up the back of my neck and the world spins with me. The thoughts won't leave me alone, flashing images of them both turning. Being faced with the decision to end their suffering or imprison them for life until a cure is discovered terrifies me.

Those thoughts are poison to my soul.

When she reaches the door, she cuts me a quick look for help as she can't open the door with her injury while holding the fairy. I dash over and tear open the door for her. Once we're both inside, I take the lead and head directly to Deimos' chamber.

From a distance, I see that his door lays open and hear voices stream from inside.

My heart clenches, and I can't get there quick enough. Suddenly, I'm running.

Don't let him be turned into a Bloodcursed. Gods, please.

I burst into the room. Ahren twists toward me, his face grim and pale with a look that carries a dark burden.

I lose all semblance of composure and march up to the bed, where four healers hover around my brother. Maids are rushing out of the room.

"Get the fuck out of my way," I bellow to the healers, who just stand there. They're useless, and I shove myself past them.

Deimos lies on his back in bed, his eyes shut, his shoulder bandaged. He isn't moving, but I notice the rise and fall of his chest.

A golden transparent haze encases my brother.

"What is this?" I choke out.

"A temporary device to keep him alive until a cure is created," a deep voice speaks, belonging to the dark figure who emerges from the shadows across the bed from me.

Jasion Crow. Another mage from the palace, except he works closely with Ahren. He stands tall, his shoulders broad, dressed just like the other mages with a skull hanging down the middle of his bare chest. He's powerful, terrifyingly so, but he remains under the king's command. No matter what he says about doing his own thing, I highly doubt he truly does. He'd do the king's bidding without question.

"How long does he have?" I ask Jasion, and he doesn't blink or show any form of emotion. Not much scares this mage. He isn't too much older than Ahren, yet he and my brother bonded after we first arrived at the palace. Both were young and new in the kingdom, both in roles where a lot was expected of them. They formed a friendship as they went through training together. Many, including Ahren, say Jasion should be positioned as head mage. The king doesn't seem to agree.

"A week or two," Jasion answers.

My blood ices in my veins. "How the fuck are we meant to find a cure in that short of time?"

"You need to give me a day or two, Your Highness," he says.

"I'll run more tests to see how fast his blood is changing to give you a better indication. But you know the truth about this toxin." His hooded eyes intensify, and I know exactly what he's talking about. We've tested so many Bloodcursed, their blood, different spells...everything one can think of, we've tried. But nothing helped because it came down to one thing. The only way to break a curse is to use magic from the creator.

I growl in response and turn toward Ahren, but it's Guendolyn my eyes settle on.

She stands there with red eyes. Fresh tears keep falling down her cheeks as she glances at Deimos, and she's still clutching onto that damn fairy.

My heart rips in half, grieving for my brother, terrified for Guendolyn, and confused by so many things I don't understand.

I move closer and cradle her in my arms without squashing the fairy. Guendolyn softens against me. In my mind, I picture her lying next to Deimos, both of them taken by the infection. Breath catches in my throat.

"How are you feeling?" I whisper.

She doesn't respond, but her breaths turn to sobs.

I lift my attention to Ahren.

Fury burns behind his gaze. "What the hell happened back there?" he growls.

I lean in closer and whisper, "Somehow she opened the portal in the palace while she was in the mansion."

My brother turns to everyone else in the room. "Everyone, leave now. Out!"

The maids scurry out while Jasion strolls past us. His pale gray eyes fix on Guendolyn, showing too much interest for my liking. Nothing good comes from piquing a mage's curiosity.

With the click of the door, Guendolyn pulls away from me.

"What is that?" Ahren snaps, staring at the fairy in her clutches as if seeing it for the first time.

"They helped us defeat the Bloodcursed," she answers with confidence. "And this little one hurt her wing, so I promised to help her."

"Promised whom? The vermin who attack fae?" Ahren asks.

"We have a bigger problem," I say, interrupting. "Guendolyn's been bitten too."

Ahren's face pales, his gaze scanning her body and landing on her arm. Blood is dripping onto the floorboards.

"Gods no. We need Jasion back."

"No," she says. "Please just wait a moment. I need to catch my breath since so much has happened so fast. Yes, I got bitten, but I'm not feeling sick yet. I saw how quickly the infection took Deimos, but all I feel is the freaking pain shooting up my arm." She lifts her arm and whimpers. "Please help me with the bleeding and pain first, because it doesn't sound like your healers have any real solution."

I pivot on my heels and dart into the bathroom, where the maids left buckets with hot water and material for cleaning wounds. I collect what I need and am back by her side in moments.

Ahren has her sitting on the couch, and next to her is the fairy looking pretty miserable as well. One of her wings sits twisted and broken.

I kneel in front of Guendolyn and lay her arm on her thigh with the wound facing upward. Dunking one of the rags into the water, I wring it out and dab her messed-up wound.

She winces, but I press on and wipe the injury, needing it clean before I bind it.

"Talk to me," Ahren begins, drawing her attention from what I'm doing. "What happened today?"

She licks her dry lips and keeps glancing over to Deimos and back at us. "When you left to visit the king, Deimos and I started talking." She swallows loudly, struggling to find her words.

"And then?" Ahren encourages her to speak.

"Then I kissed him. He kissed me." Her cheeks blush furiously, but she never looks away, knowing how I feel about her.

My thoughts are stuck on the word *kissed*. It shouldn't bother me. I've seen the way Deimos and Guendolyn are both drawn to each other. We three have shared girls before. I won't deny jealousy roars through me, igniting my insides like an inferno. I still haven't had a chance to spend time with Guendolyn. To help her remember our past. I taste her deeply on my lips and want more.

"The whole room started shaking," she continues. "I felt the magic in the air. Last time Deimos and I kissed, we were transported from Earth to this realm. So I think this time, it opened the portal. I'm so sorry. I don't even know how I did it or why it was different from the last time."

I lower my head and keep cleaning her wound, finding it's a lot more superficial than it first seemed. I start bandaging it and will have to disinfect it later, but I need to stop the bleeding first.

"The kingdom is encased in magic to keep the Bloodcursed out, so maybe it's distorting your portal ability," Ahren suggests, which makes sense.

"And I think when I tried to close the portal, I somehow opened a second doorway for the fairies." She looks down to her new friend and smiles.

I take a seat next to Guendolyn.

"And how are you controlling the fairies?" Ahren's thinking it all through, trying to piece everything together and make sense of her power. How to keep it from happening again. It's what Ahren is good at.

"I don't know," she admits. "They just seem to like me."

The fairies don't like anyone unless they're tearing into them and sucking the marrow out of their bones.

Silence falls heavily across the room, and everything seems to shut down inside me. Everything but the instinct to fight.

Every time I look over to Deimos, a sledgehammer smashes into my chest. How the fuck did we end up here?

"All right, so we know the following," Ahren begins, counting on his fingers. "Guendolyn can't control her power, and it's triggered by kissing, perhaps?"

"Well, not completely true," I interject sheepishly. "I kissed her earlier in the corridor, and there was no transportation between realms."

Ahren's brow arches, studying me. I can't work out the look in his eyes. "Does that mean the power responds differently to certain people, or is it just a state of stress? Jasion told me his power can fluctuate depending on what emotions he feels on any given day."

"I've never heard of that before." The times I've worked with the king's mages, they share information easily, so to never have heard this is a surprise.

"We need to account for what we're dealing with. We know that fairies seem to respond well to you, Guendolyn, and they help you, so there's something there."

She nods.

"And for some reason, you're not reacting to a Bloodcursed's infectious bite."

"We don't know that yet," she murmurs.

"True, but we'll know by the end of the day, as I've never seen an infection take long to spread." His brows pinches with the look he always gets when he doesn't believe what he's hearing.

"You missed the most critical part," I announce, lifting my chin toward Ahren. "Deimos has limited time left in that magic haze before the toxins transform him and we lose our brother for good."

CHAPTER 5

GUENDOLYN

*A*hren stands before Luther and me with the light from the window casting a glow around him. His long, white hair is pulled into an alluring man bun at the back of his head, a few strands hanging messily around his face. Those pale green eyes look right through me. Ahren is spectacular. Tall and broad-shouldered, he stands with confidence. I can easily see him sitting on a throne, leading this realm. He has a way of reminding you he's the heir and will never take no for an answer.

In truth, all three of the princes leave me swooning. But that doesn't make them any less frustrating or dangerous.

Everything has become more complicated since arriving in this kingdom. Things were messy enough as it is... I'm a fae from the Unseelie Court, the princes' mortal enemy, apparently. My parents are in that court, but no one can tell me anything more except I might get killed by the Unseelie if they find me.

My head hurts just trying to make sense of it all. Now, Deimos has been bitten, and I can somehow command fairies. If things weren't crazy before, they sure are now.

"Guendolyn," Ahren whispers, and I can tell by his tone he wants something of me. "When we stopped in that backwater town, you healed my bite mark. Do you remember?"

How can I forget? Those wolves almost killed us, but I know exactly where Ahren is going with his question.

"I don't know how I did that, but I'll try on Deimos. I'd do anything to help him." I stare down at the fairy, who's sitting with one blue wing wrapped around her and the other kinked outward. I have to help her as well somehow. I get to my feet and take quick steps to Deimos, remembering how Ahren's bite mark vanished when I touched it, leaving behind my handprint on his skin. I hope he's right, as I can't stop worrying it won't work in this case.

The transparent haze over Deimos glints like golden jewels beneath the sunlight pouring in from the windows.

"Can I touch it?" I glance over my shoulder at Ahren, who steps alongside me.

"The magic holding him won't affect you." He studies me as if I'm about to perform some kind of awe-inspiring trick.

There's no doubt the whole situation is a shitstorm waiting to happen. Luther stands by the window, not saying a word, and I can feel the tension rolling off him in waves. I don't blame him. This is a fucked-up position to end up in.

Facing Deimos, I try to push aside my fear, and with a deep breath, I lower my open palm to his bandaged shoulder. The magic feels cold against my skin. With my eyes shut, I imagine my energy pouring through me and into Deimos.

I seize my power.

The floor shakes beneath my feet, and I snap open my eyes to find the walls trembling. Wobbling backward from the movement, I lash out a hand toward Ahren to steady myself.

He snatches my wrist and wrenches me against him as the walls quiver and groan.

In moments, the shuddering settles. Everyone freezes, and no one says a word as we wait.

"Was that you?" Luther stares right at me.

"I'm sure that was her power," Ahren responds on my behalf.

Quickly pulling free from Ahren, I rush back to Deimos' side to inspect his shoulder. Please, please be healed. I pull at the bandages eagerly, my heart banging.

The white fabric peels away from his flesh, bringing with it blood and the sight of the open wound. So much blood pools up around the bite mark.

I cringe and want to scream. Hastily, I reapply the bandage tightly to stop the bleeding, then look toward Ahren and shake my head.

"I felt the power, but it didn't work," I murmur.

Luther sighs. "The only thing to counteract their magic will be a cure from the creator," Luther explains.

I jerk my head toward him. "Then why am I still not feeling the symptoms of my bite?"

"I can speculate," Luther says, his voice matter-of-fact, as if he's been pondering this already. "You have Unseelie blood in your veins, and the curse on our court is from Ash Court, where the Unseelie live. I'd say that makes you immune, and the spell targets Seelie blood-lines only."

There's a coldness in the way he delivers those words, like he almost resents me for being Unseelie. I didn't even know fae existed before these princes brought me here, let alone that there are two factions.

"I'm going to collect Jasion," Ahren grunts while crossing the room for the door, his footfalls thumping the wooden floorboards.

"Shouldn't we wait until I show symptoms?" I say, seeing the worry on Ahren's face, his impatience.

Each time I glance over to Deimos in the bed, I want to cry. We've been running non-stop since he first took me from the nightclub back on Earth. Somehow, during all the complications and fighting for our lives, I found myself drawn to him. I believed with time I'd discover what my emotions for him really mean, if the tender-ness he showed me is real, and now I don't know if I'll get the chance to uncover the truth.

"Jasion might know more about Unseelie magic and perhaps even something about fairies so we can work out why you can control them," Ahren explains. He doesn't wait for a response, just marches out of the room like he can't stand still doing nothing while his brother lies unconscious.

Luther crashes on the lounge, on the opposite end of the little blue-winged fairy. He leans forward, his forearms on his thighs as he stares out the windows at the spectacular view of the mountains.

He's devastatingly handsome, and I feel so many mixed emotions for him, things I don't understand. Confusion seems to now cross his face. Since meeting him, he's been patient with me when it comes to remembering our past together, but I can see the pain behind his eyes when he looks at me. Now, he's miles away.

I'm still jittery from the day's events, and my insides are frayed.

"I think what you said before about why I'm not feeling the infection might be right," I say to eliminate the silence.

Luther meets my gaze. "I already know what Jasion will say. He's said it before. We need to find a cure from the creator in Ash Court, and that's not going to fucking happen."

The corded muscles in his neck pulse, and I feel the pressure on my shoulders, weighing me down. What he's saying between the lines is that Deimos is fucked. What I hate more than the guilt flaring through me is seeing it across Luther's face.

"You know, I didn't do this on purpose," I reply.

"Never said you did." He lifts his chin and lets out a breath. "I'm not blaming you, little wolf. I'm trying to work out how to save my brother."

I give myself a shake to dislodge the sadness in my thoughts and walk across to Luther. Sitting next to him,

I reach over and place my hand on his to let him know he's not alone in this. Grief has a way of bringing out the worst and best in people, my foster mom used to tell me.

I don't know what to say, but when Luther twists his head my way, all I see are those vibrant dark eyes with a golden rim around the edges. They almost seem to glow when the sunlight hits them.

He clears his throat. "When I was fourteen, I fell off a horse. My foot got stuck in the stirrup and I was dragged by the startled animal. I was going to die, and I knew in my heart that this was how everyone would remember me—as the prince who couldn't ride a horse. Except I didn't realize that Deimos was galloping along-side us, determined to stop my steed. He managed to leap onto my horse's back and calm him down. I remember him jumping down and staring at me as I lay there beaten and bleeding. The first thing he said to me was, 'This proves I'm the better rider.'" Luther chuckles softly to himself at the memory. "He's always been competitive, but he's never let me down. So I can't lose him or let him be known as 'the prince taken by the Bloodcursed.'"

My heart nearly spills out of my chest at the realization of how much he's hurting.

He studies my hand in his lap before glancing back at me. "I haven't the headspace to show you the kingdom and help you remember our past as I promised. At least, not until I know my brother is safe."

I swallow the unease forming in my throat. "I wouldn't expect you to, not with this going on." My voice comes out ragged, making me sound like I lied. I smile at him to show him I understand, not revealing the disappointment in my gut. That makes me sound selfish, but I'm trapped in this realm away from family and friends, and there's danger at every corner. And I want Deimos to heal with every ounce of my being, but I'm supposedly from this realm, and this place would feel a little more home-like if I remembered what happened before.

"So what happened to you after the horse incident?" I ask to pull myself out of my sinking thoughts.

"We never told a soul. We explained the cuts and bruises by telling our mother that Deimos fought a boar that tried to attack me."

"You two are super close, right?"

He nods.

"What about Ahren?"

Luther shrugs. "Unfortunately, as the eldest, he was forced to take responsibilities from a young age and didn't spend as much time with us while growing up. While Deimos and I rode horses, he was forced to work with tutors on the etiquette of being a king."

"That's kind of sad for him," I say. "He lost his childhood."

"You may think it's sad, but he's been dreaming of being king ever since he could speak. So his king lessons were a dream come true for him, a promise of what will come."

Thinking back to my conversation with Ahren in Swindon, I know his real father had beat him senseless.

Of course, he'll aspire to be as different from him as possible.

"I have a younger foster brother, and he's a little snot on good days."

Luther's brows pull together in confusion.

"He's just annoying and likes to irritate me," I explain.

The hinges to the door give a small groan, and we both turn around. Ahren marches inside the bedroom with no sign of the mage on his heels.

"Change of mind?" Luther asks.

"Jasion is occupied and will join us later."

"So what does Jasion do in the kingdom?" I ask.

"He's a mage and has a stronger affinity to the magic all fae possess," Ahren explains. "Usually, they carry control over four or five abilities. As soon as they show such signs at a young age, they are taken to temples for training, and most end up working for one of the four kingdoms in Wandering Realm as protectors and advisors."

"And to carry out the king's dirty work. Everyone knows they practice with dark magic," Luther announces automatically.

"Jasion is not like the rest of them," Ahren snaps.

Luther shakes his head. "I get that he's your friend, but if the king gave him an order, Jasion would carry it out like all mages, no matter the consequences. That's the part that I have problems with."

Ahren's jawline clenches, but he just shakes his head and moves toward Deimos as if they've had this argument too many times before. I don't know what to make of the mages, as this is all new to me, so I say nothing and sit next to the fairy before collecting her into my hands. She lifts her head and gives a small yawn, her mouth filled with dozens of tiny sharp teeth. She shifts in my hands and winces, glancing at her injured wing.

I place my palm over her wing, not touching it, and concentrate on driving what energy I have in me to the wing to help heal her. She has no curse on her that I am aware of, so this might work.

"Put that thing in here," Luther says.

I lift my head as he pulls open a drawer on a mahogany chest located across the room. It's elaborately engraved with spirals and looks like it belongs in an antique store.

"Deimos' clothes will make perfect cushioning for it to sleep," I suggest.

"You're not keeping that thing in this room with Deimos," Ahren growls. "Fairies attack and eat fae, and he's defenseless right now."

Luther clicks his tongue, and rage flares over his face. Before he explodes, I interrupt.

"How about the fairy sleeps in the drawer just while we stay in this room? Then I'll take her with me to wherever I'm staying."

"Sounds perfect to me," Luther responds eagerly.

Ahren watches the way I hold the fairy against my chest, and as if in a gesture of good faith, he nods.

I hastily tuck her in and leave the drawer open. "Sleep, little thing."

She curls in on herself on a blue, soft fabric. Her

kind saved us, so I intend to care for her until she's ready to join her family once more.

"I'm going to arrange for food and drinks." Luther heads across the room. "I'm fucking starving."

The tension between him and Ahren fills the room, but I remind myself of what my foster mother said about grief.

Luther heads out of the room, his chin high and held confident as always. Though today, I saw a crack in his tough exterior.

Ahren leans against the windowsill, his hands deep in the pockets of his pants, his legs crossed at the ankles.

"Luther brought you to this realm two years ago," Ahren says, breaking the silence. "He found you through magic and never should have looked for you or carried you back to this realm."

His words don't make me feel wanted in the slight-est. I don't know how to respond to that. Typically, I would answer his passive-aggressiveness with my own. Except I can feel Ahren's eyes on me as if expecting nothing less. "I never asked to be brought here."

Ahren's mouth flattens in a thin line. "But he did, and by doing so, he started the tragic events that led to you unleashing the curse on Shadow Court. The reason I'm telling you is so you know that he lives with that guilt every day."

His explanation takes me off guard. Here I thought his intention was to insult me, but all along, he just wanted me to see that Luther is hurting. Maybe he meant to do both. Since meeting Ahren, he's worn a grizzly exterior around me, infuriating me. Though I've seen snippets of what lies beneath that tough mask, so he's not who he pretends to be. He's aggressively caring and always thinking about everyone else. His past is horrifically tragic; his real father whipped Ahren whenever he disobeyed him. The past pain from the scars criss-crossing his back might give him the strength to keep fighting for what he believes is right, but to me, they're bruises on my mind, a reminder that those memories will always be with this strong, confident fae. No one deserves such a terrible upbringing.

"I didn't realize Luther blamed himself," I mutter.

Ahren pushes off the windowsill, his posture stiff. "I wish you knew how much it destroyed him when you disappeared back to Earth for two years."

He saunters over to Deimos and stands over him, watching him silently.

My stomach sinks right through me. Luther's heart lies damaged, and I need to talk to him. Some needy part of me wants to clear the ache from his soul and comfort him. But most of all, I wish the missing memories would just flood back already.

As I sit on the couch, I curl my legs under me. Ahren truly cares for both of his brothers, even if they growl at each other, and that touches me deeply.

A light breeze sweeps into the room and across my back, sending shivers down my spine.

I turn toward the door as a man pushes it open. He's large, intimidating, and scowling. A golden crown sits crooked on his head. He marches inside like a charging bull, and he's coming straight for me.

fierce instinct drives me to stiffen. My head screams to run, but I can't move. What I want to do is disappear into thin air, but instead, I curl in on myself on the couch.

The king swings in my direction, each step striking the floorboards like a drumbeat counting down to my death.

He must remember me from the throne room. Shit! He must have seen me there…but how much did he witness? Me trying to close the portal? The princes protecting me? The fairies?

Ahren darts between me and his stepfather in a heartbeat. "King Tibout." He fists a hand to his heart two times. "We weren't expecting such an honorable visit." His voice sounds as strained as he looks.

"Stop fucking groveling and get out of my way. And I told you to not be so formal when we're not in the throne room."

King Tibout's frustration almost makes me think he

wants Ahren to call him "Dad" or something more personable. Maybe the princes need to give their stepfather a chance?

But I somehow doubt the king will be that lenient with me when he realizes I opened a portal to the Bloodcursed in his throne room, and oh yeah, released the curse on his kingdom.

Nudging Ahren out of the way, the barrel of a man looms over me. He's changed his clothes and now wears a silvery blue coat tightly buttoned from his navel to his throat, as well as black pants and black, shiny boots. He stares at me as wildly as his unruly short, white hair.

"Who are you?" he demands, giving nothing away as to what he might have seen me do in the throne room. What exactly drove him to seek me out? Does he recognize every person living in his palace?

I feel overwhelmed and can't find my voice. I've just dealt with Bloodcursed and figuring out how to close portals, now this.

"Do you have a voice or are you mute, girl?" he persists.

"G-Gainy. That's my name," I mumble, hating that the first thing to pop in my head is that stupid name Deimos gave me.

"And where are you from, Gainy?"

I watch the wheels spin behind his eyes as he pieces it all together. A new person in his palace on the same day that Bloodcursed mysteriously break into the throne room. I would come to the same conclusion. But I can't let him know the truth. The frown sliding over his face doesn't belong to an understanding man.

My heart beats frantically, preparing to rip out of my chest and escape.

"I—"

"She's just a healer from the village in the kingdom. Why are you interrogating the poor girl?" Ahren remarks. "I would have thought you'd be more concerned with Deimos being bitten."

The king's head jerks toward the bed, his posture straightening. All the color drains from his face.

"For fuck's sake," Tibout snarls and storms across the room to Deimos' bedside. "Your mother is going to be devastated. Fuck!"

I slump back into the couch and can breathe again.

Ahren gives me a reassuring look and joins his step-father. They talk to one another trying to figure out how Deimos must have gotten bitten, considering he's an exceptional warrior. I picture the scene in my mind. One Bloodcursed catching him off guard, then another moving fast to take him down. But talking about the past isn't going to fix the problem. All I care about is that they try to help Deimos, who's languishing in front of them.

I roll down the sleeve of my dress over my bandaged arm.

"Update me the moment you hear from Jasion," the king grumbles and sweeps toward me, sending a swarm of shivers up my arms. "I may still have a connection or two in the Ash Court."

Ahren clears his throat and meets the king's stare with one made of sorrow. "I've received grave news about the Master of Game," Ahren responds. "Gabel

Wulfe passed in a terrible battle in the woods recently near Ash Court."

The king's features weaken, his grief deepened by the news. "How did I miss the message?"

My heart clenches at the memory of Gabel. He was a fae who believed in being fair and truthful to the people. It hurts to remember his death, which occurred while helping us battle Bloodcursed in the forest.

"Can't say." Ahren shrugs and steps toward the door, guiding the king out. Except the king turns back to me. He doesn't miss a beat, does he? I can't say I'm surprised, but I appreciate Ahren's attempt to get rid of his stepfather.

"You look familiar," the king addresses me. "Have we met before today?"

"You might have seen her down in the city," Ahren answers for me, his voice a lot smoother and convincing now.

"Your Majesty," I say quickly, "Luther encountered me healing my neighbor and asked me to come talk to your healers about a potential position to work here."

They both look at me strangely, and maybe I should have just let Ahren do the talking. But I've found if there's going to be a lie, it's always more convincing when two parties bounce off each other with the lie. Except with the way Ahren studies me, I'm guessing I must have said something out of place.

"Luther is hiring staff for my palace?" the king asks.

Ahren snorts a condescending laugh. "You know the locals; they'll say anything to be hired by the palace.

Luther simply asked her to join us so he could ascertain how effective her healing actually is."

The king doesn't seem to buy it as he scrutinizes me with a stern gaze. I wheeze in a breath.

"That's me. I'd do anything to work here." God, I hate how desperate I sound.

With a scratch of his white beard, the king's lips tilt into a frown. "Is part of your healing capacity to consort with fairies and carry them around? You are aware they attack and devour fae?"

Ah, there it is. He'd seen me with the fairy in my grasp, and that bit of knowledge gives me the confidence to speak freely.

"If a person or animal is hurt, I don't discriminate, Your Majesty," I respond. "The fairies were clearly helping us defeat the Bloodcursed, so the least I could do was aid one who had her wing damaged."

"You mustn't be well versed in etiquette around royalty, or my sons have misled you to believe that meeting my gaze so freely is acceptable." There's a tightness in his voice.

Considering I looked him in the eyes before, I'm guessing what he really doesn't like is having anyone correct his assumptions. I swallow roughly, lower my head, and begrudgingly submit. I don't want him pushing for more answers and discovering I caused the breach today. "My apologies, Your Majesty."

Footfalls tapping the floorboards recede toward the door. I lift my gaze and turn as the king tosses over his shoulder, "If I find any more vermin fairies in my kingdom, girl, you will be held personally accountable."

I want to argue back, but I bite my tongue instead.

Luther barges into the room and skids to a halt at seeing his stepfather. Luther's panicked gaze flicks from him to me, then Ahren.

"You two, we need to talk about today," the king snarls at the princes. "Follow me," he orders as he storms out of the room. "We also need to move Deimos to the palace. Your mother will want him close to her."

Luther frantically looks at Ahren, who whispers something to Luther I can't hear, so I can only imagine he's bringing him up to speed on what we told the king. Then both of them head outside the room, shutting the door behind them.

I collapse on the couch and gasp for air. "Fuck!" Will my heart ever beat calmly again?

A knock comes at the door, and I leap onto my feet. What the hell now?

"Come in," I say.

The door swings wide and an older lady with brown, bouncy curls walks in backward. She's wearing a floor-length burgundy dress with a white apron tied around her waist. Wheeling a wooden food trolley covered by white fabric, she drags it across the room and places it next to the couch.

The maid's eyes sweep over to Deimos, and she does a small double tap to her heart, mumbling what I guess is a prayer under her breath.

When she looks at me, her eyes widen, and a smile tugs her lips upward as if she recognizes me. She waits for me to respond, but I don't know her. "My lady, you have returned. It has been years since I have seen you last. The princes wouldn't tell me what became of you, but blessings, you are safe."

One interaction with her, and I already like her. "I don't remember things too well," I admit.

"Oh, my lady, I had no idea. I'm sorry." She bows. "My name is Dana."

"Don't be sorry. It's wonderful to meet you, Dana. Again, apparently." I can't bring myself to tell her my name, as I have no clue what I called myself the last time I was at the mansion.

She quickly turns to the trolley and unwraps her goodies, a ceramic teapot and several stacked cups. Next to it is a large platter filled with what looks like scones and jam, triangle pastries, strips of dried meat, and a bowl of chopped fruit. My stomach responds with a growl. It feels like forever since I last ate.

She sets out the cutlery and napkins along with a gold plate for me.

"Enjoy, my lady." She bows and heads out of the room.

"Thank you," I call out after her. The moment the door clicks shut, I dive into the food and don't even bother with the cutlery. I taste a bit of everything. The triangles are cheese and spinach and taste divine. The beef jerky is a bit too salty for my liking, but the scones just melt on my tongue.

When I think I might burst, I collect the bowl of fruit made up of apples, pears, grapes, and a pink thing that looks like melon, then return to the couch.

Still no show from the princes, so I help myself to

the fruit while staring outside at the snowflakes drifting downward.

It isn't long until a thick blanket of white has fallen over the green landscape. With this spectacular view, I can easily forget where I am. I glance over to Deimos, and my heart squeezes. "Please get well."

A sudden rush of cold air surges into the room as the door is shoved open, stealing with it my small reprieve. I twist around in my seat.

Ahren and Luther shut the door and march inside. Before they say a word, they're gorging on the remaining food, using their hands just as I had.

"Is everything all right?" I ask, embracing the fruit bowl in my lap.

"Yes," Luther answers. "Just had to convince our stepfather that I hired you temporarily to be my healer for the agonizing headaches I've been experiencing. I told him you'll be staying in the mansion with us while I require your services."

The way he said that almost made it sound like I'm offering him different services, and I can't stop the smirk from spreading across my lips.

"And we convinced him we knew nothing about the breach," Ahren adds.

Has Jasion come back?

Luther's low voice sweeps over my mind, smooth and dangerously sexy. His ability allows him to speak in people's minds. Though he told me that it's prohibited in the kingdom under the command of the king, he apparently doesn't care.

I meet his gaze and shake my head, even if my

insides quiver from the intimacy of having his voice in my head.

He grabs more food and wanders over to Deimos. I don't say anything for a long moment and remember Ahren's words about Luther's pain.

"Are you all right?" Ahren asks, drawing my attention to him.

"I feel wrecked. This has been the most insane day of my life. I can't even remember how many times I almost died."

"Little wolf, I'll take you to your room. Maybe you should have an early night." It's more of a statement than a question.

Exhaustion ripples over me, and while I have no idea what time it is, I'm guessing it's late afternoon. "I'd like that," I answer.

Luther turns and walks right past me before leading me into the hallway.

"Good night," I say to Ahren as I quickly go and collect the blue-winged fairy from her drawer and take her with me. She's half-asleep and hardly notices I'm carrying her again.

Luther doesn't say a word to me as we travel down the corridors. Left and right, we turn so many times, I completely lose track of how to get back to Deimos. Not that he'll be there by tomorrow, as the king will have him moved to the palace. Luther stops near a huge black door and opens it for me.

"This isn't the room you brought me into when I first arrived at the mansion. Why are you changing my bedroom?" Paranoia spikes my question.

"This room is safer. Lock the door from the inside," he tells me as he stands tall near the doorway, making no attempt to lean closer and steal a kiss or remind me of what we once had.

"Sleep well." He reaches over to slide a loose strand of hair out of my eye. For those few moments, I expect more from him. Words that everything will be alright, a hug—damn, anything but this cold demeanor.

Instinctively, I lean against his touch, but he pulls away. I blink at him, my heart skipping a beat.

"See you in the morning, little wolf." He starts walking away, his head bowed forward, and the shadows swallow him. When he vanishes, the hallway stands silent. Too silent for my liking, so I quickly shut the door and lock it. Then with the fairy in hand, I step deeper into the enormous room. Black velvet curtains cover the windows, and the walls are made of dark granite. A huge stone fireplace cracks and spits embers into the metal grill, throwing light over the two long couches facing each other, and a wooden coffee table sits between them.

To my left stands a doorway to another room, and inside I discover a generous bed with a mahogany headboard and dozens of frilled pillows on one end. Near the bed is a chamber pot, and I cringe at the idea of using it, but I'm no longer on Earth. Gotta do like the locals.

"Well, looks like this is our place to share for the night."

The fairy looks at me from half-closed eyes. She

looks worn down, and I worry about how much she's sleeping. But what do I know about fairies?

Using the pillows, I make her a little nest in the corner of the room and lay her in the center, where she curls in on herself and is already making tiny snoring sounds. I don't for a second have any concerns that she'll attack me during the night. I trust her, which I know is strange, but I do.

Considering there's nothing else to do in this room, I yawn and climb into bed only to find a deep blue nightgown tucked under a pillow. I get changed, jump into bed, and curl up under the blanket.

I don't want to overthink everything from today.

I need sleep, and I pray tomorrow makes up for today being an asshole of a day.

I wake with the driest mouth in the world. I gasp as I try to swallow, but it's impossible.

Golden flames from the fireplace in the other room chase away the shadows in the bedroom.

Getting out of bed, I stretch and somehow feel semi-normal. When I peer past the heavy curtains, night has claimed the landscape but I can't see much else. I look down to my bitten arm and pull back the bandages to find the mark completely healed over. Running my fingers over the skin, there's not a bump or bruise. How in the world did that happen? How did I end up immune to the Bloodcursed's bite?

I pad on bare feet into the main room, still dressed

in the nightgown. I remove the bandage from my arm before placing it on a side table. I search the room, but there are no water bottles or glasses or any indication of water. Swinging toward the door, I unlock it and stick my head out. It's dark, and the globes of light dangling from the ceiling illuminate the walls and an array of animal statues. The kitchen is bound to be somewhere nearby, so I pull the door shut behind me and decide to go left, the direction Luther headed after leaving my room.

I wander through the mansion corridors quickly, trying random doors, but they're all locked. From what I've seen, only the princes live in the main rooms and the helpers stay in their own quarters, probably downstairs.

The next door I try ends up being a small medieval-looking bathroom. There's a long bench against the back wall with a wooden lid located in the middle. I open it and find a hole like outhouses. To my surprise, it doesn't smell, so I shut the door and ease the buildup in my bladder.

Once I'm back out, I continue my search until I bump into Dana around the next corner.

She leaps back, startled by my presence. "My lady, what are you doing out here and in your nightdress?" That part seems to shock her the most.

"I'm thirsty and looking for water."

She tsks and rushes into a room behind her. Inside, the light is bright, and I spot a small kitchen with a counter on one side and a cast-iron stove on the other.

Moments later, she re-emerges and hands me a smooth silver goblet filled with water.

"Thanks." I drink the whole thing down in several mouthfuls, and it's the best-tasting water ever. I'm guessing this is what real mountain water should taste like, not the stuff in grocery stores.

She collects the goblet from my hand. "Now quickly return to your chamber. No respectable lady would ever be caught in her nightdress."

Not sure I can ever call myself respectable, but I give her a nod. "Thank you." Then I pivot on my heels and hurry back the way I came.

I don't know how long I've walked around, but I'm certain I've gone in a circle a few times as I eye the same statue of a roaring lion.

Clunk.

I flinch and tear my gaze from the lion and look farther down the hall to where the sound came from. One of the doors sits slightly ajar, and curiosity has me padding towards it on bare feet. Inching closer, I peer through the sliver of a gap into a room not too different from Deimos'. I shift to see more of the room, and Ahren comes into view. He's sitting on the couch in front of a blazing fire, and my mouth drops open at the sight.

He's not wearing a stitch of clothing.

CHAPTER 7

GUENDOLYN

*A*hren is reclined on the couch, his long fingers wrapped around his heavy cock. Head tilted back, eyes shut, he's oblivious to me watching him. The golden hue from the fireplace illuminates his insanely perfect body—his strong chest muscles, his muscular bicep flexing with each stroke. His shaft seems to tremble in his grip, as if he's barely holding back from climaxing. Excitement ripples over my body at having accidentally stumbled over this scene, and I know that I will never forget it.

I see every delicious inch of him, and God, he's hot as hell. Long, powerful legs lead up to tight balls and an almost golden blond thatch of hair at the base of his cock. A drizzle of light hair runs down the middle of his abs. He is completely absorbed, and seeing such a powerful man succumb to this desire undoes me.

I should run away embarrassed and not invade his private moment, but I can't move. I can't look away.

How can I when I have a front-row seat to a dirty fantasy that has crossed my mind more than a few times?

My heart is practically in my mouth, and I am utterly fascinated. My mind imagines what it would be like to be with a fae like him, to have him strip me of my clothes. Would he be rough or gentle?

I clench my thighs together, intensifying the ache building inside me, but nothing helps when this is the hottest thing I've ever watched. Gnawing on my lower lip, I'm struggling with the intensity pulsing through me. I reach down and push the bunched-up fabric of my nightdress between my thighs. My fingers press up against my heat, and I imagine him touching me there.

His hot skin against mine, his kisses on me.

My heart pounds in my ears, and I'm breathing rapidly. I'm turned on, and everything is spinning within me.

There are so many things wrong with this situation, yet I can't convince myself to go. Everything about Ahren captivates me. His hand moves faster, and my breaths match his rapid actions.

This is actually happening.

My mind screams to get out of here. To run back to my room and lock myself inside.

I squeeze my thighs even more as I'm imagine him inside me, while my nipples harden and press against the fabric of my nightdress.

What is wrong with me, and why am I enjoying watching this? This isn't me. Except, who am I kidding?

I am lapping up the sexy scene in front of me and nothing will make me turn away.

Then he growls, and his chest arches. A small moan presses on the back of my throat, the heat inside me melting into liquid fire. It drips down the inside of my thighs. If I had worn my underwear before I went to bed, they'd be soaked now.

All I can picture is Ahren and me naked, doing filthy things.

How can this fae be so incredibly tempting when most conversations with him leave me frustrated as hell? Yet here I am imagining myself with him. Thinking of what Ahren would be like makes it so I can barely breathe, and a thick lump lodges in my throat.

I stare at this prince palming his cock, pumping his hand up and down.

A keening, satisfied groan spills from his lips. His dick stiffens and his balls contract, then thick ropes of cum spew from the head.

Sucking in a sharp breath, I clasp my hand over my mouth.

Ahren jerks his head forward as if hearing me. I jolt back, turn, and run. I don't stop, don't dare stop.

God, please don't let him have seen me.

I look behind me as a shadow spills from inside the room. Throwing myself around the corner, I sprint, unsure exactly where I'm going, but somehow I find my way back to my room. I rush inside and close the door silently, then lock it.

Running to my bed and jumping under the covers, I lie there, my whole body thumping with each heartbeat.

The reality that he might have seen me blasts through my mind like a storm. My cheeks are burning with the shame of being caught. I'm breathing so hard, I might be hyperventilating. I lie in utter silence, expecting a knock at my door, but it never comes. All I can picture is him filling me, stretching me to the point where the pain twists with pleasure, where I scream for more.

The image of his hand stroking the thick length of his cock stays with me. It never leaves me, even when I fall into sleep.

Sitting on a balcony with the three princes sends shivers up my spine. I barely know them, yet they stare at me hungrily from their seats in front of me.

A servant comes in carrying a silver platter and hands Ahren a drink in a jewel-studded crystal goblet, the rest of which he hands to the other two princes, then me. I accept and drink two mouthfuls, quenching my dried throat. "So, I'm a lost girl from this world, you say." I press the goblet to my lips, finishing the refreshing minty iced tea. The man refills my drink from a golden pitcher.

"Something like that," Luther adds.

I shift in my seat. They might be the most beautiful men in the world, but they lie through their teeth and keep secrets. The truth hides behind their gazes and their clipped responses.

"If I'm from this place, where are my parents?" I ask.

Something shifts behind Ahren's eyes but vanishes as

quickly as it came. "There's no news on your parents. We've searched." The corner of his eye twitches.

Liar. Big, fat liar.

My breath comes too fast, and I can't hold back the words. "If you don't intend to tell me the truth, don't mock me with lies," I retort. "Speak honestly."

Never insult them, the maid told me earlier.

Ahren bristles, his nostrils flaring as he glares at me with narrowing eyes. "Do not challenge me," he roars, his hands gripping the arms of his chair. "On your knees."

Fear strangles me, and I look to Luther for help, but he sits back with a curious expression, like he's goddamn enjoying himself.

I shouldn't have said anything when I have absolutely nothing nice to say, but the response flew out. "Like I told your brother, I'm not yours to control. You hide so much behind that smile, but like someone once told me, we all have shadows. I'd rather we speak the truth."

Never say no to the princes, the maid also said.

Ahren shoots to his feet, his expression twisting and warping. It darkens, but his gaze never leaves me. He marches closer, and panic soars through me. I jolt to my feet, but he moves too fast. His hand juts out and seizes me by the throat, squeezing.

I grasp for his hand, pulling at the fingers that block my breathing. Terror... real terror locks around me like a straitjacket. This is real, and this madman will kill me. Tears spring to my eyes.

"Little girl, you keep pushing me," he spits. "Next time, you'll learn how to fly off my balcony."

My eyes flutter open to a loud banging at the door. It takes me moments to remember where I am and what happened last night. My mind is still drowning in a dream I had of the princes. Like previous visions I've had since arriving at the kingdom, this one stays crisp and clear with me. I remember the moment like it just happened… I can't remember the context of how we came to be on the balcony, but the moment definitely happened.

Why doesn't it surprise me that when I met Ahren for the first time, he was a standoffish ass who threatened to kill me? I know those visions are snippets into my past and memories that refuse to completely unlock for me. Now, I can't get the image of him naked out of my head.

Sunlight pours in from the gaps around the curtains on the windows and even more floods in through the doorway from the main room.

Knock. Knock.

I flinch.

God, please don't let it be Ahren.

I scramble quickly out of bed, pushing aside the blankets, and drop my bare feet to the cold floorboards.

"Who is it?" I call out as I rush toward the door.

"My lady, it's Dana. I've come to take you for your morning bath."

"Bath? I don't need a bath." I unlock the door and pull it open.

A huge brown dog leaps at me. I scream from the shock and reel backward as the animal bowls into me. My chest heaves for air as I scramble away, unsure if this thing is friendly or wants to eat me.

"Do you remember Sir Wolf-A-Lot, my lady?" Dana asks from the doorway, her smile wide as if she planned this so-called surprise.

"Is he going to eat me?"

She laughs and claps her hands. The dog sits in front of me obediently. He's larger than a big German Shepard. He stares up at me with black eyes, his long sharp ears upright, and his thin tail swinging side to side. The end is tipped with a barbed club.

"Is he a hellhound?" I ask, gaining myself a puzzled look from Dana.

"He's an ordinary dog, my lady."

Ordinary my ass, but I smile regardless.

"He belongs to Luther. On your last visit, you and Sir Wolf-A-Lot bonded."

We did? I look down at the dog, who seems to be waiting for a response. I reach over gingerly and pat his head, his dark fur feeling coarse under my hand.

"Hey, boy, do you remember me?" At my voice, he's on his feet and nudging his head into my arm to keep scratching him. Okay, maybe he's not so bad after all.

"Are you ready for a bath now?" Dana asks, impatience growing in her voice.

"Give me a moment."

I hastily dart back into the bedroom and check on my little blue-winged fairy.

"Hey, little one. How are you feeling?" I cross the

room, only to find her little nest is empty. I stiffen. Where is she?

I scan the walls and ceiling, then kneel next to the bed and look underneath. Nothing.

Maybe she went into the other room. Frantically, I rush back out, worried about the dog spotting her.

Dana looks displeased in the doorway, arms folded over her chest, but the room shows no sign of the fairy. My gut tightens as I remember the king's warning. *If I find any vermin fairies in my kingdom, girl, you will be held personally accountable.*

Just great.

"Are you ready, my lady?"

I turn to Dana. "Did you see anything rush out of the room while you were standing there?"

Her brows pinch together. Of course she'd remember seeing a fairy fly out of here. God, what if she snuck out last night when I went for a drink of water? This is all I need. The only positive is that the king doesn't live in this mansion. I pray the little fairy didn't leave this building and get caught up where she shouldn't.

"This way," Dana commands as she hurries me with a wave of her hand, being rather pushy. I shut the door once Sir Wolf-A-Lot comes out, just in case she's hiding somewhere in there.

The bathroom is across the mansion. Inside the small room is an elaborate white freestanding tub with golden clawed feet, half-filled with water, but my first thought goes to the princes.

"Any news on Deimos?" I ask as I step into the room,

which smells like burning incense. Two light globes dangle from the ceiling, illuminating the space.

"No change yet," Dana answers. "It's so tragic. Deimos is the most mischievous of the princes, but also the one who jumps into any battle first. Poor boy. He might lose his life, and all before he finds a princess to share it with. You know, my lady," Dana continues as she picks up several towels from the shelves on the wall and places them on a table near the tub, "before the curse was placed on our kingdom, the king was arranging a grand ball for the princes to find their prospective wives. He invited all the other royal families. It was going to be the biggest and most elaborate celebration."

I'm lost for words as my mind bounces back and forth like a tennis match between the potential of losing Deimos to the infection and his marriage plans if he survives.

"Once the mages find a way to eradicate the curse, the king will marry off the princes. It's how he secures his allegiances to other family houses."

After a long pause and hesitation, I say, "I'm happy for them."

Except in all honesty, I'm not. The thought of the king finding the princes future wives carves through me like a blade. I shouldn't be jealous, as they are royalty. I'm from the enemy court and don't even belong in this realm. And it's not like I can have all three of them. Even if I could marry one, that's still only one of them, and I'm not sure I'd be okay with that, based on the feelings I seem to have for all three.

I'm barely getting to know them, but I can't ignore the way my heart bangs in my chest in their presence. How I can't stop thinking of Deimos' and Luther's lips on my mouth, how my mind fills with images of Ahren naked.

"Quickly now, before the water gets cold," Dana reprimands me, and I begin to undress.

"What about Luther or Ahren? Have you seen them this morning?" Just saying Ahren's name floods me with a burning desire. I'm not sure I can ever look at him again without picturing him with his hand on his huge cock. My cheeks burn from the memory alone, so how am I meant to act normal around him now? Worse, I'm still praying he doesn't know it was me spying on him last night. I know I'll see the answer the moment I look him in the eyes, but at this moment, I decide on three things.

One, I won't hide from him.

Two, if he did see me last night, then I'll act like it never happened.

Three, no more sneaking around the mansion at night.

"Only Luther, my lady," Dana replies. "He instructed me to bathe, dress, and feed you."

I may as well do as she commands and enjoy it while I can.

"*H*oney with your porridge?" Dana asks as she fills my silver cup with more orange juice.

"Yes, please."

She pours some thick honey over my porridge and then heads back into the kitchen while I sit alone in a dining room at a large, round table in the middle. The surface is polished to a shine while the edges are carved with tiny wings. Silver vases overflowing with flowers fill the shelves against the walls.

A fire roars in the fireplace. Across from the table, the windows are floor-to-ceiling with no curtains, just the most spectacular view of mountains coated in white. Pine trees sparkle in the sunlight from the snow dusting them. I eat the porridge while staring outside, daydreaming that I'm not in a dangerous place.

"Gainy, what an opportune moment to catch you," a man murmurs.

I twist around in my seat as Jasion walks into the room, his presence making me stiffen.

His long, black robe-skirt sashays around his ankles, and the crystal eyes in the skull hanging from his chest seem to glint in the sunlight. He's bare chested and not a masculine man, but toned. Just looking at him bare-chested makes me cold.

I'm wearing a long-sleeved dress with buttons running from my cleavage to my stomach, cinched in around the waist, and my skirt flows to my ankles in soft waves. The fabric is thicker than it looks and comfortably warm. Still, I feel cold at the thought of being as exposed as this fae.

"Can I join you?" he asks.

"Of course."

He sits one seat away from me just as Dana returns. She freezes in the doorway to the kitchen after seeing him.

"Tea, please," he calls out, lifting his chin in her direction.

She nods nervously and darts back into the kitchen.

"She seems scared of you," I say.

Jasion laughs softly, like my comment somehow makes him proud of the maid's reaction. He's a handsome man with dark eyes and long lashes, full lips, and a wide jawline. Tiny black feathers twist through white hair cut short that sits messily around his face, and his pointy ears poke upward through it.

"And you look at me like you've never seen a mage before."

"I've seen you around, but many down in the city know that it's not wise to approach a mage," I lie, going purely on instinct and Dana's reaction.

"Are we that horribly thought of in the city?"

"I wouldn't say horribly, but you have to admit your image alone is intimidating."

Maybe I've said too much, as he raises a brow. "The ritual garb can make others wary of us. But it also lets them know we are here to keep the kingdom safe from the curse and Bloodcursed surrounding our home."

I bite my tongue in response. As a supposed local, I should watch my words and perhaps play the meek female.

Our gazes lock.

Does he see through my thoughts?

The door slaps shut, and I flinch as I look up. Dana rushes over carrying a tray with a teapot and two cups. She sets them before us without a word. I catch her cutting me a side look before she hurries away, her eyes holding a warning I can only imagine relates to Jasion.

"Thank you," he says, watching her head back into the kitchen before taking his time to pour us each a cup of tea. It smells overly sweet. "You're a fascinating woman, Gainy."

I cringe on the inside at the way he says my fake name. Instead of letting him see my discomfort, I stare at this dangerous man who sends shivers over my skin. Ahren trusts him, though I doubt the man's loyalty would extend to not reporting an enemy in their court to the king.

"You don't have to compliment me." I reach for my cup of tea and blow over the top of it. My attention lingers on the symbols inked on his cheeks.

Catching me staring, he says, "They are ancient runes, and each one represents an ability I master."

I look closer, having no clue what any of the patterns mean. "It must have hurt getting them."

"Rewards don't come without pain."

I hadn't planned on getting into a full-on conversation with him, but the questions keep rolling off my tongue. "So you're saying the markings are more than just decorative?"

A smirk touches the edges of his lips. "Correct."

I raise the cup to my lips and sip the honeyed drink. The mage watches me as if trying to decipher me.

"Does it ever worry you that your enemies can learn of your power by reading the runes before a great battle?"

He breaks out laughing again. "You have a tremendous imagination. Mages never go to battle. We are the foundations behind the scenes." He leans closer. "Excuse my bluntness, but how does a simple healer from the city attract the attention of the princes? These are deadly times, and trusting the wrong person can be a horrible mistake to make."

There's so much being said between us without words.

"I've known Ahren for a long time, and he's never held back secrets from me...until now." His gaze burrows through me. What I see reflected back at me is determination and jealousy.

I swallow the thickness in my throat. "Luther saw promise in my ability. And he offered to pay me to help him." I lower my eyes to let him think he's intimidating me. Hell, I am squirming in my seat, but he's trying to get me to tell him the truth.

"Perhaps he saw a few things in you." The corners of his mouth quirk as he implies I am more than a healer to Luther. I seethe on the inside but say nothing.

He reaches his hand over, palm side up. "Please, may I have your hand?"

I swallow hard. "Why?" My voice comes out as a whisper.

"I saw you handling the fairy, and I haven't yet met anyone capable of doing so. I want to feel the strength of your healing ability."

When I don't offer him my hand, he says, "Legends tell us the fairy race is older than fae and their magic comes from the gods themselves. The power was given to them by the gods back in the days when fairies ruled this world."

My interest is piqued. "Then why do they attack fae?"

"There's an old account I read in an ancient text that told one version of the story. When fairies first appeared in the Wandering Realm, they were full-sized, like you and I. Many centuries later, the first fae came into existence. The king of the fae was said to have fallen in love with the queen of the fairies. When she rejected his offer of marriage, he kidnapped her and raped her. But it wasn't enough for him, so he kept her imprisoned as his own."

"What a fucking monster."

Jasion nods. "It wasn't long before she fell pregnant, and on the day her daughter was born, she used the child's placenta to cast a deadly curse on the fae. She hexed them to be forever hunted down. But curses born of fury are temperamental things, and the curse turned the queen and her people into the fairies you see today. Ferocious creatures who live off fae flesh."

"That's a tragic story," I say, so captivated by the story that I only now notice my hand sitting in his grasp.

"Legends usually are."

I jerk back, but his grip tightens and holds me still. "Luther is right—your power is incredibly strong."

Suddenly, his eyes roll back into his head, leaving

behind only white. A spark races up my arm. Blue lines erupt and jump from my hand to his.

Flinching, I rip my hand from his with such force that I fall backward out of my seat. Scrambling quickly, I get to my feet. My heart is beating too fast, and panic claws at my insides. I can't have this mage know I can open portals.

He's on his feet, his eyes back to normal, and the look on his face is indescribable.

Confusion.

Fear.

Determination.

He scans me head to toe as if he's seeing me for the first time. "Who are you?"

"I-I told you already. I should go." I back away toward the kitchen door, not lifting my gaze from Jasion.

He moves with such speed, all I feel is the movement of air buffeting into me. Towering over me, he brings his mouth to my ear. "Gainy, there are fae in this kingdom way more dangerous than me."

What does he know about me? Has Ahren said something to him? I can't bring myself to ask without somehow sounding guilty, though the questions bubble in my mind.

"Don't do anything stupid. You can trust me," he says.

I want to laugh in his face at the idea that he'd think I am that foolish. If someone needs to ask to be trusted, then my alarm bells go off.

Just then, Dana walks into the room. Sighing with

relief, I use that moment for my escape. I spin toward her and take fast steps into the kitchen.

I just need to get away from the mage before he learns the truth about me.

CHAPTER 8

AHREN

"*D*eimos has a week," I announce as I march into the council room.

The king stares at me with frustration in his eyes. He's alone, sitting on a golden chair behind a round desk. It's made of timber from Alethian trees. The wood is as black as the night and said to be as ancient as the fae race itself. These trees only grow in the east in a secured woodland where chopping them is prohibited. Queen Titania runs one of the two kingdoms in the east. She gifted my stepfather the table as a gesture of expectation that we would continue trading for our precious stones. Shadow Court's riches come from the wealth under our feet. In exchange, our court receives a constant supply of farm animals, food, and spices for our growing population.

Titania also has her eyes on bonding our courts and is known for collecting husbands. Those poor suckers have a tendency of mysteriously vanishing after a few years of marriage.

"A fucking week," the king growls, his lips twisting. "Fuck."

There are moments when King Tibout surprises me and shows he cares for us. Like now, his level of anger isn't what I expect. Not from the king who's been known to not speak to us for a month, or sends us orders through advisors, or goes on visits to other kingdoms that we don't find out about until weeks into his trip. He's not the most thoughtful of stepfathers, but seeing him give a fuck about Deimos gives me hope that he's not another asshole like our biological father.

"There's only one solution," I respond. I've been thinking about this most of the night, and it's the only way.

The king locks eyes with me. "You're talking about going to Ash Court, aren't you? It has crossed my mind as well. With Gabel gone, I know only one other person in that court who can possibly help." He sighs heavily and gets up from his seat. Pulling down on his gold, embellished tunic, he sighs once again as he turns his back to me. A black cloak with fur lining hangs from his shoulders. He stares out the enormous arched window at the royal gardens that include a small hedge maze. Snow covers everything in sight. Only the king and my mother frequent the location, but even during winter, the paths are swept. No one else would dare go into the royal gardens.

"Who's your contact?" I ask.

The king turns to me abruptly, his nose wrinkled. "You aren't going on this mission."

"Like hell I'm not. My brother's life hangs in the

balance. I'm not trusting anyone else." I hold his stare and see the fury burning behind his eyes. "Who else do you trust to go into the enemy court and not fuck it up or change allegiances if they're caught?" I'm not backing down.

He grits his jaw. "You're just as infuriating as your mother. I'll think about it."

"I'm going on this mission, no matter what you say," I declare, standing my ground.

His gaze narrows, a determination washing over his face. No king accepts being challenged, but I don't give a shit. Not this time.

"Fuck! Fine, but take Luther." He huffs loudly. "That boy can fight better than my best soldiers. But if either of you get killed, your mother will cut my balls off, and I'll come after you in the underworld. Understood? Just don't get hurt."

"We'll try not to die." I hold back the gloating grin tugging the corners of my mouth. There are only two other times where the king showed us concern. When we first arrived at the kingdom and he offered us anything we wanted. And when my real father threatened to kill us because he's a fucking asshole.

"Sit," the king orders, and we sit across from each other at his table.

"In the Ash Court, there's a woman by the name of Relle." His mouth tightens, and the way he licks his teeth, delaying the information, tells me everything.

"You keep a lover in the enemy court?" I growl.

He scrunches up his face as if I insulted him.

"Nothing like that. Relle is someone who helped me when I visited Ash Court."

I have so many questions about why he'd risk going to the enemy kingdom, but I don't ask.

"Relle used to provide me with some insider information," the king says, "but it has been years since I last heard from her. I don't know what happened to make her fall silent."

"Would she still help you?" I ask.

He pauses, thinking my question through. "I'll arrange to send her a bird carrier. If she responds, then she will be your key to get into Ash Court. If not, then you'll need to break in. Speak to my mages for a masking spell for concealment when you enter the Ash Court." He reclines in his seat. "So once you get inside, what's your plan? Find the mage who cast the spell and bring him back here so he can create a cure?"

I stiffen. "I'll cut open his throat after he gives me the cure then and there."

"Risky." The king clicks his tongue again.

So is kidnapping a fucking mage, but I say nothing. "I'll ask Jasion for a trapping spell, something to help me incapacitate the mage while I find out where he keeps an antidote."

Jasion told me once that Shadow Court mages keep cures of every spell they cast as backup should anything go wrong, so I just need to pray Unseelie mages follow this rule as well, then track the potion down and bring it back home.

"And what about the girl who unleashed the curse two years ago? Guendolyn. Any news on her whereabouts?" He cuts me a hard stare. The king's eyes narrow, and I know the look.

Everyone knows of the fae girl who was taken from our world as a child, along with her prophecy. There are so many theories about who exactly she is, but no one knows the truth except that she came from Ash Court.

But revealing that Guendolyn is in our kingdom comes with too many complications. My stepfather will imprison her until we find a cure, then kill her afterward for being an Unseelie and cursing his kingdom. The mages, including Jasion, won't stop until they have her to experiment on. They are obsessed with magic, and Guendolyn has a rare power I haven't seen others carry—opening portals between realms without the use of potions, not to mention her connection to fairies. Then there's the fae of Ash Court. They want her dead because if she dies, the curse over our kingdom can never be broken.

I look up to see the king watching me, waiting for a response about Guendolyn. "She must be hiding somewhere," I suggest. "If she's dead, we would have felt her death from the magic around us."

This is the reason we brought Guendolyn back to the Wandering Realm, the reason we risked so much. To ensure the Ash Court didn't get to her first and kill her.

I won't deny that there's also a fear I hold on to that anyone else who finds her will break her. We live in a brutal world where trusting anyone is the quickest way to get killed. And there's a vulnerability, an innocence to Guendolyn, no matter how much she fights back.

She's not used to the cruelty of our world, and part of me just wants to shield her.

As much as that girl infuriates me, I'm fucking obsessed with her. I hate that I even have that thought, but she's managed to wriggle under my skin. Just last night she spied on me, and I put on a fucking show for her. I sensed her at the door, peering in, watching me, devouring me with her eyes. Every tug, every moan came from imagining it was her sweet pussy riding me.

"All right." The king's voice rips me out of my thoughts, and he straightens his posture. "Is that all?"

I clear my throat. "Yes. I'll talk with Jasion and start arranging the trip."

My stepfather grumbles and huffs an expelled breath. "Are you certain you trust Jasion?"

"I don't understand your dislike of him," I suddenly say. Bravely or foolishly, I want to understand. If I one day take the throne of Shadow Court, I want Jasion by my side as my advisor. That means I can't have the king getting rid of him in the meantime.

"He questions everything I say," the king finally responds. "And I don't trust people who challenge me in public like they hope to humiliate me." He leans closer. "I know you think he's your friend and you two get along, but the fae who appear the most helpful are the first to stab you in the back. Don't you forget that, boy." He sits back. "I don't get close to my mages for that exact reason. Mages are starved for power. They'll do anything to get more and destroy anyone in their way. You think the ones who work for me haven't eyed Jasion and the favors you give him?"

"Maybe they need to be reminded of their place," I state, not wanting to believe Jasion is like the others. We grew up together, saved each other's asses more times than I can count. So to think I can't trust him leaves a bitter taste in my mouth. He's more than a mage, he's a good friend.

The king is notoriously paranoid, so I decide to take his advice with a grain of salt.

I stand as the door swings open and my mother walks in.

She smiles at seeing me, her crystal green eyes bleary from crying by Deimos' side. Her attentiveness over him reminds me of the times she'd lull us to sleep by telling us tales as children. My mother is strong and may not be well-liked by everyone, but after our father left her, she never gave up on us and did everything to protect us.

She spins to shut the door, her long, red velvet dress swirling around her ankles. It's a plain gown with no embellishments, and she wears no tiara today. Her white hair falls over her shoulders in curls.

"Ahren." She walks over quickly, cupping my face. "You need some sun, my son. You are looking pale today." Her thumb slides over a healed cut under my eye.

The king growls, "Don't baby him."

"I will keep that in mind, Mother," I say as I kiss her on each cheek. "I must go."

She releases me and turns to my stepfather. "Any updates on a cure for Deimos?" The pain in her voice has me curling in on myself on the inside. This is why I have to be the one to get the cure. I trust no one else.

I growl under my breath and march out of the room, my mood suddenly soured.

Guen

A flutter of movement catches my attention from down the hallway. Something blue, to be more precise.

Blue wings.

My heart skips a beat as I whip around and race after the fairy. I've been searching the halls for her most of the day, and now that night crawls over the land, she finally shows.

The light globes that hang low from the ceilings throw shadows everywhere, but her blue wings stand out amid the marble and dark marble statues.

On quiet footsteps, I hurry toward her. In moments, I'm peeking around the lion statue. Only one wing sticks out from the shadows. She's balancing on the edge of the lion's tail, leaning over, stalking something.

I lash out and snatch her, my hands coiling around her body.

She startles, jolting in my hold, and her wings beat frantically. She twists her head toward me, teeth bared, lips peeled back. Even for her tiny size, she's intimidating.

"It's just me," I say.

Her fear morphs into a furrowed brow, her nose scrunching up. She looks back in front of her just as a gray mouse scurries away for its life. The fairy makes a huffing sound as she looks up at me and hisses her disapproval.

"If you didn't run away, I could have fed you," I say. "Something a lot tastier than a mouse."

She shakes her head as if she understands me.

"You scared the crap out of me. Thank god you didn't venture into the palace. The king would have had us both killed," I whisper.

She hisses at the mention of death.

"Agreed. But the good news is you're looking much better now. Your wing has healed." Perhaps my earlier touch helped her after all, or fairies naturally heal fast? All that matters is that I found her. "Now we're going back to my room, and I'll get you some food."

More hissing.

"Is that the only sound you make? Hmm... Maybe I'll call you that from now on. Hiss. How does that sound?"

She shakes her head, hissing once more, and I laugh at how adorable she looks.

When the murmur of voices comes from somewhere down the hall, I pause and we both stare in that direction. No one's there, not yet anyway.

Bringing the fairy close to my chest, I rush us back toward my room. Through turn after turn down dark hallways filled with statues and paintings, I check for anyone around while the little fairy wriggles for escape.

"Hold on, Hiss. I'll get you food. You can't be caught, or we're both in big shit."

Her wings flutter wildly as I navigate around another corner to my room.

Footfalls strike the floorboards farther behind me, and I glance back.

Shadows emerge from a corridor. My heart is racing and I throw myself into my room and shut the door. My heart pounding, I press my back to the wall for a moment to catch my breath. Hiss takes off from my grasp and flaps wildly around the room, swooping all over the place before hovering near the window. She stares outside, pushing at the glass with her tiny hands.

"You want to go home, don't you?" I cross the room and reach for the lock. One twist, and I push open the window. A cool breeze swishes into the room, fluttering through my hair.

"Well, if you're ready, you are free, little one."

She darts closer, holding something sparkling in her hands. A nice-sized ruby.

My eyes bug out as I imagine her stealing it from the king's crown or something.

"Where did you get that from?" I reprimand.

She hisses at me, her lips peeling back as she draws the crystal tightly to her chest.

"You can't take that!" I jut my arm out as she buzzes right past me to the window.

Frantically, I grapple to snatch her out of the air

before she escapes. I catch her arm, but she freaking bites me. Those sharp teeth sink into my thumb.

Crying out, I flinch back.

Hiss zips right out the window with the ruby, like a little klepto. She looks back at me as she hovers out of reach, licking blood from her teeth. I wipe my stinging, bloody thumb.

Eirian.

The word floats over my thoughts like a cobweb, leaving me shivering.

Hiss' wings beat as snowflakes land on her head and shoulders. She stares at me with such intensity, I expect her to speak to me.

Eirian.

The word comes again.

A sudden, loud crack erupts behind me.

I jump in my shoes and spin around as Dana shoves open the door with the wheeled cart in her hands. She raises her head to see me and startles.

"My lady, you scared me. I didn't expect anyone here." Her gaze flips to the window. "It's freezing outside."

I nod and quickly turn to shut the window, searching for Hiss. But she's gone with the jewel and all she's left me with is a cryptic word that makes me wonder if it's her name.

"It looks like a storm is coming in tonight," Dana explains as she bustles inside with fresh bedclothes, a bowl of fruit, and a silver jug of water.

I stand near the fireplace to chase the cold from my hands.

"Dana," I say as I turn to face her, warming my back against the flames. "Have you heard of the word *Eirian*?"

She looks up from her cart, her eyes drifting farther upward as she thinks about it. Then she shakes her head. "Is it a location, my lady?"

"I don't know."

"Well, there's a small library in the mansion that might hold the answer."

I perk up at her response. "Where is it?"

"It sits one corridor down from the kitchen. I can take you there once I'm finished."

"No, that's fine. I can find it." I'll visit the library. There are so many things I intend to research - including the word *Eirian*, to see if it is a name or maybe it's a type of fairy. Then I want to find some background on mages to better understand their role. The conversation I had with Jasion still sits heavily on my mind. I like to think I'm a good judge of character, but with him, my instincts are all over the place.

AHREN

Most days are fucked, but today is fucked up gloriously.

I've had enough of company. Enough of royal bullshit, of mages, of arranging transport for our upcoming trip to Ash Court. The only saving grace has been Luther, who stepped in and aided with securing a brand new carriage said to be impenetrable if we're ambushed by Bloodcursed. The problem will be getting it out of the kingdom without detection.

I round the corner back to my room and pause when I notice who's lingering near my shut door. I don't hold back the smirk tugging at my mouth, or the punch of my cock against my pants.

Guendolyn doesn't strike me as the type of woman who wants to sleep with just any man she crosses paths with. Yet she's back again.

I step up behind her, but she doesn't hear me. She's mumbling in conversation with herself.

Suddenly she freezes, finally sensing me.

"Is there something you're searching for?" I say, my words growing deep. "Are you lost?"

She whips around, drawing in a quick breath in surprise. Her cheeks blush as she looks up at me.

Fuck, she affects me like no other woman ever has. All I can picture is that tight little body against mine, her legs and arms wrapped around me, and her moans in my ear as I fuck her until she begs me to stop.

When she tips her chin up, she attempts to look unaffected by me catching her. She scans the hallway behind me as though expecting someone. Except we're alone.

"I…um…" she stammers, unable to come up with a response at first. "I…I took the wrong turn."

From the moment I caught her spying, I knew there was no way I could walk away from her.

I stand in front of her as she straightens her spine, sticking to her lie. Her feistiness draws me to her more.

"I have a particular way of dealing with liars," I say.

"Yeah, and how is that?"

She's so damn good. Her comeback is delivered instantly without a flinch of hesitation, and she stares at me with a twinkle in her bright blue eyes. Guendolyn is perfect in so many ways I had refused to admit before. From the way her lips quirk when she's indecisive to how she plays with the tips of her hair, and then there're those curves of her chest, her slender neck, those lips… Gods have mercy, but I want those red lips on me.

"You will see," I mutter.

She shrugs nonchalantly. "I don't know what you're talking about."

"There you go again, opposing me. Challenging me. But in the end, I always get the truth."

Of course, she studies me with a look of determination, but all I can think about is making her mine and forcing her to submit.

"I better go," she answers, starting to turn away.

"You never answered my question," I say, leaning closer, a smile spreading my mouth.

"I'm sure you can work out whatever has you confused." She tilts her head arrogantly and walks away.

I clench my jaw and lash out, snatching her arm. I don't turn her toward me but step closer to her and press my chest flush to her back.

Her breath catches.

"I saw you watching me last night," I whisper in her ear. "And I know you came back for more."

She inhales a fast, shaky breath. When she looks at me over her shoulder, her gaze is challenging. She doesn't realize that I play to win and will never back down. I lean closer to her and rasp, "It's your turn to give me a show, angel."

She flinches against me and fights to pull away. "L-Last night was an accident. I hardly saw anything."

"You saw my cock, right?" I spin her by the shoulders to face me. Her cheeks are burning up, but her stubborn gaze is on fire as her eyes meet mine.

"Have you lost your mind?"

"Perhaps, but I get what I want."

I don't give her a chance to say another word. I drag her to me and kiss her fiercely. Part of me half expects a portal to open up like it did when she kissed

Deimos, but it never does. Perfect, as I need no distractions.

She fights me with her hands and body, but her lips kiss me back in kind. Her mouth shows me her fury as she takes sharp nips of my lips. It won't dissuade me, and I groan with pleasure.

"Now you're fucking mine."

Guen

I push against Ahren as our lips remain pressed together, his tongue slipping into my mouth. I'm weak and melt against him, even as my head screams to run. I need him like I depend on oxygen, but I also want to shove him into a wall to show him I'm not a pushover. My intention had been to visit the library, but when I spied the corridor leading to Ahren's room, I couldn't help myself. I wanted to check if he was there. The previous night has been on my mind all day, and...well, I'm clearly weak when it comes to my sex drive.

Strong hands grip my waist as he pins me to the wall, and my nipples pulse in response. He lifts me and slides a hand down my thigh, guiding it around his hip, then the other. I hold on to round, muscled shoulders, our mouths never parting. He kisses me like he's been waiting for so long to do this.

Passionate.

Dominant.

He pushes himself between my thighs, his erection pressing against my heat. Thin layers of fabric are all that stand between us, but his thrusts are forceful, his dick hard and thick.

"Is this what you want?" he growls with the deep timbre.

"I…" is all I can manage breathlessly.

"What do you suggest your punishment should be?"

"I don't—"

He grinds into me, stealing my words, and I'm left moaning. He takes that as my yes, and his tongue traces the length of my collarbone. His fingers slip under my skirt and move up the length of my thighs. They curl under the fabric of my underwear, and he rips it off me with such ease, I'm left gasping.

"Wait—"

"This isn't what you want?" he asks, his voice dark and sensual. "I think you're lying again. Each time you lie to me, it lengthens your punishment."

My body shudders with arousal, and I can't even think straight, let alone string a sentence together.

"Ahren—" My protest is cut off when he pushes his hand between us, his fingers dipping to my wetness.

I'm drenched, and his fingers slide along my slick. It feels incredible. He pushes two fingers inside me, and I arch my back and groan with desire as he enraptures me with his delightful torture. My hips move of their own accord, rocking forward with each thrust of his fingers into me.

I shouldn't enjoy this so much, shouldn't encourage

him with my whimpers of delight. But pleasure coils around me, wiping my mind clean of any thoughts other than what I need him to do to me.

His teeth latch around my earlobe, gnawing. I'm lost and high on him as he fingerfucks me, and moans escape past my lips.

"Was this what you imagined last night as you watched me? Me touching your tight, juicy pussy?" His voice gets quieter. "Why did you stay and watch?"

I have no idea how to respond. I can't speak when my only focus is his fingers plunging into me.

"It's all right. I know why you stayed." His words send me closer to the edge, my climax building inside me.

"Ahren, maybe we shouldn't," I say. All I can think is that once I've gone down this path, I won't be able to go back. Ahren is hard enough to deal with, let alone having *this* hanging over my head. How am I meant to ever look at him again without burning up on the inside as I remember the way he kissed and touched me?

"Your body tells me how much you want me."

His tongue finds my neck, and my resistance is non-existent. Instead of pushing away, I tug at his shirt. Everything about him calls to my arousal. He smells of pinewoods and fresh soap. I've come this far, and I want him ridiculously bad.

"You can't resist," he mocks me as he fingers me harder, faster. My mind is spinning with so many emotions.

"I hate you for saying that." I moan the words rather than deliver them with strength.

He laughs in my face then captures my mouth with a starved kiss. I return the passion, looping my arms around his neck and clinging to him. God, this fae infuriates me, but I crave him insatiably at the same time.

We rock together, our bodies tangled. Part of me wants to recognize how wrong this is, how I also desire his brothers, how I should resist. Except I'm too far gone to believe I have any power in stopping this. For all I know, this might be my first and last time with Ahren, so I intend to take advantage of the pulsing arousal flaring through me.

"How much do you hate me?" he insists.

"Sometimes, a lot," I admit between pants, barely able to catch my breath.

Not much else registers in my mind—just how damn good this feels. How his deft fingers work into me, how his thumb finds my clit and rubs it in small circles. I thrash and moan louder, needing that high that will take me into the heavens. I should care about the noises I make in a silent hallway, but I can't be bothered to worry right now.

He draws his fingers out of me and I groan in protest, needing them back. My skirt falls back down my legs as I stare at him bewildered. He steps away from me and opens the door to his room.

I inhale rapidly, my mind just coherent enough just to think he's taking me into his room to have his way with me. His cock tents the front of his pants and he lifts his hand to his nose, his nostrils flaring as he breathes me in.

"Hell," he curses under his breath. "Your smell alone makes me so fucking hard."

Seeing this powerful fae so turned on by me is exhilarating. I stare into those pale green eyes, at his white hair flowing over his shoulders, at the redness of his lips from our kisses, and I melt before him. Slick heat drips down the inside of my thighs.

"Your decision," he finally says. "Join me and I will fuck you, I promise you that. Or use that hate you're holding onto to finish yourself off. Think of me while you're doing it."

My words are trapped in my throat at the way he talks to me.

He turns away and disappears into his room, pulling the door to leave it ajar just as it had been last night.

I clench my jaw, left high and dry as he plays this game. I sure as hell shouldn't be kissing the heir to the kingdom, let alone allowing him to maul me out in the hallway when he's clearly an asshole. I release a long breath as I glance over to the gap in the door.

Think of me while you're doing it.

He's such a prick! Still, my lips buzz from our kiss. I squeeze my thighs together, and a rush of heat shoots sparks of desire through my body.

The intensity of the moment crawls up my spine. My mind yells at me to get out of there while my body and heart tug toward the door. I'm not prepared for this moment, and shock clings to me. I have to get out of here.

My heart pounds fast like it might explode out of my chest, and I don't wait for a second longer. I turn and bolt down the hallway. This never should have happened. I glance over my shoulder, but Ahren doesn't come after me.

I trip over my own feet on the way, but I don't stop until I reach my room. Shoving the door open, I step inside and slam it shut behind me. Shaking all over, I hug myself and move toward the fireplace that does nothing to get rid of the shivers.

And that's when I realize something that leaves me completely confused. I'd been so caught up in Ahren and what he made me feel that it never crossed my mind until now.

Why didn't anything magical happen, like a portal opening when I kissed him?

LUTHER

"So what's the plan to help Deimos?" Guendolyn asks before eating another mouthful of venison served with a side of roast vegetables. She's on her second helping, and I admire a girl who isn't shy to eat, but I wonder if she's being fed enough during the day.

She lifts her gaze to me, waiting for a response, but she doesn't give me the chance to speak. "I spent most of the day with Deimos, and I didn't see any healers or mages come to check on him. I'm worried."

The bridge of her nose creases slightly, like it does every time she tries to hide her emotions. Anyone can tell with a glance how much she cares for Deimos, how much the two bonded when he went to Earth to collect her. To say I'm not jealous is a fucking lie, but I have no issues with sharing with my brothers. We might very well be all her mates. My issue is her not retaining her memories of the two of us and staring at me like I'm a stranger. That is a dagger to my heart.

Ahren eats his dinner, not having said a word since we arrived in the dining room. A dark shadow seems to sit over him tonight. Something is going on with him, but he isn't the kind of fae one can push for answers. He'll talk when he's ready.

"We have plans to obtain a cure," I explain.

Her eyes widen as a smile captures her gorgeous mouth. "That's fantastic. Where do we get it from? Can we go tomorrow?"

"You're not going anywhere," Ahren responds sharply. "And it's complicated. Leave it to us."

She glares at him as he returns to his food, and the tension ripples in the air. What the hell happened between them? My brother can be fucking infuriating, but Guendolyn has a fiery side to her as well. Since the portal incident, I've kept my distance from her and come to the grave realization that me chasing her like a lovestruck kid is fucking pathetic. She barely remembers me from two years ago, and as much as that stings like a bitch, I'm not going to chase her or live in a dream world. The priority is healing my brother, then sorting out the mess of the curse on our kingdom. Until then, I'll be sure to show her the real me, and if that means starting over, so be it.

Guendolyn fills her silver cup with peach juice before setting the jug back on the table. "Surely there's something I can do to help?"

"Stay in the mansion," I respond, sounding matter-of-fact because there is no way she is leaving the building until we get this mess sorted out.

She brings the cup to her lips and glances at Dana as

the servant walks into the room, carrying a plated cake with white icing and decorated with wild berries and figs.

"That looks delicious." Gwendolyn eyes the cake as Dana smiles proudly and sets the dessert on the round table already filled with plates of food and drinks. One of the other female kitchenhands with short blonde hair rushes in after her and begins collecting our plates. I haven't seen her before.

"This recipe belongs to my grandmother, Gods bless her soul," Dana says, the joy evident in her voice and her beaming grin.

"I can't wait to try it," I add as she places a plate with a large piece in front of me. I eye the layers and smell vanilla cream. Dana serves Ahren and Guendolyn with slices.

The smile Guendolyn offers me is a temptation sweeter than any cake. She starts eating, and her eyes widen with surprise, after which she hurriedly eats more of the cake. She's making a satisfied moaning sound that has both Ahren and I staring at her like a pair of wolves stalking a lost deer in the woods.

Guen

The memory of my time with Ahren has haunted me all day. Not even this heavenly cake distracts me. Well, maybe a little.

He sits across the table from me, watching my every move from behind his hooded eyes. Tonight he's dressed in all black—tight black pants and a shirt with shiny matching buttons. Against the darkness of his clothing, his white hair seems to almost glow. He has it tucked behind his ears today, showing off his very elven facial structure.

He takes a drink of his wine, then licks his lips. On a scale of one to ten, he is easily a fifty, but there's something scary about him too. The way he needs to control and dominate, to prove his point. If I were back home, my best friend, Nickie, would talk some sense into me. Who am I kidding? She'd tell me to fuck his brains out, then walk out on him. And the thing is, I probably wouldn't fight her that hard.

Not when I think of his perfect body, his kiss, his touch. All of it flashes through my mind as I sip more of my juice. My heart thumps faster, and I can't help but wonder if someone can have a heart attack from being constantly turned on.

I can still feel his fingers inside me, and a shiver of excitement lashes over me. I hate him for walking out on me like that, but I also crave his touch. Hell, I'm all over the damn place. I scold myself for having such thoughts about him, for the raw desire surging through me.

Looking up at him through my lashes, I see the storm in his eyes. I eat another bite of cake and try to pretend he's not in front of me. I spent the whole day in the library to avoid Ahren and do research. Except, the books available were limited to history of fae royalty and their entire boring life story. No mention of fairies; it's as if the fae don't want to admit they exist. Nothing on the word *Eirian* either. So that was a waste.

The priority is helping Deimos, then uncovering who my parents are in Ash Court are. Lastly, I want to get a handle on my ability, then I can work out where in all these worlds I actually belong. If portal opening is my thing, there has to be a way to activate it and determine where a portal should open. Oh, and work out the small complication of why that only happened in Deimos' company. I really like the idea of being able to touch and kiss him without worrying about letting in a horde of Bloodcursed.

Luther sits between Ahren and me at the round table, quieter than normal. My gaze searches his ridiculously handsome face. I have never met a man this gorgeous in real life. As far as I'm concerned, they exist only in fashion magazines and are completely photoshopped. But Luther is real, primal, and intimidating. His impeccably straight dark hair falls to his shoulders, framing piercing, fiery eyes and a hard jawline. Everything about him is brooding and sexy. I feel a pull to him, and in truth, it terrifies me to have such an attraction. To not remember our past is like having to live with a blade permanently stuck in my chest. When I look at Luther, I can't take a deep enough breath and my emotions confuse me, so I pull away, scared of the depth of feelings he stirs inside me.

Mael, Ahren's advisor, enters the room. The candles in the orbs hanging from the ceiling flicker from his hard, fast steps toward us.

"What is it?" Luther asks, as if sensing his unease.

"His Majesty requests the lady's company." He gives the princes a small bow of his head, then looks my way.

"What for?" Ahren mutters.

"He didn't say." He doesn't say anything else but stands there, waiting for a response to give the king.

"Then I will attend with her," Ahren announces.

"Your Highness." Mael bows his head. "The king specifically said he wants to talk to her alone."

I stiffen, the cake in my stomach swirling, and I shove my spine against the back of the seat. "I-I don't know if that's a good idea," I murmur.

"You can't deny his request, my lady," Mael explains to me with a gentle voice.

"What does he really want?" Luther asks Ahren.

A shiver races up my back at the thought that the king knows who I am.

Ahren tilts his head up, his lips thinning. "Mael, please advise the king that Gainy will join him after her meal. Perhaps imply we have just started eating."

The advisor nods vigorously and retreats quickly back into the kitchen.

I meet Ahren's stormy irises and ask, "Is this a good idea?"

Ahren

"*I*f you don't go to the king, things will end badly for you," I explain, my words clipped and fast. I'm agitated about why he wants to see her. Did he see something during the battle? I shake those thoughts away. I won't panic. The king has always been an inquisitive man and often invites new people in his court for a casual conversation to get to know them.

I look over to Guendolyn, who's studying her half-eaten cake slice.

Ever since last night, she's been on my mind. In my veins. In my dreams. I can't get her fucking out, and sitting so far from her has me knotted up. I want to roar the anger out of me.

I expected her to follow me into my room, to finish what we started. Instead, she left. Now I meet her stony stare while an inferno blazes in mine.

Her scent still clings to my nose and fogs my mind. All I can think about is imprinting myself on her, biting her, anything to remind her she's mine. To rip that pretty blue dress she wears off her body before I sink into that sweet pink pussy and fuck her balls-deep.

I huff out a deep, frustrated breath, then take my chalice and down several mouthfuls of wine. Luther watches me. He knows I'm agitated. Hell, I've been so fucking horny since yesterday that my balls are swollen and aching for release.

Guendolyn shifts in her seat uncomfortably. "What if he suspects something, asks me questions? God, what if he insists I'm to do…stuff with him?" Panic surges like a tidal wave in her eyes, and she pushes the plate of cake away from her. "I can't do this. I say lots of shit when I'm nervous."

A nerve ticks in my neck at the thought of the king touching her.

"He's not going to touch you," Luther says, drawing me out of my thoughts. "He can be a bastard, but I've never seen him hurt women. Stick to the story we discussed about why you're here. Ask him questions, as he loves to talk, and then he'll forget to pry into your affairs."

I slide my gaze to her as she nods enthusiastically. She wears a crooked smile, that vulnerable side of her coming out, touching me. A nerve pulses against my temple at how much she distracts me.

She'll hate my pity, but right now, she only has us two to help her in the Wandering Realm. "Look, I'll walk you to the palace and give you some more tips along the way."

Her chin raises, her eyes opening wider for a moment, looking at me as if I have an alternate motivation. "You don't have to."

"I insist," I reply.

"I'm sure you have better things to do," she sneers, looking me up and down. This firecat challenges me again, and I lick my teeth, staring at her with so much promise of what's to come.

"When I make a promise, I keep my word."

Her brow furrows. "There were no promises made. Just an offer for me to decide."

She is seriously getting on my nerves to the point

where I will tan her ass until it blushes with my hand-print. "And you decided wrong."

She gasps, stunned at my response. Did she really assume I didn't want her to join me? Had I not made it clear enough? I search her expression for an answer, but I'm interrupted by Luther clearing his throat.

"Am I missing something?"

I huff and snap to my feet. "It's nothing." I swing my attention to Guendolyn. "I'll be in the hallway when you're ready." She blinks at me, but I turn and make my way to the door before I say something fucking stupid.

I'm letting her get under my skin.

I press my back against the wall in the shadows of the hallway. Around her I react purely on instinct, shoving aside all rational thoughts. This isn't who I am, and especially not when I need to keep my head straight. Except she's gotten to me and has become my obsession.

After a long moment, she steps out of the room and walks right past me without a second thought of where I might be. I snag her wrist, and she flinches around in surprise before tugging her hand back.

My grasp tightens. "You're with me." I stride forward, dragging her alongside me. We march down the hallway and are swallowed by empty corridors, the maids' voices sounding in the distance. We leave the dining room far behind us as my boots thump on the black rug leading us across the mansion.

"What the hell is your problem?" she snaps at me.

"You speak with such disrespect. You talk to the king this way, and you'll lose your head."

"You demand too much of me."

I glance around and haul her across the hall and into an empty room. There are so many barren rooms in the mansion with only my brothers, me, and the servants living here. The intention is to fill this place once the three of us find brides and marry. Fuck, that's the last thing on my mind right now. I can't imagine marrying someone else when *she's* right here in front of me.

As I kick the door shut behind us, the globes light up the large room. I swing Guendolyn around, pushing her back to the wall, and a small squeak escapes her mouth. Her hands instinctively fly up to my chest, pushing against me. I feel the tension in her as her surprised expression dissolves to anger. Bracing my hands on the wall on either side of her head, I lean in, giving her no chance to escape. I inhale her sweet scent, and my cock hardens.

"What part of last night didn't you understand?" I ask.

She stares at me, bewildered.

I endure a moment's hesitation as she inhales sharply and exhales out a long sigh. I smell the peach juice on her breath as my gaze falls to her full lips.

She licks them, staring into my eyes. "Are you always this rude and pushy?"

"When you don't listen to me I am."

Her teeth dig into her bottom lip. "There's nothing to tell. I—"

"Don't lie to me."

Her eyes narrow, and the corner of her mouth quirks, her every move calculated.

"Do I need to remind you of my punishment for lying?"

"I—" She struggles to talk, and fuck, that drives me wild. I want to give it all to her, and now. To rip away that smug look on her face and replace it with one of absolute ecstasy.

"You want to know the truth?" she blurts out.

"Yes," I growl.

"You scare me. The things you made me feel scare me."

Her words catch me off-guard like a slap to the face as she tells me the truth—how her desire for me leaves her frightened. Has she never been with a man before?

She suddenly pushes forward, and her lips graze mine. I breathe against them, slide my hand to the back of her head, and kiss her hard.

I lose myself, a growl rolling over my throat, and I let myself fall to the savage hunger inside me. Around her, I'm losing my mind. I taste her swollen lips and explore her mouth. "You make me crazy with need," I murmur.

She kisses me again and slides her tongue into my mouth. I wrap my arms around her petite frame, pressing her to me, feeling the swell of her breasts, the tremble of her body. I move my hands down her back and over her perfect ass. The new blue dress she wears tonight is long and has too much fabric for my liking.

The small sound in her throat pushes me closer to the edge where I won't be able to stop. I suck on her tongue, on her lips. I'm so fucking starved for her. No woman has ever done this to me before.

"How much do you want me?" she whispers against my mouth.

"I'd climb into the heavens and carve the moon out of the sky for you," I admit, as corny as it sounds in my head.

Her hand reaches between us and slides over my cock in my pants. I growl as my pulse zaps through my veins.

Our kiss deepens, and I'm falling so fast and deep, I'll never find my way back out.

Loud footfalls resonate on the hallway floorboards outside the room. "Where the hell is she?" Mael's voice pierces the perfect moment. "Find Luther; I'll search for Ahren. The king's patience runs low."

"Fuck," I whisper under my breath as I break from Guendolyn.

Those gorgeous lips are bruised red from my hard kisses, her eyes imploring me to continue, her parting mouth demanding I fuck her up against the wall.

"I need to take you to the king," I mutter.

"Right now?" Her cheeks glow.

"Yes, now. We need to hurry," I growl, fucking frustrated that we have to leave this unfinished.

CHAPTER 11

GUENDOLYN

The walk to the palace is silent.

Ahren leads me over the bridge between the two buildings. The night is icy and snow falls feathery soft, covering everything. By the time we reach the palace, I'm trembling. Warmth encases me as soon as the doors are shut behind us, as though the building has insulated heat. Unlike the dark colors of the mansion that remind me of a gothic church, everything here is elegant with gleaming white marble and polished gold. Golden framed portraits of fae fill the walls, each subject more spectacular and gorgeous than the last. Is there such a thing as an ugly fae? I have yet to meet one.

Guards are posted at every turn, standing tall in their midnight blue uniforms, their fitted jackets with gilded buttons running diagonally from their waist to a shoulder. An insignia of a golden wing pierced by an arrow sits on each of their left arms.

Finally, we reach two grand doors the color of snow

with ornate golden handles. I assumed we would go to the throne room, except this is a different room. Uniformed guards draw the doors open, revealing an opulent sitting room that has me frozen on the spot, as if I just walked into Disneyland.

Arched mullioned windows with golden frames cover three of the walls, and the corners are laced with frost from the frigid night. Dozens upon dozens of the glass globes hang from the lofty ceiling, each glowing a different color. My insides beam at seeing the rainbow of turquoise, magenta, marmalade, and so many other colors across the ceiling overhead, and I can't stop looking at them. It feels like I've walked into the kind of fantasy world I'd expect in movies. At the end of the room is a golden fireplace, intricately carved and flanked by two giant statues of beautiful women with wings. They seemed to be reaching for the sky. There are four guards near the fireplace and couches, watching over the king.

Ahren places his hand on my lower back and ushers me inside. I stumble forward, my shoes tapping at the golden path that will take me to the semi-circle of black leather couches facing the fire. The door shuts with a decisive thud, and I whip around to find myself closed in here without Ahren.

"Come over already, I don't bite," the king barks from over at the fireplace. Looking closely, I can only see the top of his head from where he sits on the couch.

My insides twist as I walk closer, and I feel like I'm heading to the slaughter.

I'm worried that he suspects something of me. That I

might not be from his kingdom, or he knows who I really am and is planning to offer me an ultimatum. Considering the outcome of that, part of me wants this to be as simple as him believing he can make a move on me. That I can deal with.

I swallow past the lump in my throat.

Just get this over with. I march across the room, my steps echoing like hands clapping. I keep looking up at the colors that twinkle with every move I make. As I step alongside the couch, I suddenly find it's not just the king waiting for me, but Jasion too.

My mouth dries.

Alarm bells ring in my head at the possibility that the mage knows something and now they're about to confront me. The princes told me the king doesn't think highly of Jasion, so what reason can there be for both of them being together?

"Ah, Gainy, good of you to join me. Take a seat." The king jerks his chin to the couch adjacent to his.

My feet refuse to move at first, as my gaze sweeps from the king, then to Jasion.

"Evening, Gainy. It's good to see you again," Jasion states formally, his attention dipping to my lips. Can he tell I've just been kissing Ahren? Is my face blushing wildly? When I meet his stare, all I see is hunger—a fae who believes I'm a stepping stone for him to grow his power and standing in the court.

He turns to the king as he straightens his back. He's still wearing the robe-skirt and no shirt with heavy black boots too.

"Your Majesty, I will take my leave, and we can resume our discussion on the morrow."

"Yes, yes." The king waves him off, his eyes locking on me.

Jasion bows his head and walks away toward the door. As if sensing his presence, the doors open and the guards are there to greet him as he marches past them and vanishes around the corner. Then the doors shut once again.

"Sit," the king reminds me.

I do so on the next couch, sitting in the corner closest to him to avoid looking like I am scared by keeping my distance. Even though I'm shaking, I hold myself still since I don't need the king to suspect me of being afraid.

The king is handsome for his age, and has a slight ruddy glow on his face, which is framed by white hair. Unlike the previous time I met him, now he wears a simple deep burgundy loose shirt with a lace up tie at his chest that's sitting undone and black pants with lace-up boots. He sits with his legs wide, arms by his side. In front of him is a small golden table with two golden wine chalices on top and a matching jug behind them.

"Don't look so frightened, girl." He shuffles forward in his seat and collects the jug before filling both of the cups. He hands me one. "This should warm you up. Winter seems to have sprung on us early this year."

I accept the cup, my hands trembling.

"Well, drink up," he says, then presses his chalice to his lips and swallows several mouthfuls.

I look down at the deep red wine, the strong aroma of berries and fermentation filling my nose. It smells like normal wine, so I tilt the chalice back, and the liquid rolls into my mouth. Sweetness and honey hit me first, then a strong peppery punch at the back of my throat. I cough, and the king laughs at me.

"Weren't expecting that hit at the end, were you? It will warm you on nights like tonight."

I nod and finish the drink, which is growing on me, despite the heated aftertaste. "Your Majesty, what would you like to talk about?" I figure the quicker we start, the quicker I can leave. It's awkward enough as it is.

"The cold weather always brings on pain from an old injury on my shoulder, and nothing the healers do helps. Jasion suggested I give you a try."

I stiffen, confused by Jasion's actions.

"I can definitely try. My touch seems to have helped others."

"Good." He leans over and takes the jug before filling the cup in my hand.

"Oh, I think that's enough for me." Last thing I want is to end up drunk... but maybe that's the king's intention.

"Nonsense. I need your hands warm before you touch me." He winks like that's a joke, or does he mean something else?

I am struggling to make sense of the king and what his intentions are. In his position, he is probably the master at holding a poker face, having dealt with lots of royals.

He watches me, so I sip down the second helping of

wine and set it on the table before he fills it up once more. Heat rushes down my throat and into my belly, kindling my insides to a warm blaze. I rub my hands together to ensure they are heated too.

"You know what's strange," he begins, "is that none of my healers have sensed you in the city the whole time you've lived here."

Shrugging, I put on a small smile. "I mostly keep to myself. I only help a couple of neighbors who need it." What little Ahren's and Luther have told the king about me comes to mind about what they've told the king about me. The less I say, the better. Just get this over and done with, then I can get out of here.

"The healers do a regular sweep of our population for anyone with abilities. We coud use every able hand in our kingdom in the current circumstance. Perhaps they missed you, somehow."

"They must have." Nerves kicking me, my knees start bouncing, so I inch to the edge of the couch. "Would you like me to try healing your shoulder, Your Majesty?"

There's hesitation in the king's response. He's watching me, and I can see the thoughts swirling behind his eyes. I suspect he doesn't believe the story of my abilities not being picked up.

"When I spoke to Jasion, do you know what he told me?"

I freeze all over and hate where this is going, hate that I feel so trapped. I don't know how many lies I can make up without trapping myself in a web, as I don't know much about this kingdom or realm.

"He told me your power is unlike anything he's felt

before. Something he'd like to better understand... And he can't for the life of him understand how he missed you in the city, as he regularly walks through there to detect any strong powers. You know what he thinks?"

I shake my head, not trusting my voice right now.

"He insists that the princes brought you into our kingdom from elsewhere." He tilts his head to the side, studying me, leaning closer. "So, my question is, who would my princes bring into our home unannounced, and why would they lie about it?"

I suck in a ragged breath as fear pummels me, and I grasp onto every ounce of bravery I have. I loathe Jasion, I decide at that moment. And to think, the last time we talked, he asked me to trust him. But this isn't the time for me to lock up and freeze. Instead, I push out a laugh. It helps that I feel super relaxed from the wine.

"It sounds to me like Jasion is looking for a way to cover his tracks for not detecting me in the first place. You can ask the princes. They stumbled into me about two years ago. Before that, I usually kept to myself and didn't go out much. I'm sure you place more trust in them than a mage." This time I shift closer, leaning my arms over my thighs, holding his stare. The wine's gone to my head and fills me with bravery.

He watches me with a gleam in his eyes. "That so?"

"You know what I believe?" I ask.

"What's that?"

"Jasion is threatened by me."

The king huffs as if surprised, then processes the information. All the while, I'm wracking my brain for what else I can say to turn the tables on Jasion and still sound legit.

"But he's not a healer. Why would he care?" The king fills our cups once more.

Sweat rolls down my spine. The king is indeed inquisitive, and I can tell now this summoning is much more of an interrogation about the red flags Jasion raised about me. I remember everything Jasion said to me over breakfast, well-aware that if he hasn't told it all to the king yet, he will soon enough. So, I'd better to be one step ahead.

"Because of my affinity with fairies." I hold my breath.

He doesn't respond or show any sign of shock. That tells me Jasion has already told him, which I can work in my favor.

"Jasion asked me how I handled the blue-winged fairy who'd been injured during the battle. He was pushy and anxious. He mentioned he hasn't met anyone else who can do that before." I shrug and reach for my chalice. "I can only imagine that's what he's threatened by." I drink down the wine, chasing the lies on my tongue, and set the cup back on the table.

He blinks at me. "Did you call the fairies into the kingdom?"

I gasp on purpose, though on the inside I'm squirming. "I have no idea how they got in, but it's a good thing they did, don't you think?"

The way he studies me sends a shiver up my arms.

I'm suddenly burning hot, and my face feels like it's glowing. Why did I drink that third round of wine?

Finally, he nods and reaches for his cup. "Come, try your healing on me and tell me more about how your affinity with fairies works. Do they listen to your command?" He collects his wine and reclines back on the couch as he pushes down on the fabric of his shirt to reveal a broad shoulder. He grimaces, clearly in pain. There are healed scratches across the white flesh.

"Oh, it's nothing elaborate at all, but more of a coincidence when they seem to help me." I laugh a bit as I get to my feet, and the room tilts around me. Note to self; no more wine.

Navigating to stand alongside his couch, I try to concentrate and remember what I did with Ahren when I healed him. Not much, so I'm going to try the same tactic.

"Is it alright if I sit next to you, Your Majesty?"

"Of course, girl. Tell me how you first encountered fairies."

I slide down on my bent leg so I'm facing him. Lifting my hand, I gingerly set my palm and splayed fingers over his shoulder. His skin is fiery to the touch, but he doesn't react.

For a few moments, I focus on the room to try and stop it from revolving around me. Then I begin making up a story about the fairies...keeping it simple and as close as possible to the truth.

"When I was much younger, I was collecting wild mushrooms outside our walls. Suddenly, two Blood-cursed came out of nowhere and attacked me. I was running for my life when I bumped into the fairies' nest. They swarmed over me, but in all honesty, I was too scared of the Bloodcursed at the time to be too afraid of the fairies."

"Two demons coming at you at once," the king says, nodding his head as though he understands, and drinks his wine.

"But here's the thing. As soon as the Bloodcursed came at me, the fairies turned on them and devoured them down to their bones before my eyes down. Then they let me run back home without coming after me. And ever since, if I see them, it's like they acknowledge me and leave me alone."

"Fascinating. You've heard the story of how fairies came into existence?"

"Of course. Haven't we all?" I snort a laugh then curse myself for snorting in front of a king.

He raises a brow in my direction. "Personally, I've always wanted to believe they are benevolent creatures. They are spawned from revenge after an injustice." He grunts and finishes his wine. Then he leans forward to grab the jug for a refill, and I pull my hand back as he does. When he returns, I don't miss the reddening handprint on his shoulder.

Hopefully, that works on his injury. Ahren's mark vanished after a short while.

"The queen of fairies didn't deserve to be treated the way she was," I say. "And I also think if the fairies can feed just as easily on the Bloodcursed, what if there's a way to make them focus on eliminating the infected?" The room suddenly feels like it's swaying around me.

He turns to me, a grin tugging the corners of his

mouth upward. "I like the way you think. Maybe there's something here you can help us with besides healing."

I nod, strangely eager to make this man smile approvingly. I've clearly had too much wine.

"My first encounter with fairies is embarrassing," he begins. "I was using the outhouse when they burst in on me to hide from a greater danger. You can imagine all of our surprises."

"There's a greater danger to fairies?" I ask, half grinning at the image he just described.

"Definitely." He drinks half his wine, then breaks into his story about fighting off underground beasts that sound like goblins. I'm utterly captivated at learning more about this world. He reminds me of my foster mother's boyfriend, who loved telling tales, but what he loved even more was having an audience. So I provide that for the king, pushing away all other concerns—including my worry that the king thinks I am anything but a local from his kingdom.

CHAPTER 12

"You waited for me," I say to Ahren as I step outside the king's room, the guards shutting the doors behind me.

He greets me with a grin, leaning a shoulder on the wall with his arms folded over his chest. Maybe I've had too much to drink, but to me, he looks like a god...a sexy-as-hell god.

"I wasn't letting you go back alone." The firelight from the torches attached to the wall dances across his gorgeous green eyes.

My knees tremble at the thought of being with a fae who takes so much pleasure from being in my company. Back home, I struggled to get a date, so this feels surreal, overwhelming, and exhilarating. Now I'm feeling all kinds of warm fuzzies on the inside.

"I—" Licking my lips, I step toward him, only to trip over my own feet, so I hastily straighten myself. "I wasn't sure if you would be here."

He arches an eyebrow at my misstep. Then again,

my mind is spinning like a tornado. Whatever wine the king gave me is now in full effect.

Ahren reaches out and takes my hand in his, then pulls me into a walk. "Let's go."

I take quick steps to keep up with him. There are are watching us everywhere, and Ahren doesn't say a word, not until he leads me straight to his room. Which is just as well, because it's taking all of my focus to keep from stumbling again.

Ahren lets go of my hand and shuts the door. "I expected you last night, so I had to make sure you didn't run out on me again."

I swallow hard. "Well, I'm here now. Why dwell on the past?"

Ahren strolls over to the fireplace and bathes in its warmth, studying me.

Like my suite, there is another doorway that leads to the bedroom. In this room, swords and shields cover the walls, along with paintings of a valley with a smaller mansion. It's surrounded by woodlands with a river winding behind it, and there's something simple and calming about the scene. I move closer to one of the paintings, concentrating on each step to avoid falling over. It's taking every ounce of strength to hold it together and not just sit where I am until the room stops whirling.

"Where is this location? It doesn't seem familiar," I say, proud of myself for asking a real question without slurring my words.

He steps up behind me, looming over me and burning me up with his heat. Suddenly, I can't breathe.

All I can think about is how close he stands, how my skin tingles with anticipation of his touch. I'm no fool, and I know exactly why I allowed him to bring me back to his room.

"It's a painting of the home I grew up in," he explains with a melancholy sound in his voice.

"So you didn't grow up as a prince?" I glance over my shoulder at him.

"Oh I did, but Mother insisted we stay there instead of the palace. But that's all in the past." His hands go to my shoulders, and I let out a tiny whimper of need, then he turns me around to face him.

I can't think, I can only see this god-like man staring down at me while my insides soften in his presence.

"Please," I whisper, unsure exactly what I'm begging for. His kiss? For him to take me already? Or for his kindness? Maybe all three.

I reach up and loop my hands around his neck, my fingers interlacing, while I lift myself onto my toes. He tips his head forward, and our mouths clash. Chest to chest, I push my body against him, my nipples hardening.

His hand splays wide over my back and sweeps down to my ass. The size of his palm easily covers a decent portion of my asscheeks, and I shiver at the memory of his fingers inside me, stretching me. His other hand glides to the back of my head, fisting my hair and holding me in place. His beautiful assault on my mouth sends desire through every inch of me. I return the kiss, desperate to jump right back to where we ended yesterday. I shift to slide against him, and his huge erection presses against my lower stomach, pulsing in response.

It tickles me, and I can't stop the laughter from bursting out.

He breaks from me, pulling my head back, and stares at me. "Is something funny?"

I gasp for air between my laughs. "It's just your cock is tickling my stomach." I reach down to touch him over his pants, but he seizes my wrist.

His eyes narrow. "How much have you had to drink tonight?"

I lift my hand and show him all my fingers, then frown. "No, that's not right." I bend two down. "Three chalices."

"You're drunk," he accuses. "I need to take you back to your room. I won't spend a night with you if you're drunk."

"Am not!" In one swift move, I pivot away from him and saunter to his couch before throwing myself down on the soft cushions and rolling onto my back. "Gosh, is the ceiling twirling?"

"Fuck, Guendolyn," he hisses. The way he looks at me is one of judgment.

"Come to me. I have something to show you, something you'll want to see." In my head, I am sounding sexy as hell, yet this fae stares at me with that arrogant demeanor he often wears.

"You need to go get some sleep," he growls, clearly disappointed in me.

"Take me to *your* bed, Ahren?" I plead. "I don't want to sleep alone."

His shoulders soften, and something washes over his face at my request, making him look at me with endearment.

"You know, I like this side of you most of all," I say. "There's no furrowing brow, and that brooding look you usually have is gone."

He steps closer. "Brooding?

"Yeah, where you look permanently angry or constipated…and like you're ready to punch someone."

He huffs heavily, then sweeps me off the couch and lifts me into his arms. I laugh out loud at how fast he does that as he carries me across the room and toward his bedroom.

"Now, that was fun. Let's do it again."

"You don't hold your drink well," he reprimands me, as if that's meant to be insulting.

"Hello, I'm the queen of being a light-weight drinker. I even got drunk at my friend's party on two shots of her vodka."

"Not sure why you think that's a good thing."

"Wow, you are a master at insults, aren't you?"

He shakes his head, exhaling louder.

"You're not perfect either. What you did last night was a dick move," I blurt out, shoving my free hand against his muscles. Oh, so many of them. I run my hands up his rounded shoulders and biceps as I slip my lower lip between my teeth. "You definitely work out."

"I told you there'd be punishment, but apparently, that will have to wait for another night."

"Your punishment is teasing me, then taking the

supposed discipline away." The words rush from my mouth. "It's not just me you're punishing then, is it?"

"The difference is, I have control."

"Hey, I came here because you made a big deal of it. Plus, I've been so freaking horny since last night." My eyes pop open wide. "Oops, I wasn't meant to say that last bit out loud."

Something flashes over his gaze that looks like, a primal hunger, but it's gone as fast as it came. "If you weren't so drunk, I'd tan your ass for drinking so much."

I wave my hands in the air. "Well, your father—"

"Stepfather," he growls.

"He's a great man who has the best stories and made me laugh so much. He told me he loves you and your brothers as much as he does your mother." The king has grown on me, and I can't help but feel differently about him.

"You don't know what you're talking about," he mutters, and walks us into his bedroom.

We enter an enormous room with heavy velvet curtains parted over arched windows. Moonlight streams over the king-sized bed with a monstrous headboard carved into the shape of a huge oak tree.

"Is that made of gold?"

He doesn't respond but lays me in the bed, then covers me in a red blanket. I soften into the cocoon of the mattress and puffy pillows.

"This is so comfortable." My eyes flutter closed and open, and I'm struggling to think as sleep crashes over me.

He brushes the hair off my brow. "Sleep," he orders in a husky rasp.

"No, I..." Dreamland tugs at me, and I can't remember what I was going to say.

"You're going to be the end of me, Guendolyn. The sweetest, most tempting end."

***

"Have you been watching me sleep? It's kinda creepy," I murmur, trying to wake up as I turn onto my side in bed to face Ahren. He's lying on his side on top of the blankets, still fully clothed, studying me.

"If keeping an eye on you is creepy, then I'll accept the title," he responds in a soft tone, as if he's just woken up himself and his walls haven't locked into place yet.

I study him through hooded eyes as the silvery hue of moonlight lights up half of his gorgeous face. I shake my head, clearing up my thoughts this time. "No. That was wrong of me to say."

He reaches over and strokes the back of his fingers down my face. I can't help myself, and my hand automatically goes to his chest, his muscles flexing against me. Something about him makes me want to always touch him.

We've had so many confrontations, and he isn't the most patient or understanding of men. He's quick to speak his mind and criticize, not to mention his issues with being controlling. He is the opposite of what I've always thought I wanted in a man.

Except, I was wrong. So fucking wrong because he is exactly what I desire.

"What are you thinking?" I ask.

"How I never thought I'd have you all to myself," he answers bluntly without any hesitation, but that's Ahren in a nutshell.

My cheeks burn at his confession.

He leans closer to me, his hand on my neck, his gaze sliding to mine. "How's your head feeling?"

"Much better. The wine completely knocked me out."

"Its side effect is heavy sleep. The king drinks it most nights."

"Good to know," I say, our faces so close now. He bends forward and captures my lips with his, soft and demanding at once. His delicious tongue plunges into my mouth almost instantly, and I press myself toward him, kissing him back. He tastes of honey and whiskey.

I'm utterly lost under his spell, knowing where this is going, and I hungrily grasp onto his shirt to hold him in place. Too much has come between us, and I need this. I need him. So I let myself fall, forgetting where I am and the danger all around me, the worry for Deimos, the confusion with Luther. All I care about is about Ahren and me. The other stuff can wait.

Right now, there's only us floating together. It's incredible. Addictive. And I need more.

His hand slides down my shoulder, feather-soft, then

peels back the blankets covering my body, and a chill encases me. His large, warm hand finds my breast and squeezes. Flesh to flesh…

Whoa, wait up!

I break from his melting kiss and look down to find I'm not wearing anything, then I shoot a glance back up at him. "Did you strip me?"

"Of course. You can't sleep with clothes on comfortably. Is there a problem?"

I raise a brow. "You can't undress a woman while she's sleeping! Now, *that* is creepy."

He grins mischievously, his eyes almost darkening when he looks at me as if he took a lot of joy in getting me nude. "You worry about strange things. Now will you let me have my way with you and do as I please, beautiful?" His voice carries a longing.

There is no way I can say no to such an offer, so I nod. "I'm yours."

He takes my hand and presses it to his mouth. His tongue traces the length, from the base of my palm to the tip of my fingers. I tremble with exhilaration, wanting that tongue all over me.

"It's only fair that you take your clothes off too," I murmur, my voice barely a whisper.

There is no hesitation in his actions as he climbs out of bed. He stands tall, staring at me the whole time as his large hands pull at the buttons on his midnight blue shirt and part the fabric. My gaze dips to his washboard abs, then to that sexy as hell, sharply-cut V at his hips while his shirt cascades off his shoulders and to the ground. He pops open the button on his pants and bends down, dragging them to his ankles, then kicks them aside. When he stands, my attention falls to his cock.

Erect.

Large.

All mine.

The tip glistens with pre-cum, and he strokes himself a few times, his upper lip curling up as if he's barely holding on.

I shuffle across the bed to his side and reach over to grasp him. He lets go of his hardness, and I wrap my fingers around his thickness. It's so warm to the touch, and the skin is silky soft, yet hard as rock underneath. I slide my hand over him, and he hisses, his eyes rolling back. He moans, and it sounds so incredible. His noises alone have me shivering with need, and the apex between my thighs pulses in eagerness to have him.

One swipe with his hand, and he nudges my hand away. "Enough. Tonight is going to last. With no more interruptions, you are mine to do with as I will." He moves to stand at the end of the bed, facing me.

He's tall and broad… Seeing him standing over me reminds me just how much larger he is than me. How small I actually am in comparison. Bending toward me, he grasps my ankles and yanks me down the bed.

"Whoa!" My stomach lurches from the movement.

Moonlight catches on the healed scars that run over his shoulders from where he was whipped as a child. My heart clenches as I remember his past, except the man standing before me is fucking powerful despite what his asshole father did to him. I can't help but admire someone who can go through so much shit and still hold it together. Half the time, I feel twisted on the inside after growing up and moving from one foster family to another until I found my forever family. Still, I always felt like I didn't belong with them…or anywhere. Until I arrived here. A strange sensation coats my insides, like somehow, this is a homecoming.

"I can see your mind spinning with thoughts. What distracts you from me?" He lays his hands on my knees, forcing them open as he drops to his knees before me at the end of the bed.

That gesture covers me in goosebumps, and I forget everything on my mind.

I gasp as his breath finds my slick heat.

"Fuck, you're so beautiful," he mutters and leaves a trail of kisses down my inner thighs, his lips as soft as feathers. "I'm going to eat you now."

I'm not sure how to respond, but the word "Yes" slips from my mouth. I chew on my lower lip, my heart thumping in my chest faster, louder.

This gorgeous fae, a freaking heir to the throne, is going down on me!

His mouth seals over my pussy, ,then he sucks, and I cry out from the pleasure crashing into me. He licks me over and over with the hard tip of his tongue, and I spread my legs wider, my whole body quivering. Relentlessly, he tugs at my inner lips, keeping his focus on my clit.

I arch my back as he savagely helps himself to me, as he satiates himself. With one hand, he reaches up and grabs my breast, then plucks at my nipple. His other hand presses a finger inside me, and I run my hand through his hair to the back of his head, then push him deeper into me. Arousal aches deeply in me with such intensity, I can barely hold myself together. I'm going to explode any moment.

My body shudders, my hips rocking back and forth. He takes my eagerness well and lashes his tongue over my silky length. When he adds a second thick finger into me, I lose it. I'm shaking, and all I see is white as I scream through the most incredible orgasm I've ever experienced.

Ahren tugs on my clit, elongating the climax and teasing me. I shut my eyes, clasp the bedsheet, and convulse as he takes me into his mouth. I don't know how long I'm floating, but I try to hold on to the pulsing sensation for as long as possible. I'd give anything for more moments like these, when I can't remember real life.

Finally, I float back down to reality and open my eyes, my body vibrating with elation. I can't stop smiling, and find Ahren watching me from between my legs, grinning. His lips and chin glisten in the moonlight, and lust fills his eyes.

I shuffle back on the bed as he climbs on and crawls to me on all fours. Lingering over me, his arms plant on either side of my shoulders, and he smiles down at me.

"Guendolyn, I'm going to make you forget about everything in the best way possible." He leans in and kisses me, tasting me, claiming me. I can feel it in the way he takes control so possessively. I taste myself on his mouth, my sex smell intoxicating.

"I need to know," he begins, whispering in my ear. "Am I to be your first?" He pulls back and looks at me.

For a long pause, I'm at a loss for words, as that's the last thing I expected to hear from him. With me beneath him, it's a bit too late to feel shy about these things. "No," I say. "You're my second."

He nods. "I wanted to make sure, angel, because I don't want to hurt you and—"

"Please stop talking," I manage. "Just take me. I'm stronger than you think, and I won't break. I promise."

The growl in his throat makes me smile.

"Fuck me," I plead.

"I love when you speak to me that way. Now let me make that pretty pussy of yours purr."

He guides the tip of his cock against my heat. His flesh is scorching hot, and I moan from the touch alone. He presses his cock into me slowly, and I hold on as he inches in deeper and deeper, widening me. God, he's big, and pleasure washes through me at the feel of him inside him. He presses his face to my neck and inhales me.

I gasp loudly and grip onto his muscular arms. I crave this fae who bucks his hips, sliding smoothly in and out of me. Flooding me, stretching me, owning me as he swings back and forth into me. The faster he goes, the more the friction between us ignites. With each plunge, he presses against my clit, as if he does it on purpose. He drives harder, his balls slapping against me.

"Fuck!" he grits out, fucking me so hard, my whole body jerks, my heart matching the rhythm. "You see what you do to me, angel?"

He's so hot, and I'm breathing quicker, practically panting. He growls, and I can tell he's going to come any moment now.

"Come for me again. Scream for me," he whispers in my ear, his hips pounding into me, never stopping his gorgeous assault.

A wave of explosions slams into me, dragging me under. I shake uncontrollably as my whole body contracts, and I groan from the pleasure wrapping around me. My muscles clench around his dick, squeezing him as he shoots hot cum inside me, and he roars like a lion as he comes. I scream my own pleasure, and our voices twist together into something beautiful. I don't know how long we stay locked that way, but when he finally pulls out of me, my body feels tender and a bit sore. I sag back on the bed, sweating and breathing heavily.

With a devious smirk, he stands up from the bed and turns to walk out of the room.

"Hey, where are you going?" I tilt my head up, staring at that firm ass.

"Be back soon." He glances at me over his shoulder. "I'm getting something to clean you up, then I want you on your hands and knees. Ass in the air, legs spread, and your tight little pussy exposed. We're going again." His words undo me, and already my heart beats in the pulse between my legs.

I may never walk again after tonight.

CHAPTER 13

LUTHER

I swallow, my throat growing dry. Deimos lies in bed where the magic keeps him alive, but for how long? His time is ticking, and we're still waiting for the damn message from the king's contact in Ash Court.

I'm losing my grip, because my brother has one week and we've already lost three days. If we don't get a response today, Ahren and I will depart for Ash Court tonight. I'll tear down the entire Unseelie palace if needed to find a cure for Deimos.

He's so pale. All I want is to hear his voice and for him to tell his stupid jokes. I swear if he survives this, I'll laugh at every one of them.

Worry strangles me. What if we're too late? What if...? Fuck, Deimos can't die. I can't lose him. Barbed emotions drag through me, cresting easily, and too many things come at me, overwhelming me. I clench my hands and grit my teeth, lost in my thoughts and staring down at the floor, when the door behind me creaks open.

"Luther, there you are," my stepfather says with impatience in his voice.

I don't turn to face him as his footsteps close in. He joins me, staring down at Deimos, and says nothing at first.

"The bird carrier just arrived from Ash Court," he states abruptly.

With the realization of what he's implying, I glance at him, locking my gaze on his face. He's not smiling but not frowning either. I bristle on the inside, wishing that maybe for once, he could just show some fucking emotions.

"What did it say?" I ask rapidly.

He lifts a rolled-up piece of parchment in his hand and opens it to reveal a few words, which he reads aloud. "'East entrance to servant quarters.'"

"That's all? You sure this isn't a setup?" I ask. The king's delivered letter could have been intercepted by anyone at Ash Court.

"It's Relle's handwriting, and the location is where we always used to meet. She is most likely expecting me, as I only sent her one word, which was our code for when I had to see her urgently."

I nod, processing everything he's telling me, though I have so many questions. Questions we've been told never to ask him, as we must always let a king keep his secrets. But if we're going to risk our lives, I want to understand the relationship he has with those in Ash Court. "I don't understand why you used to visit Ash

Court when the Unseelie would kill you if they found out."

He snorts, completely frustrated with my question. "Concentrate on the mission. My friend Relle is helpful, and you will need to give her this." He sticks his hand into the pocket of his gold and purple surcoat and pulls out a diamond-studded bracelet.

I frown when I look up at him, my eyes narrowing.

"She's not my lover. Fuck, Luther, focus! I've always gifted her jewels to help her provide for her family, and this will also let her know you are with me. Explain to her what you need, and she can demand her price. I'll pay it if she gets us the cure for Deimos from their mages."

My mind races with scenarios of who this contact could be. The darkness sweeping over my stepfather's eyes tells me he won't reveal anything, so maybe we'll uncover the truth from Relle.

"Anything else we should know?" I ask, thinking of the carriage I arranged earlier for our trip, the horses selected, supplies and weapons packed. "Does Ahren know?"

"I can't find Ahren, so let him know and head off this morning. No delays, understand? Tell no one where you two are going. I have asked my mages to create a cloaking spell for your carriage, and one for you and Ahren to enter Ash Court grounds." He pauses, staring at me but seeming to look right through me. "There's a huge tree along the east wall that allows for an easy climb up and over."

I nod and straighten, my mind going over anything else we might have missed for the trip, but we're ready.

"Of course." Part of me plays on the notion of visiting Guendolyn for no other reason than to see her one more time...just in case. Just in case the worst happens. Hell, that's a terrible idea. She will ask questions, and I'll cave. "I better go."

When I turn away, my stepfather seizes my arm.

I face him, expecting him to have forgotten something crucial. Except he's staring at me with a strange look in his eyes. Is that concern swimming in his gaze? I must be imagining things.

"Luther, I may not have been the best father to you and your brothers, but I've only ever wanted to give you all the best."

"You don't—"

"Just fucking listen for once," he growls, then exhales loudly, the anger fading from his face. "I screwed up when you all were young, by not spending time with you and pushing you all aside. But I'm going to fix that. When you return and Deimos is healed, I want us to spend more time together. I want...I want to be a real family."

I'm lost for words. Utterly lost. This isn't the king I've known most of my life, but a man eager to make amends. Before I can respond, he hauls me against him in an awkward hug and slaps my back twice before breaking away.

He clears his throat. "Good luck, my son."

Then he marches out of the room.

I'm left standing bewildered for a few moments,

then I look over at Deimos. "Did you hear that? Maybe the bastard is getting soft in his old age."

***

Ahren

"I don't trust Gainy," Jasion mutters with such distaste in his voice that it sickens me. "She's lying and can't be trusted. What if she's here from Ash Court? I know she's not from this kingdom, so she has obviously lied to you."

Jasion marches back and forth in front of the window in my study. I remain in my seat, as the hearth nearby keeps me warm. Shelves full of books line the walls, and I often use this room to take my time away from everyone.

The snow has stopped falling and the sun peeks out from behind the heavy cloud cover. Maybe today will be a day of good fortune and we'll finally hear news from the king's contact. Luther insists we are leaving tonight if we hear nothing, and I can't agree more.

"Ahren, are you even paying attention to what I'm saying?" Jasion growls, and I groan under my breath at his rant.

"You don't need to worry about her, trust me on this. She is safe. Now, is there something else you need to speak to me about?"

My patience wanes today, and concentrating on the mage's skepticism is wearing me thin. He's too close to the truth of discovering who Guendolyn is, which annoys me. He's always been paranoid about every small thing, watching the other mages, believing they were conspiring to kill him, scrutinizing anyone I speak with. I have accepted this is part of his personality, but maybe his behavior is my fault for not putting an end to it when it started. By letting him think I tolerate his paranoia, he's crossing the line right now with Guendolyn. I want him the fuck away from her. There's enough shit going on without dealing with a neurotic mage.

He huffs and fiddles with the skull around his neck. I've always disliked that thing, but I also know the mages use some of the fairy skulls' energy to enhance their own. There's magic in their bones, ancient sorcery from times long ago. That's the real reason Jasion has suddenly been paying so much attention to Guendolyn—he witnessed her ability to control a fairy. And in his eyes, he sees the potential of power she might possess, and that's exactly why I want him away from her.

"You can't trust her," he reiterates. "I'm going to find out exactly who she is and her intentions."

I stand up from the seat and approach him. "I'm saying this as your prince, not your friend, Jasion. Don't go near her. Don't talk to her. Don't let me hear you did anything foolish." Fury burns through me, and I grind my back teeth. I've never seen him this worked up before about anyone. Usually, if I tell him to leave something alone, he backs down. What the fuck is wrong with him today?

His upper lip curls with a hatred I've never seen before. "You trust that whore because she spreads her legs for you, when I've been by your side from the beginning."

My anger nearly explodes through me, knowing he's spied on Guendolyn and me. He must have caught us in the hallway, but I don't fucking get why it bothers him so much. "Be careful, Jasion." My hands curl, and I'm seething.

His face screws up, his chest rising and falling fast. "I don't understand why you're so protective of her. I've told you that I'll always have your back. I'm just trying to protect you. Let me take her into questioning. You know I can be very persuasive." His deplorable smirk has me loathing him. I've seen him enjoy interrogating others before and taking it further than it needs to go.

I get in his face and lower my voice to a growl. "Listen carefully, because you are having problems hearing me. I'm telling you to back the fuck off. Touch her, and I'll kill you myself. Is that clear enough?"

He flinches at my threat, his brows pulling together into an angry knot. Fire flares behind his eyes, and I can physically see him warring with himself in his expression.

With tight lips, he gives me a perfunctory bow of his head. "Of course, Your Highness."

My heart is pounding in my chest at how furious he's made me. I'll set a guard outside Guendolyn's room and ensure she no longer walks around the mansion on her own. Something about Jasion is off, and I can't risk him doing something stupid. There's enough shit to worry about without this added to the heap.

Jasion tilts his head up, meeting my gaze. "You would tell me if she's anything but a local healer, wouldn't you?" His neediness grates on my nerves.

"Get the fuck out of my room," I growl.

He nods and starts to turn away, but looks at me once more. "She's just a whore you're infatuated with. I know plenty more who are better and—"

My fist flies at him, clipping him in the side of the face. I'm furious and can't hold back any longer.

"Get the fuck out!" I bellow before I murder him.

He snarls under his breath as his hand goes to the blood trickling from beneath his eye, staring at me defiantly for a moment. Then he marches out of the study, shutting the door behind him with a bang.

"Fuck!" Jasion has always been loyal, so what the hell?

The door swings open, and I jerk around with fury, only to find it's Luther.

He gives me a weird look, but still asks, "What the hell's up with you?"

I heave each shallow breath and calm myself. "What do you want?"

"I have good news, brother." He crosses the room.

"About fucking time, I could use some."

"We received a response from the king's contact in Ash Court, and we need to leave now." He speaks quickly, reminding me of the times he went hunting, full of adrenaline and fueled to fight. "Deimos only has four days left, so we need to hurry."

"About damn time. I have something I need to do first, so I'll meet you down in the stables."

Luther nods, eager as fuck. "Oh, and the king said not to tell anyone where we're going. I don't think we should let Guendolyn know either, in case she lets it slips to someone."

"Agreed." Plus, she'll insist on coming with us and I don't want to leave on a bad note with her. It's crappy enough I left our bed this morning without saying a word. I should have woken her with a kiss, except I'm just fooling myself thinking there can be more between us. I don't fucking know where my mind is. It's bursting with so much information about what's going on, I'm not coping with the emotions as well as I usually would.

First, I need to help Deimos. Then I can sort out things with Guendolyn.

"Alright," Luther throws over his shoulder as he charges out of my room. "We leave as soon as possible, so get your ass down there immediately."

He vanishes, and I'm left in the room, stewing over Jasion, over needing to keep Guendolyn safe while we're gone...and then reality finally sinks in. We're about to break into the enemy court, and should anything go wrong, it could spell our deaths.

CHAPTER 14

GUENDOLYN

"Are you ready for your surprise?" Luther teases.

"What is it?" I squeak.

Something looks different about him tonight. Why is he so excited? He's smiling too much, and his touch warms my body. I long to sit with him and just talk about us, learn more about him, but when he excitedly burst into my room in the mansion, insisting we had to leave right away, his exhilaration was like a fever enveloping me. Talking could wait, I guess.

"You'll see," he says, his grin captivating as we run through the woods. With him, I don't feel scared. Maybe I should, but not tonight.

When he finally comes to a stop, we stand in front of a square wooden platform with railings on three sides. It's big enough for two or three people inside.

"What is that?" I'm breathing heavily, while he's barely broken a sweat.

He steps inside and guides me to follow him. "Welcome to my Ferris wheel."

I eye him suspiciously, but on the inside, I'm squirming with joy. Not only did he remember what we'd talked about when he spoke to me in my mind, but he made one. It looks nothing like the ones back home, since this is a simple platform that I assume just takes us upward, but he's never seen a Ferris wheel. He based his creation on my description, so I am excited to see what he made, and my stomach somersaults at the notion that he created this for me.

"I'm at a loss for words." I step onto the platform.

"That'll be a first." His hand finds my lower back, drawing me closer, and I sag against him. "Now hold on."

He stands so close now, I can feel the hard muscles of his chest and smell his breath, honey and blueberries and all masculine. He tugs hard on a rope with one hand, and in a heartbeat, our platform lurches and catapults upward. A whirring sound buzzes, like rope running over a metal wheel. My stomach pitches, and I shudder while clutching on to him, my hands bunching up his shirt as I plaster myself to him.

He laughs as the wind brushes against us, one large hand holding me in place the other gripping the wooden railing. We might end up soaring through the skies with how fast we travel as we slide up alongside lofty pine trees, their scent wafting on the breeze.

"Do you like my Ferris wheel?" he asks, his voice buffeting against the rush of air.

I hold on to him for dear life, the heat of his body pouring over me. "It's fantastic."

***

I rush down the mansion hallway in yesterday's dress, and morning sunlight harshly cuts across my path from the windows of open rooms. Last night's dream of Luther's homemade Ferris Wheel still clings to my mind. The memory from the dream comes alive in me and leaves behind a tenderness from the reminder that he did such a thing for me. I just want to remember everything so I stop feeling so lost. I promise myself to ask him about it when I see him next.

The open rooms I pass are empty—no sign of the princes.

How long did I sleep in? I woke up in Ahren's bed, and his side was cold. After the most incredible night of my life, I expected to wake up in his arms, but maybe I was fooling myself.

No, I refuse to go down that rabbit hole, thinking that this was a one-off thing for him. Sure, he's the heir to the throne and there are expectations for him. That must be why he left me alone in his bed after a night of unbridled Kama Sutra.

Seriously, Ahren was insatiable, and every step I take now brings a delicious ache between my legs. It reminds me of him devouring my body for hours last night, and fucking me in so many positions, I lost track. If that was the typical libido of the fae, I am in for a massive roller-coaster ride.

Darting into my room, I've just shut the door, when seconds later, someone knocks on it. I pivot and run to it, expecting Ahren.

Dana stands in the doorway, and my heart sinks when I realize it's not Ahren waiting for me. It annoys me how much he's affected me after one night of sex. I should know better, because from everything I've learned about us, we can't be together, yet I fell prey to my sex-driven body.

"My lady, your bath awaits you." She delivers the words with a delighted grin, as if she loves to boss me around.

I blink at her, trying to calm the disappointment jabbing at my insides. "Have you seen Ahren this morning?"

Dana shakes her head, her brown curls bouncing across her shoulders. "We will find him after your bath, now come with me. You can't see the princes looking like that." She takes my wrist and tugs me to follow her. Reluctantly, I cave in and go because a bath sounds perfect. I glance down at my wrinkled blue dress and can only assume my hair is a mess.

"I have a surprise for you," she says, glancing across to me as she fights to hold back a smile.

"What is it?"

"I have filled your wardrobe with over a dozen outfits suited to royalty. The princes ordered them so you will have a selection to pick from."

My eyes widen. "Really? They did that for me?" Then the thought crosses my mind that Dana must have come into my room this morning when I wasn't there.

"I could never save enough money to afford to purchase such a wardrobe in my entire life, so count yourself lucky."

All I can think is that she's been in my room and noticed I didn't sleep in my bed last night. What does she think? That I'm the girl the princes are enjoying for payment in the form of clothes? "Dana, I'm only here to help heal Deimos."

"Of course, my lady." But she won't look at me when she talks.

I grind my back teeth, well aware she doesn't believe me. All the staff in the mansion must be gossiping about me as the princes' latest conquest. Fuck! I shouldn't care because it's better than everyone here knowing the truth, but it makes me wonder how many females the princes have brought into their mansion. A fire flares in my chest at the mental images the thought creates.

In the bathroom, we make a beeline for a tub filled with water. Wisps of heat curl upward, and the air is ripe with a pine scent. I'm ready to wash myself clean and start a new day. I swear I can still smell Ahren and his musky cum on me.

"I hope it's not too rude of me to say," Dana begins, "but I see the way the princes look at you, my lady."

After undressing, I climb into the tub, then slide down into the hot water and wrap my arms around my bent knees. "I'm sure they're just being nice, Dana. They are royalty, and I'm just a commoner."

She laughs and moves to stand behind me before starting to wet my hair with a pitcher. "I've seen them with other ladies, and they never looked at them this way. What a heart wants doesn't follow the rules made by a king."

***

Breakfast comes and goes, and there's still no sign of Luther or Ahren. Now I'm in a sitting room with two walls of windows that overlook the picturesque mountains coated in snow. I stand in front of the spectacular view to try to distract myself, except it takes everything in me not to burst out of this room and demand someone tell me where the princes are.

Dana promised to track them down…that was over half an hour ago. If I hadn't spent the night with Ahren, I probably wouldn't care, but something at the back of my mind nags me that the night means something different to him than it did to me. I hate thinking that way.

I turn abruptly on my heels when Jasion strolls into the room. His shoulders are broad, chest bare, and his robe-skirt sashays around his legs. My heart bangs loudly in my ears. What's he doing here? Ahren wouldn't have told him what we got up to, would he? I lick my lips nervously.

"Morning," he says with a grin. "How are you feeling?"

"I'm fine." I look around, avoiding eye contact so he gets the hint that I don't want his company.

"Dana is worried about you," he says. "Saying you were frantically asking for the princes."

I jerk my head up. He moves to stand in front of the

fireplace, warming his hands. I watch him suspiciously, convinced he's making up crap. He's trying to get a reaction out of me.

"You know Dana, she's always so dramatic." I half laugh, hiding my nervousness. "She reminds me of my mother. Always thinking the worst of any scenario, but I know it comes from a place of caring. Anyway, what brings you here?" I'm talking too fast and breathing quicker. There goes trying to play calm.

He doesn't respond right away. When he does, his voice is inquisitive. "You have a different dialect than others from this region," he says with his back to me.

"My mother isn't from this kingdom, so guess I picked up her way of speaking."

"And where is she from?" He turns to face me, the skull on his necklace swinging across his chest.

He's so predictable. I expected him to ask that question, so I use the same lie Deimos told Gabel. "She's from Waverton, a horribly dry place, apparently. They all speak a bit funny there."

He scans me head to toe. The more time I spend with this fae, the more he scares me. "Have you visited Waverton?" he asks me.

I shake my head. "Have you?" I'm not used to this back and forth war of words, and it makes my stomach ache.

He straightens. "No. The heat doesn't agree with me." Such a weird comment.

Silence sweeps between us. "The princes will be gone for a few days, and if you—"

"Wait, they're going away? Where?"

A smirk quirks the corners of his mouth upward. "That's not my place to say, but they may have already left."

They must be going to find a cure or something for Deimos. Ahren didn't even wake me up before leaving this morning? Heaviness sinks through me. "Where are they going?" I repeat.

"Why is that important to you?" Jasion's brow raises, impatiently waiting for me to respond.

Ahren seems like a good judge of character, and he trusts Jasion, but my gut tells me not to.

This time, I pull back my tense shoulders and shrug. "Curiosity, I guess." I'm tired of sparring with this fae who stares at me like a bug. My mind is frantically swirling at hearing Ahren and Luther are leaving the kingdom. I don't want to be left alone in this place.

I move toward the door when Jasion mutters, "I know you are not who you say you are."

My insides tremble, and his warning hits me hard. He's never going to give up… and while the two princes are gone, what's going to stop this asshole from going to the king and convincing him to imprison me, or worse yet… kill me? What if he has a way of finding out I'm from the Unseelie court? The thought of him talking with the king about me last night haunts me, echoing in my mind.

"I refuse to keep arguing with you about this. If you don't believe me, then take it up with Luther and Ahren upon their return."

My gaze locks on the door as I march forward, but

shivers crawl up the back of my legs as I sense Jasion watching me.

"There are eyes everywhere in this kingdom, girl. Especially on you."

Shock rattles through my system. "You're having me watched?" Spinning around, I face the mage, tired of his threats. I don't even know him, but he treats me like a criminal. My gaze searches the darkness behind his eyes, leaving me feeling uneasy. There is something not right about him.

"Of course." He snorts. "And do you know what my priority is?"

I don't respond as I study this monster who wants a reaction out of me.

"Ensuring Ahren isn't harmed. All I ask is that you're open with me before this escalates. If you care for Ahren, you will tell me the truth and let me help you."

The only person who will take this further is Jasion. I don't trust a single thing about him.

"Help me with what?" I snap as a shiver slithers down my spine. How much does he know? Or is he simply bluffing? "Sorry, I thought you were Ahren's friend, not his bodyguard."

He tilts his head to the side. "I assumed you wouldn't cooperate." His gaze lifts to mine, and the warning is plain as day in his expression.

I suck in a breath, feeling like I've been punched in the gut.

"Have a pleasant day, girl," he patronizes me, then marches out of the room.

Alone with my drowning thoughts, I drag a hand

down my face and sigh, feeling sick to my stomach. Jasion's threats swirl in my mind.

There are eyes everywhere.

What have I gotten myself into?

I glance at the door where he left, and my skin crawls. Staying here spells disaster for me, as Jasion seems to know so much more than he's letting on. The threatening nature of his words lift the hairs on my arms. I'd be an idiot to think I'm safe here on my own, and that means I need to catch the princes before they leave.

Marching across the room, I know this is the right decision. I run the rest of the way to my room, and grab a long coat and boots, then I'm off toward the kitchen, where I remember seeing a back door that leads outside. With no one in sight in the hallway, I dart left and into the main dining room. It's empty, and in the kitchen, I find the cook with his back to me, stirring something on the fire stove that smells like stew. Quick feet carry me to the back door, and I inch it open, then slide outside where the snow is coming down like a curtain. I can't see or hear anyone, and I pray I'm not too late.

CHAPTER 15

LUTHER

Gusts of wind barrel into the carriage, but the cold is kept away by the fur blankets on our seats, our coats, and the sealed doors. We jostle from the bumpy terrain, but otherwise, it's an easy ride so far. Two horses harnessed to the coach wear a protective spell to aid with the freezing temperatures, and they have instructions on where to take us, so no need for a driver. Courtesy of one of the king's mages.

We've traveled for most of the day, cutting through the forest, and my ass is fucking numb from sitting so long. Ahren, who sits across from me, stares out the window at snow-covered trees.

"Any Bloodcursed out there?" I ask with sarcasm in my voice. The king's mages created a diversion on the opposite side of the kingdom to aid our exit. A few stragglers came after us, but we moved too fast for them.

Ahren shakes his head but doesn't look my way.

"What's wrong with you? Are you scared?" I throw at him.

He sneers at me, his nostrils flaring.

"Look, I tolerate you most of the time, but I'm not dealing with your moody shit today," I explain. "This mission could get us killed, so whatever's gotten to you, spill it."

Ahren responds with an intimidating frown, and I stiffen. If we were anywhere else, I'd push those buttons until we fought to get him to talk, but we don't have that luxury here.

"I've got lots on my mind."

"This isn't the time for distractions, brother."

He nods, almost conceding. This isn't Ahren. He stares out the window, his profile a mask. The air is tense around him, filling our carriage.

So I change topics to take a different approach. "Heard anything about the king's meeting with Guendolyn?"

"He got her drunk." Ahren looks at me, his lips thinning with disapproval.

My pulse races at the news. "He didn't try to—"

"Fuck, no," he answers with confidence. "The girl just can't hold her wine. I bumped into her in the hallway."

"You ended up making sure she got to her room safely last night, right?"

"What's with the interrogation?"

I bristle but don't jump back down his throat. Something else is going on here. "What the hell's up your ass?"

He turns away from the window to face me, his arms stretching out on either side on the back of his seat. "So much could go wrong. I'm just trying to get my mind into that headspace."

The wind howls again, buffeting the carriage and sending the whole vehicle into a sideward sway.

I cross my legs, an ankle over a knee, and run a hand through my hair. "I told Mael to keep a close eye on Guendolyn while we're gone."

"What if we don't make it back? What happens to her?" His voice is gentle, like he's given this a lot of thought, and he lets out a frustrated sigh. So it's fear that distracts him today—fear for Guendolyn.

My brother's feelings for her are stronger than I realized. Did sharing her company in the mansion affect him so much?

"You really like her, don't you?" I ask, locking my gaze with his. If my brothers are drawn to Guendolyn, there's nothing I can do about it, but I want to know. His expression turns thoughtful, as if considering my question for a sliver of a moment.

Then his upper lip curls. "Why the fuck are you asking me so many questions about her?"

"I'm not pissed, if that's what you're thinking. Hell, you know I'm head over heels for her. Have been even before I met her two years ago. Deimos lost his heart to her when he went to collect her from the human realm. So why are you so reluctant to admit it?"

"Since when do you openly talk about emotions?" he growls, his eyes narrowing.

I break out laughing and slouch back into my seat. "Touché, brother."

That rouses a smile out of Ahren, and he stretches his legs out at an angle so he doesn't hit mine.

"What's our backup plan?" I ask. "You fly us out of there?" I arch a brow and gain myself a grumpy look. "I don't remember the last time you used your wings."

"And you're not going to, so leave it the fuck alone." He clears his throat. The wings hidden inside his back are a touchy subject, but where we're going, any option to escape should be on the table.

"If shit goes south, then we fucking run for our lives. I've got explosive spells that will help us escape."

I nod, well aware that the Unseelie have their own range of powers, and there's a reason most fae keep their abilities private. Once the enemy knows, you are easily overpowered, but none of that matters if we can't find a cure for Deimos.

"Do you trust the king's contact that we're meeting in Ash Court?" I ask.

"How much do you trust any fae?"

"Fuck, not at all."

"Then you know what we're dealing with. Our guards stay up. In and out fast."

A short, explosive sneeze echoes faintly in the carriage. Ahren's brow lifts.

I frown and look all around us. "What the fuck?" My thoughts fly to those damn fairies. Could they have hitched a ride with us?

The sneeze comes again, directly below me. I jump

to my feet and shove aside the fur blankets. I grab the edge of the velvet seat and push it up to reveal the storage compartment.

Bright blue eyes stare up at me, face swallowed by shadows, and she sneezes again.

"Guendolyn? For fuck's sake." Fury barrels through me.

Bent low so as not to hit my head on the ceiling, I turn to Ahren who shuffles into the corner of his seat to give me space. He's seething.

"You told her, didn't you?" I bark. "We agreed not to tell her for this exact reason, but—"

"I didn't tell her anything," Ahren snaps back.

She pushes herself up to get out of the tight confinement, and I reach down, sliding my hands under her back and knees, then lift her out. Ahren shuts the lid, and I set her down, then squeeze in alongside Ahren. Both of us are staring at her.

Groaning, she stretches her arms into the air and twists her back until a bone cracks. She was squashed in there for a while, no wonder she's all cramped up, and possibly bruised, from the bumpy ride.

"Surprise!" she says, half smiling, half nervous. "And for your information, Jasion told me that you were leaving." She glares at Ahren more than me.

"We couldn't tell you for this reason," he reprimands.

"I—" She licks her lips and pulls the black coat tighter around her throat. "I didn't want to be in the kingdom alone. Jasion threatened me, and I didn't feel safe. Plus, I don't see why I can't come with you to get whatever is needed for Deimos' cure."

"Wait, what did Jasion do?" Ahren leans forward.

She reclines in her seat, glancing outside momentarily. "He said I was being watched and that he didn't believe my story about who I was."

"How is that a threat?" I ask.

Guendolyn rolls her eyes. "Really? When a man says that kind of shit, that means one thing—someone wants to hurt me."

"I have to agree with Guendolyn on this one," Ahren says. "Jasion is by nature a very paranoid person. It takes him a long time to trust anyone, and he goes out of his way to find out the truth when he thinks he's being told lies. He won't harm you, though. I've spoken to him already about needing to keep away from you, to ensure you are not harmed."

She folds her arms around her middle. "I guess you had to be there to feel the evil vibes shooting off him. And he wasn't keeping his distance. He might be nice to you, but he hates me. I saw it in his eyes."

I butt in. "Jasion has always been attached to you, brother. And I've seen him get jealous when you spend time with women."

Ahren stiffens. "No, you're wrong. We're friends. We've always been friends and he's just protective."

I shake my head. "Brother, I should have seen this earlier too. It makes sense as to why he'd have tantrums when he couldn't find you, and why he's constantly in our mansion and not with the other mages. You know he once secretly paid the seamstress several gold coins to leave and never return or there'd be consequences? I thought he was just being a prick, which is normal for him, but he did that after the woman spent the morning with you alone to measure you for a new coat."

He broods and shifts his angry stare from Guendolyn to me. "Why the fuck are we talking about me?" Ahren swings his attention back to her. "You can't come with us."

"How do you know you won't need me?" She smirks in mischief, and if I wasn't so furious that she joined us on this perilous trip, I might sit back and enjoy the show. She's quite the performer.

Ahren's glare deepens. "I don't want you hurt. You're not coming."

"So what, you're going to turn around and head back to the kingdom and waste precious time Deimos doesn't have?"

He shakes his head. "We're dropping you off in the next Seelie town to wait for us."

Her mouth drops open. "You wouldn't!"

"You think that's a smart idea?" I ask, unsure I want to leave Guendolyn with strangers right now.

"It's better than her joining us," Ahren snarls.

"I'm not getting dumped in some town. I bet all the men there leer at females like that last town we stopped at."

Ahren sighs, and I'm not sure what the fuck to do.

"Fucking fine," my brother growls. "You stay in the carriage this whole trip. If things go bad...well, then we're all pretty much fucked anyway."

Her gaze widens, stunned at his reply.

Exhaling a heavy breath, I offer her a half-smile. "You being here is a really bad move, little wolf."

She studies me for a long pause. "Well, so is being stalked. I'll hedge my bets and choose you two over Jasion. You can't blame me for not wanting to end up in prison." Sullen, she curls toward the window.

Except she has no idea how wrong she is. She's joined us on a trip that might be our last.

CHAPTER 16

GUENDOLYN

I don't know what to feel.

They clearly aren't happy to see me, but I don't care. I'm not being left behind. Eventually, Luther moved to sit on my side, while I have my legs curled in under me. I lean against the carriage window and stare outside, though I keep sneaking glances over to Ahren who has that angry look on his face. I can sense him watching me. Is he thinking about us last night or what a douche he was for not even coming to see me this morning? They're both asses for heading off on a hazardous journey without saying goodbye.

Forests and mountains fill my view, and half the time, I still can't believe I'm in such a beautiful place… but even a rose has thorns, right?

The carriage suddenly comes to a halt.

I straighten in my seat and swivel around. Ahren pushes open the door on the other side, and a gust of icy wind rushes inside, biting into my flesh. He climbs out and sends the carriage rocking.

Luther turns to leave as well, but I grab his arm. "Hey, can we talk?" I ask.

He pauses as if considering my question, then sits back down. "What is it?"

"I get you're both pissed at me, but I was seriously scared for my life with Jasion. That's why I came. I figured I could help if you're just picking up ingredients or something for the cure. I had no idea you were going to Ash Court."

"This trip is perilous, especially for you." A touch of paleness touches his cheeks.

Deimos' words from when we first arrived outside the Unseelie castle come to mind.

They find us on their land, they'll kill us in the most painful way possible.

But with that memory comes another from the Unseelie who attacked me in the elevator back on Earth and what he said.

The King of Ash Court has called for you.

Why would the king send those monsters to bring me to their court if they intend to kill me?

"My parents live there," I say. "This could be a chance for me to find out who they are."

Luther shakes his head and laughs hysterically, but it's fake. "Do you have a death wish?"

"It's not funny. My whole life, I've wanted to know the truth of who I am."

"Little wolf, listen carefully. Whoever your parents are, they are not nice fae. I'd give my right arm to say otherwise, but they gave you up so the mages could use you as a carrier for a curse to destroy Shadow Court."

I try to swallow his words, but they punch me straight in the chest. My parents sacrificed me, that's what he's saying. That I wasn't important enough.

"Then why did they send me to Earth? Why not just release the curse and be done with it? Why this elaborate show?"

He runs a hand through his hair, a softness sweeping across his expression as if he pities me.

"Don't feel sorry for me," I argue. "Help me understand what happened."

"The Unseelie liked to have a constant reminder of the curse they placed on us and the threat of unleashing it if we didn't submit to them. They were the ones who spread the rumors of your prophecy in the first place, to scare everyone."

I nod, my throat thickening, and I swallow past the growing lump. "I'm a nobody then. A throwaway child."

I glance away, and he touches my hand in my lap.

"Not true."

I blink away the tears as my stomach sinks. Am I really just a pawn in a game between two kingdoms? With a tilt of my head, I look up at Luther, this gorgeous fae who whisked me from my oblivious world and brought me here. "Maybe it was a mistake to bring me to the Wandering Realm."

"You didn't have a choice, little wolf. The spies from Ash Court had found you. It was the only way I tracked you down, or we might never have crossed paths."

"Then why would they still kill me if I return to their kingdom? I've unknowingly completed whatever mission they sent me on me, right? So why not embrace me back into their court?"

He sighs heavily, lifting his attention to the window and away from me.

"What do you know?" My voice deepens. "Please, Luther."

His big hand reaches over and strokes the side of my face, but I have no patience today. I push him away. "Tell me!"

He huffs a loud breath. "If you die, the curse on our kingdom can never be removed. We will forever be plagued by the Bloodcursed until every last Seelie fae is killed."

My head feels heavy, and my chest aches. I'm consumed by the horrible thoughts that my own parents used me and are now happy to dispose of me. "The final nail in the coffin. Fuck!"

He starts saying something, but I don't hear the words. I just keep thinking over what he's told me and everything that's led me to this point. All the information amplifies my curiosity. If the Unseelie wanted me dead after I unleashed the spell, why send me back to Earth with no memories? Why not kill me then and there? Hell, why not kill me as a child? What am I missing?

But part of the answer forms over my mind like a cobweb.

I swipe at the tear sneaking out the corner of my eye and interrupt Luther. "I think someone at the Ash Court tried to save me. Maybe they botched the spell." I give Luther a rundown of my thoughts. "Why else would I forget my past? It's so they couldn't find me on Earth. Except, I was lucky that you and your brothers found me first."

His brow furrows as he prods a finger at his chin.

"You think it might have been my parents?" I ask. "Maybe they were forced to give me up." I feel hope creeping into my chest.

"Oh, little wolf." Luther's face falls, and he gathers me into his arms.

I soften against him, inhaling his woodsy, masculine scent that carries a splash of clementine, as if he'd eaten them for breakfast. He holds me so tight, making me feel safe.

"What's going on?" Ahren's words slice through the moment.

I break away to find him watching us from outside the carriage and expect some kind of jealousy, but he stares at us with admiration. I have been way off base with these princes since I first met them. They all confuse me with their emotions and reactions.

"Where are we going?" I glance out through the windows and see nothing but forest.

Ahren stretches out a gloved hand toward me. I pull myself out of Luther's arms and take Ahren's offered hand as I step outside into the cold. Tugging my coat tighter around me, I stare ahead at the enormous bronze fence woven intricately with swirling patterns. They open before us, revealing a dirt road and more trees that layer the land beyond the gates.

A man in a black coat with a hat pulled down low on his head waves us in to join him.

"Where are we?"

"Lockinge, a small town aligned with Shadow Court. We send them protection and whatever else they need," Luther explains. "In exchange, they provide us with information on what they see in the woods. Most living here are scouts or forest wardens."

"What's that?"

"Fae entrusted with the oversight of the forest and its animals."

"So like rangers. That is really impressive."

"You two go ahead," Ahren orders. "I'll take the carriage and horses inside."

Luther and I move forward, the snow crunching under our feet with each step. "Is this town similar to the other one we stopped at when we traveled to the kingdom?"

He shakes his head. "Nothing like it. Here, people work for the good of the fae, and we are always welcome without payment."

It warms my heart to hear that for once we're not looking over our shoulders.

"The local tavern serves the best deer stew and fresh poppy seed bread."

Considering I haven't eaten at all, I'm ready to eat anything they put in front of me. "Sounds good. I'm starving."

Luther walks tall beside me. From the way he carries himself, it's easy to recognize that he's royalty. He pushes up the collar of his deep blue coat, and we stride quickly down the path, fighting a horribly icy wind.

Up ahead, there's a small wooden hut that's round

with a pointy roof. The whole thing is a deep green color. There's a front door and two windows, along with a chimney pumping out smoke from a fireplace. Amid the trees, I find more homes similar to that one, but no one's around, and I don't blame them. It's too cold.

Luther directs me to another enormous round hut. No windows, just a large arched door.

I glance back but see no sign of Ahren. "Do you think your brother will be alright? Maybe we should wait for him?"

"He's more than capable. Plus, he has to meet the town leader."

Luther doesn't seem worried about the fae living here, so I breathe easily. "That doesn't sound like fun," I answer.

"Not that much fun, not when it comes to royal requirements and etiquette."

A wall of heat smothers us the moment we step into the building. Rows of long wooden tables and benches fill the large room. At one side is a bar-like counter and a door that goes into what I assume is a kitchen. On the other side is a monstrous fireplace made of black stone, flames snapping and crackling within.

The man behind the counter lifts his chin to us, his mouth dropping open, then he bows his head. He sets the dishcloth in his hand on the counter and rushes over to us, running his hands down his white apron.

"Your Highness," he says. "I didn't know you were paying us a visit today."

"Bracken," Luther greets him. "It's great to see you again. How long has it been?"

"Two years." He lifts his head to look at the prince, not even noticing me. There's admiration in the fae's eyes, as though he's fangirling over the prince. "The king paid a visit several months ago, but it is wonderful to have you join us. Unfortunately, this weather does not permit for a hunting challenge like on your last visit."

Luther breaks out laughing and slaps the man on the shoulder. "I believe I won that round. Do you really wish such torment on the locals again?"

His smile is wide and contagious, and I find myself doing the same. "That you did, Your Highness. Now, please have a seat. I'll bring out hot stew and bread for you both." The man turns and hurries toward the back door.

"Make it for three," Luther calls out. "My brother Ahren will be joining us."

Bracken's eyes almost bulge out of his head, and he's practically bouncing on his toes. "Of course."

Luther undoes the buttons on his snow-dusted coat and takes it off before placing it on one of the dozen hooks on the wall beside the front door, and I do the same with mine.

He smirks when he looks down at me. "What?"

"Does everyone gush over you?"

He leans in close and whispers, "The only fae I want falling before me is you." He winks, reminding me how much he affects me. My heart races when he flirts like this. I may not remember our past, but what I feel now is a storm of emotions and attraction to this fae. I tried my best to push him away until I sorted out my thoughts, but was I just fooling myself? The magnetism between us is impossible to resist.

God, all I can think about now is Luther's remark in the carriage about all of them wanting to be with me. There was no sound of jealousy in his words, so does that mean they want to share me? It should scare me how much I love the idea of three princes ravaging me. Suddenly, I'm feeling extremely hot.

Without waiting for my comeback, Luther leads us to a table all the way at the back and sits with his back to the wall. I sit on the bench across from him.

"What did you do in the hunting challenge?" I ask out of pure curiosity and to get my mind out of the gutter. There is such a calm vibe in this tavern compared to the last one, where women had to be carried inside or they were good for all men to make a move on. I still seethe at the memory that women were for only one thing.

"Boar hunting," Luther answers as he scrunches up the sleeve of his silvery blue top to show a healed scar the length of my hand. "The bastard got me, but I got him back. He tasted delicious later that night."

The door creaks open with a gust of icy air, catching my attention. Ahren enters and spots us. I can't stop staring at him as he leaves his coat on a hook and saunters over like a god, all shoulders and power. He's dressed in black, his white hair sits ragged around his gorgeous face, and his green eyes are wild. His beauty radiates in any room he walks into, and I'd be lying if I said he doesn't affect me as much as Luther and Deimos do. My body responds to them intensely, my heart racing, my core burning up. He's so different from his brothers though…always serious and needing to be in control. Our night together revealed a different side to him…a side I longed to see again.

I turn to find Luther watching me. He's got a stronger jawline and is more rugged, but he's just as utterly sexy.

"Did you order food?" Ahren asks as he sits next to me.

"Sure did," I respond and glance back at Luther, who has a strange look on his face like he's about to ask me a question.

I pinch my lips at him and mouth, "What?"

Last night you let Ahren take you. His words flare in my mind. *Tonight, you're mine.*

CHAPTER 17

GUENDOLYN

uther grins at me so sexily that a shiver zaps south and hits me right between my thighs. A spark of electricity pulses through me at the instant arousal he stirs inside me with just a few words.

Tonight, you're mine.

The look in his eyes belongs to someone who's ready to shove aside the table between us and toss me over his shoulder. I swallow hard and look over to Ahren, who studies the room and isn't paying attention to the sexual tension about to turn me into a puddle.

You're so cute when you're startled.

I narrow my eyes at Luther to show him I'm not falling prey to his seductive stare. His grin widens as we face each other, neither of us moving. I'm at a complete loss for words. Luther likes me—more than likes me, I know this—and I'm madly attracted to him, but he's pulled away from me since we arrived at the mansion. I also can't remember why I feel so strongly toward him, but that doesn't make me less infatuated with him. We just never really got the chance to spend as much time together as I have with Ahren and Deimos.

Long ago, darkness and light came together and created beauty...a beauty that will destroy this world.

I give my head a small shake to imply I don't understand.

A proverb from the ancient fairies. It reminds me of you, except they've got it wrong. You're the beauty who will save this world.

He's definitely a sweet talker.

Ahren gets up from the table. "I'm ordering drinks. There's no one serving at this place."

"All right," I say.

He heads across the room, not glancing back.

"Why didn't you tell me?" Luther asks immediately, his voice deep. "About you and Ahren?"

I swing back to him. "He told you?"

With a tilt of his head, Luther's voice streams over my thoughts. *Brothers share.*

Heat curls up against my neck and over my cheeks. How much, exactly, did Ahren reveal? How many times he brought me to orgasm? Was it just chest-pumping bragging?

"It just happened," I whisper, my breathing growing shallow. "What do you want me to say? That I'm sorry? I won't apologize." Something isn't right with me, but my heart is pounding too hard to stop, and I don't want to apologize for something I enjoyed. Plus, I don't really know where I stand with Ahren. We haven't properly spoken since last night. "I'm sure it was a one-off thing. You don't need to make a big deal of it."

His eyes darken. Sure, he's tall, handsome, and goddamn sexy as hell, not to mention a smooth talker, but that doesn't make him less of an ass for grinning at me as I squirm.

He looks up and over my shoulder, then back at me. "One-off thing? That's not what Ahren said."

My stomach plummets right through me. "W-What did he say?"

A gleam of determination lights up in his gaze.

Just then, Ahren returns and places three wooden jugs on the table. Drops of red wine splash out over the rim and onto the table.

Remembering my night drinking with the king, I say, "Thanks, but I'll pass."

"It's not wine, little wolf," Luther murmurs. "It's a berry juice known for helping boost virility." He snorts a laugh, while Ahren shakes his head and laughs too.

I roll my eyes and push my cup away. Luther drinks his in one go, then takes mine and finishes it off while holding my stare. Oh, I know exactly what he's thinking before he even says anything.

All for you, little wolf.

I want to smack that smirk off his face. He's such a smartass today.

Bracken turns up at our table with a tray and places bowls of stew in front of us, along with a wicker basket filled with sliced bread and butter, then he sets down a cup of water for me. Another waiter, a young man with short dark hair and head held low, joins us and leaves large goblets of wine for the princes.

"Enjoy. There is plenty where that came from."

Bracken gives us spoons and a knife for the butter, then bows as he and the other server leave us in peace.

"Thank you, Bracken," Ahren responds, then he turns to his food, stirring his spoon through the stew. All business, he speaks to Luther and me. "We'll leave at dawn and should arrive at Ash Court by midday."

I stare down at my meal and take a spoonful with a piece of meat and potato. Thick and heavily spiced, the savory taste fills my senses, and I swear I'm back home eating one of my foster mom's homemade meals. "This is so good."

"Try it with the bread," Luther suggests, handing me a slice generously coated with butter. I take a bite and moan. It's still warm and salty and creamy.

"Told you it's good."

We all eat without talking until our bowls are empty. Ahren orders another serving, and I'm not too shy to hold back. But when the princes go for a third round and a new loaf of bread, I shake my head.

"That's the best dish I've had in ages." I sip my water.

Ahren glances over at me, then pauses, and I can see the wheels spinning behind his gaze. "This town is very safe, Guendolyn," he points out. "Maybe you staying here isn't such a bad idea until we return?"

"No!" Luther and I say together.

Ahren frowns at his brother, but I'm glad someone agrees with me.

"Worst case scenario," I begin, "I can try to open a portal for us to escape through."

"Except Deimos isn't here to help you with that," Ahren snaps back.

"But she activated and closed the portal for the fairies without kissing Deimos." Luther says, stealing my exact response.

"I just need to concentrate."

Ahren asks, a bit too loudly, "If you do open a portal, how will you close it quickly?"

"Well, I learned a little trick from the blue fairy for closing a portal. I think it should work."

"Think?" Ahren asks.

I don't waste a moment and reply, "If we end up needing a portal, then we're caught anyway, right? You said so in the carriage. We're fucked. To me, it makes sense that I accompany you into Ash Court."

"Hell no," Luther bites back.

Traitor. I eye him intensely, and he winks back. Something flutters in my stomach.

Ahren groans, shadows dancing under his eyes. "Fine. You can join us on the trip, but you wait in the carriage. No compromises on that."

I shrug. "Fine." It's better than being abandoned in a strange town.

The princes finish their meals just as Bracken returns. "Your Highnesses," he says with a bow. "We have a house prepared for your stay. It's the third one behind us in the woods."

"Thank you," Ahren responds, radiating waves of formality in his voice and stiff posture. "You have been too kind to us."

"There is a small matter I wanted to follow up on. The king, His Majesty, promised to send us a supply of horses and extra workers." Bracken grimaces. "I'm sorry to bring this up, but the delivery has been delayed for close to eight weeks."

"Well, that is my cue to take the lady to her room," Luther says, getting to his feet and eying me to get me to follow. "Thank you for everything, Bracken. I will let you discuss these matters with Ahren."

I'm on my feet and step over the bench. "Thank you," I say to the fae before glancing momentarily at Ahren. He's holding the man's stare, that stoic, regal expression sitting on his face, his shoulders broad.

Luther leads me across the room. We collect our coats, and I slip into mine as we walk outside. The icy wind makes me shiver as Luther shuts the door and takes my hand in his, then guides me around the side of the building. Night spreads its wings over the landscape, and the only thing visible is a flickering torch in the distance.

"Quickly," Luther says, his voice sharp.

I wrap an arm around my middle and keep my chin low as we rush down a path between the trees. We pass two homes with bright lights beaming out of the windows, then finally come upon a dark hut. Luther pushes open the door and waves me inside.

Warmth greets me, wrapping around me in an instant and vanquishing the cold clinging to my skin. The door shuts with a thump, and I step into a large living room. The fireplace floods the room with heat and light. Above the mantelpiece sits a painting of the king sitting atop a black stallion. A long couch sits in front of the fire, and two matching single chairs are on either side. I guess with no television, the fireplace is the best they have for living room entertainment in this world.

"This looks nice," I say.

Luther shrugs his coat off to hang on the hook near the door, so I unbutton mine and take it off before handing it to him and toeing off my soaked boots. He does the same. Stepping toward the fire, I head for the lush, brown rug.

Two doorways exit off the main room, leading to a kitchen and a bedroom. Looks like we'll be sharing tonight, and considering the cold, I have no problem with that. Well, and the fact that I'll be with two incredibly hot fae.

Luther stands behind the couch, his amber eyes piercing into me. My heartbeat is rapid, and I'd be lying if I said I didn't like my reaction to him. If anything, I want more. Of course, we have a history together that I don't remember, and I desperately long to… But I can't change that, and I can't ignore my growing attraction to him, either.

"How did you find the meal?" he asks to break the silence.

"Really good," I answer. "I could eat that most nights."

He leans his hands on the back of the couch. "I've asked our cooks back at the castle to replicate it, but they just can't get it right. Just like the berry drink, which you missed out on, little wolf, but I can take a bottle with us on our trip."

I shake my head and don't move from in front of the fireplace, as my back is nice and toasty. "No thanks. I'll stick to water. The last time I drank something I wasn't used to, I was left with my head spinning." Not to mention in Ahren's bed.

He quirks a corner of his mouth upward. "Spinning like a Ferris Wheel?"

I stiffen and remember my dream with Luther and the Ferris Wheel he made for me, and how he'd gone to all that trouble. I can't hold back the smile. "My dream the other night was about you showing me something you created for me in the woods. You insisted it was a Ferris Wheel based on something I'd told you."

His eyes widen, flashing with a fiery light. "You remember our past?" He's upright and alert.

I hold up a hand, not wanting to give him a false sense of hope. "It's only bits and pieces in my dreams of my past in the kingdom. Like a puzzle I still haven't put together."

He emerges from behind the couch and approaches me. "This is fantastic news." He looks at me as if he might suddenly break into cheers, which leaves me beaming on the inside.

"Can you tell me more about the scene in my dream?" I ask.

His smile is contagious, and he flops down on the arm of the couch, one foot propped up on the cushion, his arm draped over his knee. "Before we first met, I spoke to you for a long time in your mind. We talked about things you liked, your fears, your dreams, even other men you admired at your school."

"We did?" I swallow, quite unsure what to say. Did I think I was going crazy with a voice in my head? Was that why I had told him so much back then? Now, I feel a little exposed, because he knows so much about me while I know so little about him.

"And one night you spoke of Ferris Wheels." He breaks out laughing, as if he's picturing the conversation in his mind, and I can't help but grin. "You described them to me and said that's where couples go to kiss. So, when I finally found you and brought you here that first time, I created one for you." He chuckles even louder, and the sound he makes is up there with some of the best sounds I've ever heard.

"You know when I first heard 'Ferris Wheel,'" he says. "I thought it was either a weapon or a sex toy."

I can't help but burst out laughing. Those were his only two options? "So I'm guessing you built it as an excuse to kiss me?"

He studies me, tilting his head to the side. "It worked." He blows me a kiss, and my knees quiver beneath me. I'm not used to having such gorgeous men flirt with me. "I think you said I didn't quite get the wheel part right. But it was worth it for that kiss."

Part of me wants to have him kiss me and see if it sparks anything because I so want to remember more of this fae and our past. Instead I say, "The memories you describe sound incredible."

"You know, our conversations made me fall for you before I ever laid eyes on you."

His confession curls around my chest, and sorrow bites into me at the thought that I've missed out on these pieces of him. "Will you tell me more about our past?"

"Of course."

"And about your ability. There's so much I want to know. Can you go into anyone's mind anytime, including animals? What about fairies?"

He arches a brow, caught off guard by my questions. His eyes flick over me, and butterflies burst in my stomach, beating their wings. His expression denotes intrigue, like I've finally opened a door between us.

I search my mind for something to say. "I met your dog, Sir Wolf-A-Lot. He's adorable, in a if-a-hellhound-could-be-a-pet kind of way."

"I don't want to talk about hellhounds." Luther gets up and moves toward me, looking like he only wants to focus on me. I watch his every move until he stands in front of me. Without my shoes, I feel even shorter next to him, and I have to crane my head back.

He grabs my wrist and draws me to his body. My hand comes up and presses flat to his hard chest as my insides tingle. We look into each other's eyes, and his attention dips to my lips as I bite them. "What does my touch do to you? Stir any memories up?"

"No."

His expression softens. Maybe it's about time I come to terms with the fact that I may not remember my past, but with Luther's help, I can try to recreate it.

When he glances up again, he holds the sides of my face, then slowly leans in and kisses me.

"And this?"

My breath hitches, and my knees threaten to buckle. Holy hell, I'm about to swoon. "Nope, nothing. I think we need to keep trying."

His eyes search mine before he dips his head and lightly brushes his lips across mine again, making my entire body buzz. His tenderness undoes me. I kiss him back, our mouths pressed together, our tongues dancing. I want him so intensely that I forget everything else, possibly even my name. One hand pushes into my hair, and he kisses me deeper. I fist his shirt and wrench him closer, holding him tightly to me, as the hard line of his cock through his pants nestles against me.

"You are breathtaking," he whispers.

I'm drunk on his kiss, swept into another world, so far away from reality that I feel like I might pass out if he were to leave my side. My feelings for him overwhelm me and crash over me. I'm burning up as if the sun has taken residence in my chest.

He breaks our kiss, and we face each other, our foreheads touching.

"In truth, little wolf, I don't know if I'm right for you at all. Promising anything is a disaster waiting to happen. We're from enemy courts, and will never be allowed to be together," he admits, and his words sink into me like fangs.

My stomach tightens. Why is he saying this?

He continues, "I can't make you remember me, but if having you means starting over and breaking the kingdoms' laws, well...I'll risk it all to keep you."

His warm breath skates over my face, and his words tangle around my heart. An ache flares in my chest at the thought that any future I may have with the princes is rife with thorns and heartache. But staring into Luther's dark amber eyes, I realize he's offering me a chance to follow my heart. I don't care about stupid rules, only my feelings for these three princes that deepen with each passing day.

"Luther, I…" I struggle to find the right words. "That is the sweetest thing ever."

"We finally met in person two years ago, but I just didn't know how much you meant to me. Not until you stepped over the Ash Court threshold and disappeared from my arms." He kisses my nose.

"Ahren told me you blame yourself for bringing me here," I murmur.

He studies me, not showing any reaction on his face.

"What I'm guilty of is not keeping you more protected when I brought you into our realm. One of the Unseelie snuck into our mansion one night and lured you to Ash Court. They intended to have you cross the threshold into their Court, then kill you. I came after you, but everything happened so fast." He sighs heavily, shadows gathering in his eyes. "I tried to save you, but you stepped onto Ash Court during the battle, and the curse was released. Then you disappeared from my arms and back to Earth."

We fall silent after that, my chest aching at hearing the pain in his voice. He's lived with that for the past two years, and I don't know how to console him when I can't even remember the events. But with the dreams I've been having and more information from Luther, I'm starting to piece together the mystery of my past.

I cup his face and kiss him, wanting to take away his agony, and the wall I tried to put up between us comes crashing around my feet. I shouldn't rush into this, but I want to stop the hurt. I want to somehow feel like I belong here.

He kisses me back with hunger this time and drags his hands down my back, lighting me up with every stroke. His fingers trace the skin under my clothes and slide around my waist to the front of my pants. There's a desperation in us coming together, like we both want to lighten the burden we feel.

I gasp at his touch, my body thrumming. He pops open the buttons and begins to tug the pants down my hips. Our mouths draw apart, and I glance over to the door. What if Ahren comes in?

"Should we be doing this here?" I ask.

"Fuck, I don't care where we go, little wolf. I need you."

I could drown in the sexiness behind his gaze, my entire body trembling with heightened desire. If Ahren walks in on us, I don't care. Maybe he can even join us. So I pull down my pants and underwear and step out of them, offering myself to Luther because I crave him.

He reaches for me, his attention lowering, but I smirk and nudge his hand away.

"No." I fall to my knees before him and reach for his belt and undo his pants.

"Guendolyn, little wolf, you don't have to."

"But I want to do this so much." I yank down his pants, and his cock explodes out, making me gasp with delight. He's so damn erect and big, and his scent is intoxicating. There must be something to what he said about the berry juice.

I wrap my hand around his cock, and he groans as I

slide his tip into my mouth, his taste salty and sweet, then push him in deeper. My tongue runs over his shaft, leaving no part untouched.

"Oh, fuck!" He shudders beneath me.

Glancing up, I meet his eyes. I love seeing this strong fae fall at my mercy. I glide him in and out of my mouth, sucking on him. His hips start rocking back and forth, his sounds driving me to take him deeper. I want to see him lose control under my touch.

God, he is so gorgeous.

Suddenly, he nudges my shoulders back and slides himself out of my mouth with a pop. I lick my lips and take his hand as he brings me to my feet.

"Now it's my turn." He picks me up and places me on the fur rug in front of the fire. "Lift your hands." I obey him, and he tugs my shirt and the one underneath up my body and over my head. The fireplace warms me instantly. Still, my nipples harden, and I lay an arm over them.

"Don't cover yourself. You are so much more beautiful than I could have imagined." He prowls over me.

I lower my arms and lay on my back on the rug as we kiss like it's our first time, fast, exploring each other's mouths. I grasp on to his muscular arms when he dips his head to my neck and chest, licking his way to my nipples. He takes one into his mouth, drawing me deeper in.

Delicious aches pulse through my body, curling around my core. He greedily pays the same attention to my other breast, sucking on me, gently gnawing on my hardened nipple. When he comes up for air, he grins.

"You smell divine. Your fragrance reminds me of honey. Will your pussy taste like honey when I lick it?"

I quiver all over. "Oh hell, Luther."

He makes his way lower, tracing my stomach with his tongue, and pushes himself to kneel between my legs, nudging them wider.

His gaze flicks over me. "I love you like this."

Fingers slide over the seam of my pussy, and I moan, my hips automatically rising.

"So wet for me." A finger finds my heat and pushes into me.

"Ahhh." I arch my back in response.

"Good girl. Coat my fingers." He draws them out of me and pushes back in, then he leans down and licks my pussy. His tongue expertly traces my slick length while I lose myself. He wastes no time and presses his mouth to my center, devouring me as his tongue glides over my clit again and again. I fist the fur rug, moaning louder when he pulls back.

Breathing heavily, I plead, "Please don't make me wait."

The corner of his mouth tugs upward, his grin lopsided in the most ravishing way.

"Come to me." He gives me his hand, which I accept, and I'm up on my ass in seconds. Then he draws me up on the couch where he takes a seat. He pulls his top up and over his head, then tosses it aside. He has so many muscles, I am in paradise.

"I want to see you, watch your breasts bouncing in my face." His hands fall on my hips as he guides me to straddle him, then he firmly pulls me to him. We kiss as his hand slides between my thighs, sweeping over my pussy. He presses the tip of his cock to my slit, then slides it up and down.

Hell, if he doesn't take me soon, I'm going to scream.

I adjust to take him and widen my legs more to meet his movements. He sucks on my tongue as he pushes down my hips so I sit on his cock. He goes slow as I widen inch by inch for his size, but my cries of pleasure have him pushing in quicker until he's completely plunged into me.

Gripping the couch behind him, I begin to move up and down his length. His chest heaves for each breath as he watches my breasts bounce. He looks up at me as he raises his hips to meet each of my thrusts, slapping into me harder and harder. I ride him wildly, groaning, loving every second of feeling him so deep inside me.

He growls, his fingers digging into my hips, and pumps faster. I see the primal need in his eyes. He suddenly lifts me, then pivots us around so that I'm lying on the couch with him on top of me. Wasting no time, he pummels into me like a goddamn animal. He's relentless and tearing into my pussy, causing the most insane sensations to course through my body.

I cry out as he fucks me, his delicious assault leaving me filled with electricity.

I finally explode with an orgasm. Head tilted back, I scream with an insatiable release as the climax shudders through me.

Luther groans as he halts his thrusts and stays locked to me as he comes alongside me, bursts of his semen filling me. Both of us are gasping for air, smiling crazily at how good that felt.

He collapses on top of me, his breath tickling my neck. I laugh and wrap my arms around him.

"Didn't realize you were so ticklish," he whispers as his fingers find my ribs.

I burst out laughing, my body writhing to get away from him. "Hey, no fair! I'm trapped."

He pulls out and stands before me, studying all of me. "Well then, I'll give you a head start. Once we clean up, I'm going to find every part of your body that responds to my fingers."

My eyes widen. "Don't you dare."

He grins mischievously. "Challenge accepted."

CHAPTER 18

AHREN

The fire crackles and warms my freezing hands. I spent much longer with Bracken than I intended. Guendolyn and Luther are asleep on the bed, and I smell the musky aroma of sex in the small cottage. I've always shared everything with my brothers, and if Guendolyn is happy with that, I have no problem with her decision. As long as it's just my brothers and no one else.

But right now, I need some time to unwind and slow my thoughts. Tomorrow will be a big day, and I can't keep the fear away. Fear that we won't succeed, that we won't save Deimos, that we'll die.

I exhale loudly when a creak from across the room catches my attention. Guendolyn emerges from the bedroom in her black pants and top, her hair messy, but she's still as adorable as ever.

"Can't sleep?" I ask.

She nods and shuts the bedroom door. "I keep

having stupid dreams about drowning, and I'm a bit scared about tomorrow."

"Join me." I pat the couch next to me. "I'm hoping my mind stops overthinking everything."

She takes a seat next to me, and we don't speak for a little while. It's comforting to enjoy the silence with someone and not feel like I have to always perform, to be the prince always on the job.

"Did I hear right, back in the carriage, that you have wings?" she asks with excitement behind her voice.

I grind my jaw, wanting to drive Luther's head through a wall for saying shit he shouldn't have.

"It's nothing," I respond.

She fake laughs, her eyes widening. "Bullshit. Having wings is not nothing. How come I've never seen them before? What do they look like?"

She's clearly wide awake now, as she rattles on with question after question, and I can't help but adore this side of her. When she sinks her teeth into something, she picks at that thread until it comes undone. She has to know everything.

"Do you have two wings like an angel? Or four like a butterfly?" She's on her feet now, her arms animated, and as pissed as I am for her talking about a topic I loathe, she makes me smile. Guendolyn has an effect on me like no other. I don't know what it fucking is, but I feel myself soften around her.

"How about one question at a time?" I respond.

She pauses and lowers her hands. "Show them to me."

"Of course you'd ask that. The answer is no. Try again."

She huffs, and her face scrunches up before she speaks again. "I thought only fairies have wings?"

"It's quite rare for fae to have them."

"Why don't you use yours?" She shoots back. Maybe I was wrong to give her the option of asking me anything, as this can go very bad.

But with the way she looks at me, all I want is to bring back the mischievous smile on her face.

Fuck, what the hell has she done to me?

"Are you worried the wings make you look a bit girly and delicate, you know, like a fairy? Is that why you don't like them?"

I arch a brow. "What the fuck?"

She laughs at me, and I can't stop the blood pumping through my veins with the need to prove her wrong. Girly? I exhale loudly and tug my top up and over my head as I get to my feet.

I tower over her, but she doesn't back away. My shadow falls over her, while her gaze slides down my chest and lower still. She pulls her fleshy lower lip into her mouth, gnawing on it between her teeth. Last night, I took her every which way, fucked her so sweetly, and she cried my name, begging for more. Yet now, she stares at me just as hungrily, just as desperately, and something in me shifts.

"So?" She looks up at me with an arrogant little grin that I want to lick and turn into a moan. She doesn't even know what she's gotten herself into, but she will soon enough. I'm driven by adrenaline, a rising arousal, and burning rage tangling in my gut. I fear that once she sees the truth, she might change how she thinks of me. But I suddenly want her to see all of me just as I am, to see what made me the fae I am today. My pulse rages through my veins like a storm, throbbing beneath my skin.

She needs to understand what kind of world we live in and why I fight so hard to protect her against those who would harm the innocent.

She licks her lips expectantly.

"You want to see my wings?" I growl.

She nods eagerly.

I close my eyes and concentrate, reaching deep inside me. I've kept them away for so long, hidden and unused, that at this point, I don't even know if they'll respond to my call. But I sense them folded up tightly inside me.

Forgotten things.

A tingling starts at the base of my shoulder blades, then rips upward with the sharpness of a knife. I hiss through clenched teeth as my flesh tears and the wings push out of my back. Two bony shadows are cast against the wall on either side of me. They stretch outward, looming behind me like the branches of a tree stripped bare by winter.

The glint in Guendolyn's eyes vanishes, ripped away at seeing the hideous remains of what was done to me. Ironically, even in this form, their magic will still allow me to fly… not well, but it's possible. Except I refuse to use them.

"I'm broken, Guendolyn. Maybe too broken for

someone like you." She's too perfect, too good, too innocent, having not grown up in this world.

Her chin trembles, but she doesn't back away, tracing her gaze over my wings.

"What happened?" Her voice is a squeak, and agony threads through her words as though looking at me is too much for her.

Fury surges through me. Why did I show them to her? It was a fucking mistake. I turn around, tucking them against me when she reaches out. Her fingers gingerly graze over the tip of a wing.

"Who did this to you?" she asks.

I stand with my back to her, fighting the emotions punching through me.

For the first time in too many years, I feel vulnerable, and I fucking hate it. I don't need anyone's pity. I ball my hands. Somehow, I thought showing her the truth wouldn't impact me. Big fucking mistake.

All she'll see now when she looks at me is a broken fae.

Tender fingers stroke along my wing, sending a fiery spark up to my shoulder and down my back.

I run a hand down my face, lowering my head. "It was my real father's punishment. He loathed my wings and wanted them cut off my back. When he found out that would kill me, he stripped them down to the bone, and did so every time the feathers grew back."

Revulsion swirls in my chest as I remember my father's grin each time he ripped the feathers off and cut the membrane to leave me with nothing but skeletal embarrassments. The fucking asshole. The ache in my chest swallows me, and I want to kill him for what he did to me. For what he did to my mother.

"I think they're beautiful."

Her words take me off guard. I frown and jerk around, drawing my wings into their hiding place inside my back, the pain quick and bearable as my skin knits up across my shoulder blades. "Don't say that shit." I search her face for the lie, but all I find is her genuine smile.

"Your father is a fucking bastard, but that doesn't mean he's taken anything from you." She pushes herself against me, her arms wrapped around my waist, her cheek pressed to my chest. She holds me so tightly, I can barely draw in a breath, but I don't move or push her away.

I don't know how to feel.

Furious? Embarrassed?

I'm desperate to punch the wall until I no longer feel a thing, but I suck it up like I've been doing for years. That's how I deal with everything, by shoving it down, but one day, it'll all come spilling out and drive me to madness.

My gaze falls to Guendolyn. She's what I need, curled in my arms, smiling and telling me things that make me forget everything else. A beauty like her can take everything away, can let me escape the memories that haunt me, that echo in my dreams. I hate the fucking weak-ass I've become. I despise this side of me.

"You're not broken," she whispers, dragging me out of my thoughts. "You're perfectly put together for me." Her words sing in the air.

"They haven't grown back." I snarl and shake the darkness slithering over my thoughts. It threatens to take me as it has so many times before, bringing me to a place so deep I forget how to climb back out.

The only people who've seen my wings are my brothers and mother. No mages or healers. Not my stepfather. I don't even know why the fuck I showed them to Guendolyn.

Except the truth lies inside me. I've been attracted to her from the first moment we met, and what I didn't know was that I'd saved a special place in my heart for her.

Maybe we are a better match than I assumed. She's cursed, and I'm broken—the perfect mates.

She lifts her chin. "I'm sorry he did that to you." The softness of her voice clutches at my heart.

I wrap her in my arms, my eyes burning, and we don't say anything. It's not needed.

CHAPTER 19

GUENDOLYN

The ride toward Ash Court is bumpy, jolting us about. I stare outside the carriage window at the most incredible sunrise I've ever seen. It illuminates the night as if it's igniting a captivating flame.

My gaze sweeps back inside the carriage to the two princes. Luther slouches in the seat across from me, his arms folded over his chest, his chin dipped low, and his breathing heavy. He fell back asleep the moment we left the town. Ahren sits next to me, and he looks at me with green eyes so pale, they look washed out, like he's cried too many times and the color ran. Except Ahren isn't the kind to cry. He bottles everything inside, putting on a strong front. As the heir to the throne, he can't be weak.

Movies romanticize princes and princesses, but in real life, nothing is ever so perfect and easy. People are broken and have damaged pasts that shape who they are. Despite Ahren's asshole father, the prince holds on to his integrity and stands up for what is right, as do his brothers. Why else would they risk their lives for Deimos? I adore that about the three of them.

"Are you all right?" Ahren asks.

"Yeah. I'm still trying to wake up," I lie. After our conversation last night about his wings, I didn't sleep a wink. Even when he climbed into bed and I lay between two princes, I had a hard time shutting off my brain. I don't need to explain this to Ahren or remind him of the pain he lives with every day. I can't get the image of his bony wings out of my head, or banish the ache coiling in my chest at what he went through. I want to murder his real father for doing that to him.

Instead, I offer Ahren a reassuring smile and do the thing I excel at—changing the topic. "Why do the Seelie and Unseelie hate each other so much? Jasion told me the tale of the fairies and fae, so clearly, the fae all started as the same race."

"We are the same. The difference comes down to our beliefs and abilities," Ahren says, while Luther stirs, groaning. "Unseelie draw their power from the darker gods, but I believe it all stems from a huge disagreement between two kings who were brothers and ruled together. They both fell in love with the same woman, but she was tragically killed, and each brother blamed the other. So much so, that they split their kingdom— the land and the population—in half, and promised to destroy one another. That hatred has continued to this day."

Luther clears his throat from in front of us, his eyes opening halfway, studying us.

Ahren doesn't seem to notice and keeps talking.

"Details aren't precise, but one brother was once called an Unseelie, meaning 'unfortunate' in the ancient tongue, so the second king quickly announced himself as a Seelie fae, the blessed ruler. I guess the names stuck."

I absorb every word. "The history of fae is so fascinating, and there's so much I want to learn. Your stepfather told me many stories the night I went to see him. It helped pass the time as I healed him. I mean, most of the stories didn't make sense to me purely out of context, but—"

"Back up," Ahren interjects, while Luther drags himself to sit upright. "You healed the king? How?"

I shrug. "The same way I did with your bite mark." Something in his gaze makes my stomach drop. "Why are you looking at me like that?"

"Did you leave a handprint on his body?" Ahren continues, his posture stiffening. Now I'm starting to get worried.

I nod.

Luther breathes heavily and runs a hand through his hair. He and Ahren exchange a silent look, and I just know Luther is telling him things telepathically so I don't hear.

"Talk to me. What's the big deal?" I ask. Ignoring the way the corded muscles in Ahren's neck tick, I try to tell myself they're overreacting. How can fixing someone be a bad thing?

"If the king or his mages see your handprint on his flesh, it will reveal that you are an Unseelie. Only their healers carry an ability that mars the skin with magic.

We have had two Unseelie healers visit our court in the past, so everyone knows how they heal," Ahren explains.

Dammit. Why the hell hadn't he told me this before? "Oh crap!" My mind is running at a thousand miles a minute. "But wait, if they saw it, why didn't anyone come for me while I was at court?"

Luther shrugs as he says, "Maybe he never noticed the mark, or it faded."

Ahren's lips pinch tightly. "Or that could be why Jasion's been buzzing around you." He looks over to Luther. "Jasion has not been acting like himself. What if the king ordered him to uncover the truth about Guendolyn?"

"Except he was acting all suspicious with me even before I healed the king." I don't even want to think about why Jasion is interested in me. The memory of our conversations sends shivers up my arms.

"Guendolyn—" Ahren begins.

"Let's say they know. I won't be able to return to Shadow Court, will I?"

Neither prince answers because they know it's true.

"You are going to return home with us," Luther blurts out. "We just need a way to hide you until we find out what the king and Jasion know."

It's getting harder to smile and pretend I'm fine with the constant barrage of bad things happening. Ash Court wants me dead to complete their curse. Shadow Court will want to kill me for simply being from the wrong place.

Luther shuffles to the edge of his seat, leaning forward, his eyes wild. "If we tell the king her survival ensures the curse isn't permanently placed on our court, he won't kill her."

"No, but he'll imprison her for life," Ahren answers fast.

The food I ate earlier now wants to make a reappearance. I feel sick that my options are either hide for god knows how long or go into prison. If I don't want to die, of course.

I pull back and curl in on myself in the corner of the carriage, staring outside as the white landscape awakens with the rising sun.

The brothers discuss my options, hashing out a plan, but I'm struggling to deal with the news. So much has happened in such a short time. On top of everything, I'm losing myself to these princes, making me question my decisions and motives. When I arrived here, I wanted to uncover who my parents were, but now all I keep thinking about is how I don't want to lose the princes. Which is why my head feels foggy when I should be focused on not dying.

"Guendolyn," Luther says. "We'd never let anything happen to you. Believe me, we will find a way. Once we save Deimos, we'll talk to the king. He will have to understand."

Their words should encourage me, but the knot in my chest refuses to unravel. "We can try. But you're right. We need to focus on Deimos first and surviving this."

To my surprise, Ahren leans closer and drags me into his arms, giving me no chance to wriggle free. Luther joins us, and already, I feel the cold inside me melting. I believe them, that they'll make this work... God, I want this so much. I soften and curl in against the princes, feeling warm and wanted. The sensation is unlike anything I've felt before. My foster mom loved me, but this feels different, deeper and more secure. I can't even explain the sentiment that makes me believe that for once, I am truly where I belong.

The rest of the trip is spent watching the scenery, drinking and eating food packed for us by the town cook, and talking with the princes.

"The king was fucking furious yesterday," Luther explains, grinning with glee. "You know his goddamn stupid throne? It got damaged in the Bloodcursed attack, and he was yelling at everyone to find every missing shard of wood with the hope of putting it back together."

Ahren chuckles, and I can't help but admire how perfect they are. When not bickering, these princes get along so well.

"What's so special about his throne?" I ask, curiosity getting the better of me.

"It's made of Alethian wood," Ahren explains. "It's impossible to replace, as those trees are protected and it's illegal to chop them down."

"Are they magical?" I ask.

Ahren shakes his head. "The trees are said to be as old as the fae race. Only when a tree falls over from a lightning strike, can its wood be used."

"But it wasn't just the throne," Luther continues. "His precious ruby from the chair is gone."

Ahren bursts out laughing. "Fuck, if I never hear about that damn jewel again, it will be too soon."

I stiffen, remembering how Hiss flew out of my window while clutching a ruby. Of course she'd have to take something that belonged to the king. Well, thank fuck that she's gone, and no one needs to know what she did. Everything I touch in this world somehow comes back and bites me in the ass.

The way they keep laughing makes me more curious. "Why is it funny he lost the ruby?"

Luther glances over at me, stretches an arm out against the back of his seat, and draws up a bent leg. "During the first year we arrived at the kingdom, our stepfather sold all of our mother's jewels in exchange for a stone from a witch fae who passed through our court. The king was promised that the ruby would give him affinity with the fairies because the ruby was one of the last pieces in existence from the original fairy queen's crown." He rolls his eyes. "Right, because a random fae spouting lies just happens to carry an ancient relic. But the king believed her, and Mother was so angry, she didn't speak to him for a month."

"He sounds a bit obsessed," I say, offering Luther a crooked smile, while my mind whirs with thoughts of why the king didn't grill me further about the fairies earlier.

"That he is."

The ride goes on for half a day, while outside the carriage, heavy clouds darken the landscape with the promise of another snowstorm.

The carriage curves around a bend on the edge of

the hill we're starting to descend when Ash Court comes into view. I press my face to the window and stare out at the enormity of the place. It glints as though it's made of silver, and snow covers its five broad towers with pointed roofs, all connected by fortress-strong walls made of white stone. Enormous arched gates forged of gold sit at the entrance to the kingdom, and stone walls spread out from either side of the gate, enclosing the castle.

I swallow hard, unable to believe we're here. All I remember from arriving here is Deimos and me landing right inside the grounds and how quickly we ran out of there.

Suddenly, panic curls in my gut, and all I can think is…my real parents are somewhere in that kingdom. Danger suffocates this place, and yet something in my chest tugs at me, telling me that maybe I can finally find out who my parents are.

When I glance back, the princes are looking out the window as well. Their smiles are gone, replaced with trepidation.

"Ready for this?" I say.

"Fuck, no," Luther responds.

"It's going to work. It has to, for Deimos," Ahren says.

I agree. For Deimos.

CHAPTER 20

GUENDOLYN

*A*s we come to a stop at the base of the hill, trees surround the carriage and seeing past them is impossible. Ahren steered the carriage to a denser part of the woods on an overgrown path that looks unused. I've been out into the bushes to relieve myself and stretch my legs, and now I'm back inside.

"How far is the castle?" I ask, peering into the forest through the window, trying to spy Ash Court with no luck.

"Far enough that no one will find you here," Ahren answers from outside the carriage where he's guided the horses to stop.

The door sits open, and a chill flutters over me while Luther goes outside too and prepares to cast some kind of concealment spell over the carriage with me in it, so no one finds me while they're gone. My emotions go back and forth like a yo-yo. One minute, I want to join the princes, the next, I want to run as far from this place as possible. Mostly, I worry about the princes' safety and getting a cure for Deimos back in time.

If there is one positive thing about today, it's that we've encountered no problems on the trip here, so maybe we'll be lucky for the rest of the day.

Luther appears in the doorway, snow speckled over his dark hair, a few flakes sitting on his long lashes. I want to reach over and dust them away, but this isn't the right moment. He stands strong and broad, looking ready to leap into battle.

"We're going to cast the spell and get going." His words are soft, like he can't bear to leave me alone out here.

The moment he finishes talking, I'm on my feet in the carriage and rushing to the door, unable to stop myself. His arms loop around me and swing me outside, and Ahren closes in from behind me. They crowd close, and I look up at how tall they both are compared to me. Conflict swims behind Ahren's green eyes, but he never says a word, only settles a hand on my shoulder. He leans in and grasps my jaw, turning my head to kiss me with a passion I don't expect. My toes curl in my boots as his tongue sweeps into my mouth. We kiss like long-lost lovers, like we may never see each other again. Except that can't happen because I may not survive it.

He suddenly breaks from me, and I'm left breathless. There's a kindness in his expression that feels like it's reserved only for me. "Stay inside. Don't leave the carriage until we return, no matter what."

There are days when my feelings overwhelm me, when I want to stand so still that time itself stops and I can stretch certain moments out. This is one of those times. I haven't spent enough time with the princes, and it now feels like I've lost the chance. I fight the urgency tightening in my chest, the need to keep them near rising from the thought that I may not see them again. Still, I swallow the growing thickness in my throat.

"Hey, little wolf," Luther says. "It's going to be all right."

I turn to him as Ahren steps toward the horses.

"We will be back, I promise. I lost you once. It won't happen again." He cups my face, his thumbs running across my cheekbones, wiping away the stray tears. "There's a legend that says that when fated souls meet, the universe will move the stars themselves to ensure their love endures."

"Who said that? It's beautiful," I whisper, clutching on to Luther's strong arms.

"It comes from one of the ancient fairy tales."

"So much of the fae world is based on the fairies, isn't it?" I tilt my head, smiling at him.

He nods, leaning closer. The moment his mouth grazes mine, I forget everything. There's fire in his kiss, and we come together like nothing in the world can touch us. I kiss Luther, trying to memorize every last thing about him—the firmness of how he holds me, the way his tongue explores every inch of my mouth, the delicious taste of his lips.

When we break apart, worry twists in me painfully.

"We need to go, little wolf." He holds me closer and looks down at me. "If we don't return by night, say the word 'Cilhaj' to the horses. They will take the carriage straight back home."

I shake my head. "I'm not leaving you."

He kisses me, stealing my protest. "Now get into the carriage." Turning me by my shoulders, he slaps my ass hard. I look at him over my shoulder, but he's already walking toward the front of the carriage where Ahren stands. I climb back inside, my stomach churning.

When I shut the door, the whole carriage suddenly starts shaking. In the blink of an eye, a curtain of glinting dust cascades outside, vanishing as quickly as it started.

Through the window, I watch the two princes track through the woods, leaving me behind. Within seconds, they disappear into the shadows.

I slouch in my seat and wish I had my phone to at least play some games while I wait. When I get tired of watching the snow fall, I flop onto my back and stare at the ceiling. What do people do without technology? Is this why they get married so early and have half a dozen children? I close my eyes and try to rest.

Time passes. I have no idea how much, but it feels like forever.

I shuffle back up and reach over to grab the wicker basket of food the town cook packed for us, then peel back the white fabric laid on top.

Everything inside is wrapped in white cloths. I open the first one to find a block of cheese and smile. Rummaging through the basket, I find some more cheese, then a chunk of bread. There are close to half a dozen more things in here. I'm digging deeper when something sharp bites the top of my index finger.

"Ouch." I draw it back and blood is bubbling over the cut. Sticking my finger into my mouth, I pull everything out of the basket to find the culprit—a knife. I quickly wipe the blade and wrap my finger up in the cloth, then I make myself a cheese sandwich. Before I can do more damage, I place the knife back in the basket.

My finger throbs like it has its own heartbeat, but it'll heal soon enough.

Today is not going to end up as a bad day. It just can't.

I bite into my sandwich and curl up, staring outside at the falling snow, praying Ahren and Luther come back safely.

*A*hren

"*D*on't hate me, brother," Luther whispers over his shoulder at me, his grin telling me he's up to no good. "But Guendolyn thinks I'm the better kisser."

I roll my eyes at him. "Is that what you're thinking about at this moment?" We move with haste through the woods to reach the wall of Ash Court, and my mind is racing with plans for escape should we be caught.

He shrugs. "It's just something you ought to know."

I smirk and nod his way, knowing this is his way of dealing with the situation. Deflection. Even growing up, when shit got too real, too hard, he refocused on something he could control.

But I also know that once we're in battle, Luther turns deadly and will never back down. He's the perfect fae to have by my side on such a mission, and I trust him with my life.

Without another word, we move like the wind, cutting across the landscape and swerving around trees. Part of me expects Bloodcursed or guards, but there's nothing. I strain to listen for threats, but not even the birds are singing today.

Silence. It leaves me uneasy.

Luther scans the woods and scowls my way, then lifts his shoulders in a shrug.

Something feels off. Luther's voice streams over my mind.

I nod and point straight ahead to where I can already see the stone wall through the trees. My stomach tightens at where we have to go.

We're running, the snow crunching under our rushed steps, and as we get to the wall, I scan overhead and on either side of us. Nothing here.

A twig snaps somewhere behind us, and we whirl around, reaching for our blades, my heart pounding.

Not a sound.

Snow cascades all around us. When I find no movement, I direct Luther to follow me along the wall that towers over us like a giant, and I hate how trapped I feel. My mind won't leave Guendolyn, either. We left her deep enough in the woods away from the castle so she won't be found, and I pray she doesn't leave the carriage. While inside the carriage and under the spell, she's concealed from the Unseelie and warm from the cold weather.

Shuffling sounds erupt around us.

Luther seizes my arm, and I swing around. My attention catches on the three Bloodcursed stumbling out from the shadows of the dense woods. This might explain why there are no guards on the east side of the castle.

My blood runs cold, and it has nothing to do with facing them, but with leaving Guendolyn out there. She survived the Bloodcursed bite once, but can they still hurt her? Seething, I tuck my blade back into the sheath on my waist and reach over my shoulder to grab the hilt of my sword. I draw it out, Luther doing the same, and we don't waste a moment.

We charge the creatures who run at us.

Fury drives me to finish this quickly. I turn to the right, where two of them stick close together, grip my sword with two hands, and lift the blade over my shoulder. Mouths gaping, the fiends growl. Their eye sockets are sunken, their teeth missing, their clothes ripped. These poor souls were once fae just like us, but the curse ravaged them. I picture Deimos this way, and my heart clenches.

I swing the sword with all my strength. The blade sings through the air and swiftly slices through both of their necks in one move. I suck in a frosty breath as the heads topple off their shoulders, the bodies falling into the snow like sacks.

I turn to Luther, who has a monster dead by his feet. Half a dozen more are threading through the woods toward us. Where did they all come from?

Blood stains the once-immaculate snow all around us.

Luther glances at me and grins, his eyes alive with hunger for the battle.

We fight, brother, he growls in my head.

I nod, and we take on the next wave of Bloodcursed. One of them charges toward me, but I pivot out of his way and swing back around, bringing the sword down fast to the back of his head—a clean cut. Turning back around, I swipe wide, catching a fiend across his abdomen and causing his innards to spill out. When a hand slaps down on my shoulder, I drive my elbow into the creature at my back, then whip around. My free hand falls to my belt, and I grab a dagger, then plunge it right into his temple, piercing through to the brain.

A kick to the gut, and he's on the ground. The next two go down just as fast.

Luther's at my side, heaving for breath, his eyes locked on more Bloodcursed coming for us. I slide my sword over my shoulder and across my back into its sheath, then hastily collect my daggers from dead bodies.

Luther takes the lead, and we run.

Thicker snow sits near the wall, so with each step, my feet sink deeper, but there's no stopping. We have to get over the wall. I didn't come this far to fight the infected.

Up ahead, a lofty tree rises ahead of us, its branches heavily laden with snow. It's bigger than any other tree in these woods.

Luther doesn't pause as he bolts forward, throwing himself at the trunk easily, using the blades in his hands to dig into the wood for purchase. He then wrenches each one out and stabs the wood, climbing higher quickly. He's fast. Holding both my knives, I follow suit.

Behind me, I hear the Bloodcursed's shuffling footsteps, their groans.

By the time I reach the first branch that's at least fifteen feet off the ground, Luther's there grabbing my arm. He wrenches me up, and I scramble onto the thick limb and stand tall. I suck in a ragged icy breath, my heart racing.

Down below are close to two dozen creatures charging toward the wall. They hear a sound and those fuckers don't hold back, running to find their next meal. We need these things eliminated from our world, once and for all.

But not today. Right now, I want to survive and rescue Deimos.

Luther's already climbing across to another branch that stretches toward the top of the stone wall.

Beyond that spreads Ash Court, our destination its grand white castle for the Unseelie.

Between us and the castle is a scattering of trees, not dense enough to conceal us should anyone look this way. Toward the front of the enormous castle stand four guards. If the Bloodcursed make enough sounds, they'll draw the guards' attention.

"Do you have the spell?" Luther whispers, glancing over his shoulder at me. There's tightness beneath his eyes.

I tuck my blades away and pull out a small pouch from my pocket. "This has one use, so we have to make it work. And we have one for returning. It won't last long, so we have to make it across the open yard quickly." My eyes scan the lofty castle and find a small door near a garden of vegetables, tucked away near a tree. "That's us." I point to the spot.

"Let's do this," Luther murmurs.

I untie the rope on the pouch, and pour out half the contents in my palm, and the rest in Luther's. "Dust over your head while whispering, *'invisible,'*" I explain.

"Simple as that?"

I shrug and follow the instructions, stating, "It worked on the carriage." An explosion of prickles dances over my head and rains down over my body. I don't feel different, but when I lift my hand I see right through it. It still has a faint outline that looks like a heat wave, but otherwise, the spell has worked.

Luther stares at me with huge eyes.

"Hurry the hell up." I rush to the end of the branch and leap down before landing on parted legs, knees bent the snow softening the fall. Moments later, two footfalls indent the snow next to me and a hand slaps my back.

"What are you waiting for, brother?" Luther teases,

and then we're off, darting across the yard, wasting no time.

I swing my attention left and right, just in time to spot the guards racing toward the wall farther away from where we jumped. They've heard the Bloodcursed.

My heart beats faster, but I don't stop, and Luther's breaths are so loud they ring in my ears.

Rounding the tree near the vegetable garden, I throw myself toward the arched door and slam a fist on its wooden surface.

"We're still invisible," Luther grumbles in my ear. "She won't see us."

"Good, then we're covered in case someone else opens the door."

"Do you know what Relle looks like?"

I shake my head, but I'm too focused on no one answering the door to worry about that right now. A quick look over my shoulder shows more guards hurrying to the wall now. The snowfall is light, so how long do we have before they see our footprints in the snow?

I reach over to knock again when the door pulls open.

A small head pops out. It's an older woman with dark hair drawn back into a plait, her cheeks rosy as though she's been running, her eyes wide with fear. I recognize that expression on her face, the one of someone knowing they are breaking the rules. She's wearing a long, black dress with a white apron.

"Relle?" I whisper, praying it's her.

Her head swings in our direction, but she looks right through us. "Is it you?" she whispers. "Tibout?"

"It's Ahren, Tibout's son." I hold still and wait. Luther grumbles behind me at my saying son, but I ignore him.

Relle's face blanches, and she quickly draws back indoors.

I lunge after her, my hand lashing out to snatch her wrist as I say, "Please, the king sent you the message on our behalf. He said you can help us."

She's trembling against my touch, looking down at where I hold her arm as the concealment spell fades and my whole body appears in front of her.

Her eyes widen as she looks up at me, then she glances back into what a room that looks like a storage room. When she looks over to Luther, she's shaking her head. "No, this is a mistake."

"Please," I plead. "We're brothers and won't hurt you. We need your aid desperately."

For those few moments, she just watches us, her gaze swinging from us to the yard with the guards, then behind her.

"If you hurt me, I'll come after you both in the underworld," she threatens under her breath.

I smile. "The king threatened me with something similar, and now I know you two know each other well."

She sighs, her gaze frantically swinging out to the yard. "Quickly then. Enter." She opens the door wider and steps aside as she whispers, "My king and queen are on a trip to the east court, so there aren't as many guards around the palace as there normally are. This is good timing."

Luther and I slip into the dark room, and I pray that our luck holds out.

Guen

The carriage shudders.

I snap awake, my eyes fluttering open. My heart pounding, I scramble up from the seat and move over to the window. "What the hell was that?" I mumble. Have the princes returned? That would be the best news ever. When I see no movement outside, I check the other side of the carriage, where the doors are still shut. The coast is clear.

On the floor lies the kitchen towel I used to wrap my cut finger, stained with blood. My finger has stopped bleeding, though some dried blood remains on my hand. I only slept for a few moments, I'm sure.

Bang.

The sound reverberates, and I'm sent into a tumble once again as everything shakes. A shard of ice skitters down my spine.

I reach down and grab the knife from the basket. Tucking myself into the center of the long seat, I begin trembling. What the hell is going on?

A sudden explosion comes from the window, the sound ear-shattering.

I scream and flinch away, the blade shaking in my grip.

A brown bear-like animal tears right through the window, sending pieces of glass and wood in every direction. The creature snorts, scrambling to find purchase as it rips its claws through the wooden wall of the carriage.

I'm on my feet and lunging at the door on the opposite side. I rip it open, then leap outside and run, sucking in ragged breaths as I look over my shoulder. The monster lunges out of the carriage, shaking off the window frame that hangs around its neck, the kitchen towel I used on my cut in its mouth. It spits it out and sniffs the air.

Oh, hell. My blood must have drawn this thing to the carriage. So much for trying to stay invisible. Maybe the spell should have blocked out smells, too.

The creature lowers its head, its ears pressed flat to its skull.

Fuck! Brandishing the knife, I raise it at the monster. "Get the hell away from me!"

I retreat and quickly whip around to sprint into the woods.

Except I run straight into a solid wall of muscle.

My heart is going to burst out of my chest. I tilt my head back to find a man with pointy ears and white pearlescent hair that drapes over his shoulders. He's young and has scars down the side of his face. He stares at me with a filthy grin.

He greedily seizes my hand that grips the knife and squeezes. "Drop it," he snaps.

I writhe against him, crying out, but my hand gives, and the blade slips from my grasp. A flash of brown shoots past us as the animal that attacked the carriage is chased away by two other men also dressed in black uniform.

I shove my fist into my captor's arm and push against him. "Let me go!"

Only then do I see the gold on his coat, sitting above his heart. A long broadsword with wings spanning out from the hilt.

Oh, crap. I'm standing in front of an Ash Court guard.

CHAPTER 21

LUTHER

"Get inside," Relle whispers abruptly as she shoves a hand into Ahren's back, causing him to stumbles into a small bedroom with me. There's only a single bed, a wardrobe, and a dresser in here. The curtains are pulled over the window, letting in only a faint stream of light. There are no paintings or decorations of any kind on the walls, making me think this may be a spare room.

Relle rushes inside and shuts the door, then turns to face us. Her cheeks are flush, yet she stands tall. She's a plump, older woman with eyes the color of midnight. The deep lines around her eyes and hardness in her gaze tell me she's witnessed a lot of tragedy in her time, but there's also kindness in her expression, just as my stepfather said.

Suddenly standing here under her scrutiny, I suddenly feel like I'm a child about to be reprimanded for doing something wrong.

"What could be so important for King Tibout to risk the lives of his sons?"

I smile. "We come for something of *great* importance."

"Well, let's hear it then." She grips her hips, reminding me of Dana, who bosses everyone around.

I have to remind myself I'm in the heart of the enemy's stronghold and why coming here was a good idea in the first place. The king insists he trusts Relle, so we go against our better judgment. I don't feel comfortable with this decision, but I tell myself that we are stuck, so it's worth the risk of her betraying us to save Deimos.

"Our brother Deimos has been bitten by a Bloodcursed, and he doesn't have long. We all know there's only one way to save his life."

She shudders a breath, nodding.

Voices come from somewhere outside the room.

"What do you expect me to do?" she asks, her voice low. "Go into the mage's work chamber and find the potion for your brother?"

"Well, yes," I reply, still smiling slightly. My heart's racing, knowing that any moment she could call for the guards and we'd be slaughtered.

More noises come from outside in the hallway. It sounds like guards running. I guess most are going toward the Bloodcursed near the east wall, meaning escaping that way may prove trickier than breaking into the kingdom.

She shakes her head again. "I'm sorry, but you've both wasted your time."

"Please." Ahren steps forward. "The connection you have with King Tibout must be worth something."

Relle scowls. "I have no connection with your king. He came into the kingdom, and I was simply the fae who ensured his arrivals and departures remained concealed."

I slip forward, my hand sliding into the pocket of my pants. Relle isn't exactly the helpful fae I expected from what the king had said.

"I have something for you if you help us today." I pull out the diamond bracelet. "King Tibout insisted this was for you. He also said to name your price to help us, and he'll deliver it afterward."

She feverishly licks her lips, and I pull back my hand with the jewelry, pocketing it once more. "Your king knows exactly what I desire," she says.

"And that is?" Ahren asks.

"Enough gold to buy my own land away from every damn kingdom in the Wandering Realm." Shadows crowd across her expression.

Does she dislike this court that much, that she'd leave in a heartbeat?

"Deal," Ahren states. "In exchange for the antidote for our brother. No cure, no payment."

She eyes my brother for a moment, and silence echoes between us.

"Done." She draws a small knife out of her pocket, and she slashes the thick, meaty part of her palm. She lets a few drops fall onto the stone floor between us, then hands me the blade.

"Blood oath," she insists. It seems this woman is a lot more cunning than she first appeared.

It's basic magic usually done as insurance should one person not hold up their end of the bargain. Break a blood oath and Relle can demand my punishment any way she sees fit. No one can save me, not even a king because our blood connection will reveal she's right. It's one of the rules in Wandering Realm carried on from the old days and has never been changed.

I cut my thumb and squeeze a bit of blood onto the floor to merge with hers. The cut stings, but I suck it up.

She mumbles a few words under her breath, and the blood fizzles and burns up right before us, then vanishes. She then lifts her gaze to me. "You come with me. If I take you both, it'll raise suspicion."

"I'll go instead," Ahren states, and I know it's because he's spent more time with Jasion and knows mages very well. I've watched mages long enough to know exactly how they work after the king insisted he's appointed one of his mages as mine. But I've resisted and kept my distance from them.

"No," Relle snaps. "I did a blood oath with him, so he joins me. You stay here."

Ahren looks over at me and I say, "Is it safe for my brother to stay in this room?"

She frowns, as though I've asked the dumbest question in the world. "He'll be fine. When I give my word, I keep it, son. Now before we go anywhere, you need new clothes." She eyes me up and down, then rushes out of the room.

"Do you trust her?" Ahren faces me.

"What choice do we have?" I swallow hard. "Just stay hidden in case it's some kind of setup." Unease churns in my gut, because I hate the rushing, the unknown. "We get the cure and bolt the hell out of here."

Ahren nods. "This place gives me the creeps."

I blow out a long breath. "We can do this. We give her what she wants to save Deimos."

"Just be careful. And don't use your mind-reading. We don't know anyone's abilities, and they might be able to sense you probing." Ahren runs a hand through his hair, his lips thinning, and I can tell he's attempting to cover every possible angle.

"Agreed."

He digs into his pockets and pulls out two fabric pouches of magic herbs and powders from our mages back home. We brought a variety to use in case Relle wasn't able or willing to help, not fully trusting the king's contact or methods. "Just in case, brother."

I tuck them away in my pockets, remembering where I placed each concoction.

The door opens, and I draw back, my heart pounding as I finger the blade on my belt, but it's only Relle. She's carrying dark clothes and pushes them into my arms.

"Quickly, boy. Get changed. The guards seem occupied, so this is our chance."

I move to the bed and start stripping. From the corner of my eye, I catch Relle staring at me. I don't give a shit if she wants to see me naked, as long as I get my brother's cure.

In no time I'm dressed in a black guard's uniform.

The pants are too tight, and they ride high up my groin and threatening to split my boys in half. I drag the long-sleeved tunic down over my body, then tie the leather belt around my middle. I push my hair off my face and tuck it behind my ears.

"Fits you well," she says, eyeing me a bit too closely.

Ahren curls his lips upward. "Keep your head low and be quick." He claps me on the shoulder.

I tug down on the pants riding up my ass. *Goddamn.*

"Stay close," Relle says as she opens the door. She sticks her head out then steps outside and waves for me to follow.

I give a final nod to Ahren, then I'm out. He shuts the door behind us, and I'm marching right on Relle's heels down a dark corridor with lack stone on the walls, flooring, and ceiling. There are no portraits or statues of animals; only weapons adorn the walls.

There's no sound coming from around us. The place looks empty, though I can't stop looking over my shoulder as if being watched. I study everything we pass, every shadow and corridor. There's not a soul in sight. We suddenly turn and head down a sweeping staircase, making me feel even more exposed. The place smells pungent down here. There are cracks in the walls, and plants grow through those gaps—thorny vines with tiny red flowers and deep green leaves. The place is being swallowed by nature. I've heard tales that where magic is used, nature will always try to reclaim the energy it believes is hers.

My shoulders stiffen with each step I take, and my

pants ride up so high that I'm certain they'll vanish up my ass. Fuck. I shuffle as I yank at the fabric.

"Stop that," Relle scolds over her shoulder at me.

Breathing heavily, I hurry down the remaining stairs. We turn right, and coming right for us are two guards preoccupied by heady discussion, barely paying attention to us.

Keeping my head low, I march close to Relle, praying she keeps her word about helping us.

"Fucking lucky bastard. The king will reward him well for that catch," one fae says, and the other chortles like a pig.

I'm so engrossed in watching my steps, I don't notice Relle is no longer in front of me. I halt and spin around until I see her in a doorway, waving me over. She's frowning like a demon at me, so I dart toward her and into a room that smells of dried herbs and death.

Several candelabras illuminate the room. A counter runs the length of two walls, while the third is lined with shelves. Jars filled with all kinds of ingredients are crammed into every available spot.

"Is this it?" I ask.

"Yes," Relle says as she takes a seat on a wooden chair in the corner.

"What are you doing?" I whisper.

"I brought you here. Now go find the cure." She waves her hand at me.

My mouth drops open. "That wasn't part of the deal. How would I know which it is?"

She feigns insult and touches her chest with her hand. "What makes you think I know a mage's magic?"

I eye her, grinding my teeth. "Are you seriously going to just sit there?"

"Look, boy. I don't know what you're looking for, so I brought you here. Now find what you need because we don't have long."

Fury pummels into me, but I can't force her, this much I know. So I swing toward the chaotic room and think this through. I've watched mages back home work their potions enough times to understand that for each spell or curse to last, a portion of it must be kept. If I can find the cure, our mages can test it out ,and then cast it on Deimos. Also, if 'm lucky, I might even uncover the spell cast on Guendolyn that caused her to forget her past. So I dive in and start searching every damn jar and workspace and ingredient. Most of the jars have labels, which makes the task slightly easier.

I've searched half the room when I look over to Relle, who's staring at the door, chewing on her finger-nail nervously while still in her seat, her knees are bouncing up and down.

"Relle," I say. "Why did the King of Shadow Court come here?"

She doesn't respond right away, but when she does, she sighs. "If he hasn't told you, it's not my place to say. You'll need to speak with him, as I have sworn secrecy to him."

I return to searching the shelves, determined to get my stepfather to tell us what is going on. We've come this far and risked everything, so we deserve to know what he was doing in Ash Court.

"We should go," Relle whispers, her voice shaky.

"No. I still haven't found it. Maybe if you helped me, we'd be faster."

She's on her feet, her gaze swinging from the door to me. "We go now and come back later."

I refuse to leave, not when I'm so close. The next bowl I look into has half a bone and white power, and I'm curious about what that's used for.

"You don't understand. The mages in the Ash Court are dark." Relle is pacing in the room, her attention locked on the door. "They do death magic, and that comes from lives and blood. If you're caught, we're both dead. So we go now and try again later."

My response is stolen by the door opening as someone enters. My heart slamming in my ribcage, my instincts take over, and I lunge for the door, moving like the wind, drawing a blade from my waist.

Relle backs away with fright, and I don't waste a single moment.

A mage with a bald head sees me at the last moment, his eyes bulging. His mouth opens to cast a spell, no doubt, his hand grappling to one of half a dozen charms hanging from his neck.

I slam a fist right into the middle of his face, the pain racing up my hand. The mage groans and clutches his bloody nose. I snatch his arm and haul him inside, then kick the door shut. Swinging him in front of me, facing away from me, I press my blade to his throat. With my other hand, I grab the charms around his neck and rip the leather cord right off before tossing it aside. Every mage concentrates their power in objects for easier access, and the natural energy in some objects can strengthen the power the mage pours into it. None can do spells or curses without such charms or potions.

"Keep quiet, mage, or your head will roll." I growl in his ear, then I look over to Relle. "Grab a rope or something and come tie his hands—now."

The mage stills, blood dripping from his nose and onto my hand. "I'll turn you into a rat."

Relle drags his arms behind his back and ties his wrists harshly. She's shaking, her breaths racing, knowing too well that if this mage lives, her cover as a spy is blown. I'll have to do something about that.

"You're going to show me the antidote I'm after, or you die. Try anything and you die. You seeing a pattern?"

"This isn't my workshop," he hisses.

"Don't give a fuck. Find it or you die."

I shove him forward, and the bastard fights me. I press the blade to his flesh, cutting skin enough to make him groan with pain.

"Tell me where to find the cure for a Bloodcursed's bite," I command.

He laughs. "Too fucking late."

From the corner of my eye, I see Relle hasn't moved. I dig into my pocket and drag out the pouch of herbs I stuck on my right side, as they're exactly what I need. I stick the pouch out for Relle. "Open it now," I roar.

She rushes over and does so, then gives it back.

"You will pay for this, Relle," the mage warns, his whole body vibrating. The walls and floor shake with him.

My heart is pounding in my ears.

I toss the mixture of herbs over his face and whisper, "Truth."

He shakes his head.

The mage chokes, but I don't ease my hold.

"Let's try again. Where is the cure for a Blood-cursed's bite?"

He groans and shudders against me, fighting the magic. "C-corner." He splutters the word along with spittle.

I walk us to the back. "Which corner?"

He lifts his chin to the right, and I shove him there.

"Where?" I snarl, pressing the blade harder to his throat.

"G-Gold box. First shelf." He thrusts against me.

I pivot us around and reach out, shoving the other jars aside until I discover a small golden trinket box. I snatch it. "Is this the box?"

"Y-Yes!" he barks.

"See, that wasn't so hard, now was it?"

I swing him around toward the room, but Relle is suddenly there plunging a long knife into the mage's gut.

Stunned, it takes me a few moments to work out what just happened.

"What the fuck, Relle?"

The mage cries out, gurgling blood, and slumping against me. I shove him aside and he collapses to the floor. Blood spills from his wound, his body convulsing.

"You could have waited until I finished," I bark.

Relle's face is twisted with hatred as she kicks the dying man in the ribs. "Fucking pig, you raped my daughter. You killed her, so now I take your life." She shakes, her cheeks drenched with tears.

My heart clenches at seeing her agony at what this monster did.

I pocket the gold box, and while I would have liked to ask the mage for other magic spell cures, I guess that's not going to happen now. I wipe my blade on the mage's pants and put it away.

"Listen, Relle, if you want, you can come with us. Leave this castle," I offer.

She's shaking her head, swiping at her tears. She doesn't even look at me. "No, I'm not finished here yet. Go. You got what you want." Her expression focuses on the mage, her expression darkening.

I pull out the diamond bracelet from my pocket and place it in her hand. She nods, and I retreat, knowing everyone deals with revenge in their own way. And what happened to her daughter is devastating. So I walk out of the room, straighten my tunic, pull my pants out of my ass and take hasty steps along the hall and up the staircase. I keep my head low as I pass other guards then speed up until I reach Relle's room.

I knock three times fast, then add a slap at the door —a small code I developed with my brothers when we were younger. The door opens, and Ahren is standing there, gripping his weapon, so I hurry inside. His gaze bounces to the door I shut. "What happened? Where's Relle?"

"Long story, but we need to leave now. I have the cure."

His face beams. "Thank the gods something's going right for a change."

I stick my head outside the room, finding the hallway empty. Then I push open the door and slip out. Ahren is on my heels, and we're running left. I remember the path Relle used to bring us to this room, as I'd counted how many passages we traveled and rooms we passed. I rush down a set of stairs and round the corner to a long, dark corridor.

"You sure this is it?" Ahren murmurs in my ears.

"Yes. It looks the same." We're running toward the end, and I push open the last door. We step into a linen room. Shelves and shelves of folded bed sheets and towels.

No exit door to the outside.

"Fuck, we took a wrong turn somewhere." Ahren growls behind me.

"I must have miscounted. I was sure it was seven corridors we passed before—"

"I think it was six. Hell, everything looks the same in this court," he says.

I go back to the doorway and check. "All clear. We just retreat and take the other path."

We're moving with haste, when I swear the floor trembles beneath me.

Backtracking, we dart into what I hope is the correct corridor. Gods, please let it be correct.

I slam right into a guard, and ice washes down my spine.

Ahren and I are shoulder to shoulder, and we jump the fae, punching him to shut up his cries. I restrain him in a chokehold until he's knocked out, then I dump his body.

"Shit, that was close," I murmur. I totter on my feet, my shoulder hitting the wall as though I'm drunk. "Was that an earthquake?"

Someone clears their voice behind us.

"Fuck!" Ahren groans as we both turn to find a dozen Unseelie guards with swords out, standing feet from us.

CHAPTER 22

GUENDOLYN

A meaty hand slaps down on my shoulder, and I wince under the pressure. Another hand shoves me in the back, and I'm pushed through open doors into an enormous hall.

The walls are made of gold, while overhead, candle chandeliers are dripping with crystals. Pillars flank a path that cuts down the middle of the room, leading me to a woman sitting alone at one end of a grand dining table with no tablecloth, just platters of food and candelabras.

The clang of her cutlery echoes through the hall while guards stand tall along the walls, watching my every step. Marble glints beneath my feet while balconies sweep around the walls, and I suspect this location is typically used for grand announcements rather than a woman eating her meal.

"Move!" the guard behind me roars, driving me forward.

I stumble onward, unsure what to expect. Well, in

truth, I thought they'd take me to the king for punishment. But maybe they sense I have Unseelie blood. The way my luck goes, though, I'll be lucky to keep both my hands.

My heart is beating loudly, my gaze swinging between the guards and the woman, who hasn't stopped eating. Each clang she makes is a bang in my ears, hammering away. I shudder in a breath, trying to swallow the fear surging within me.

Dread flares over me as I come to a stop in front of the table filled with fruit and roast vegetables and a whole suckling pig in the middle. The woman's gray hair is drawn off her face. She appears to be in her seventies, age pulling at the lines edging around her mouth and eyes. Though she's very beautiful now, she would have been even more spectacular in her younger years.

Lowering the golden fork and knife in her hands, she lifts her head and glances at me.

"Kneel," the guard barks behind me.

A kick to the back of my knees sends me sprawling to the floor. I whimper under my breath at the brunt of the marble floor against my knees. I stay down on my heels, my head tucked low.

"Leave us," the woman cries out, her voice croaky. Maybe she'll have sympathy for me.

The marching beat of footfalls fades behind me, followed by the thump of the doors shutting.

Pointy sapphire blue boots step into my view, and a shimmering dress in the same shade cascades to slender ankles.

"What's your name?" she asks.

"G-Gainy." I hold tight, drawing on all my bravery. This isn't the time to show fear. I need to be smart and somehow get out of this tangled mess without losing my head.

"Stand."

Shudders ripple through my body, but I push myself to my feet, never eyeing her. I recall the king's anger at me looking him in the eyes.

She grabs my chin and tilts my head back. "Let me see you better."

I meet blue eyes, so bright that they might be a cloudless sky on a summer's day. They evoke something inside me...a feeling of warmth, and all I can think about is the hot days when I used to visit the beach with my foster mom. They were moments I'll never forget, filled with laughter and fun and getting sunburned. It was also the first time I kissed a boy—a surfer, to be more precise.

"Interesting." The older woman's voice snaps me out of my thoughts, leaving me feeling dizzy.

I shake the strange fog from my head and refocus on the fae, who stands at about my height, built slightly thinner, and wearing so many jewels around her neck, I'm surprised she's not weighed down. The crystals glint against the candlelight overhead, drawing my attention to the variety of colored stones.

"What is your real name?" she asks, her voice clipped and short.

I try to stop shaking, but with her question, I'm left wondering if she somehow just brought about my vision of the beach and viewed it as well—meaning she knows full well knows that scene is not from the Wandering Realm.

So I decide to take the lead, intending to live through the day. "I did nothing wrong and didn't trespass on your land."

She cocks her head to the side, her rose lips thinning into a grim smile. I already dislike the look of her expression, because something doesn't feel right. Does she know who I really am? Can she sense I am Unseelie? Shoot, what if she can read my mind… did I just let her know who I am?

"Come. Take a seat with me and let's enjoy a drink." She turns back to the table.

My feet won't respond. Instead, I glance over my shoulder, noting it's only her and me in a huge room. Arched windows made of colored glass distort the outside view, making it impossible to decipher what's out there.

My insides tighten, and I want to run from here, but the guards will be waiting outside the doors, so how far will I get? And what about Ahren and Luther? They'll find the carriage destroyed and me gone once they get back to it.

In a blinding flash of movement, the woman pounces. She's in my face so fast, I can't respond quickly enough to defend myself. She's on me like a predator, her fingers iron strong, digging into my arms, her teeth on my neck, biting. Breaking flesh.

I scream and instinctively move to shove her, but she's already back by the table, taking her place at the head. My hand clasps my bloody neck, and I'm stumbling backward. Why the hell does everyone in the realm want my blood? Bloodcursed, fairies, this crazy bitch...

She's licking my blood from her lips, her eyelids fluttering, and for those few seconds, I'm seeing someone else...a much older woman, disfigured, heavily wrinkled, and smoke wafting up from the corner of her mouth.

I don't want to be here.

"What did you just do?" Fear buckles through me, wrapping around me like a straitjacket.

"I had to be sure it was you. Now, take a seat, Guendolyn." She growls, the sound reverberating around us.

The room tilts. She knows my name from tasting my blood? Fae have abilities, different kinds. If Luther can send his thoughts to my mind, why can't this demonic fae determine who I am by tasting my blood?

"W-Who...?" My voice dies on me.

She laughs hysterically, and I already hate this woman. I loathe her.

"Do you know how long I've been searching for you? Then those idiotic princes took you from me."

"Who are you?"

"Sit!" She offers me a wry frown. "It doesn't matter who I am."

I drag myself closer and flop down on a chair. The smell of the food sickens me, and I feel like gagging. Luther told me those in this court want to kill me. I have so many questions, and I'm walking on a blade's edge as I try to determine the best way to survive while uncovering the truth.

I blink at her. "What do you know about me?"

Her eyebrow arches, and she leans forward, looking at me with those hypnotic eyes, but I look away, refusing to let her into my head again.

"I know enough," she answers.

I shift in my seat, unease pricking down my arms. I'm already exhausted from her games and just want to know the truth.

"Who are my parents?" I twist my hands in my lap. "Are you my mother?"

"Don't be ridiculous," she snaps back as she pours herself what looks like wine from a golden pitcher into her chalice.

"Then who is she? What about my father?" I sound desperate, but I've wanted to know the truth from the moment I was old enough to understand what having no parents meant. This is my one chance, because I never plan on coming back to this court if I escape.

She eyes me suspiciously. "You don't know about your father? Even after you've been to Shadow Court?"

A chill runs down my back. "What does that mean?" My mind is running at a thousand miles an hour as I try to piece everything together.

My father is in Shadow Court?

"Growing up on Earth has made you slow." She shrugs. "Doesn't matter now, does it?"

"Stop talking in riddles." It's either bravery or stupidity that makes me talk so brazenly to this fae.

She sips from her gold chalice, then places it back

down on the table. Standing, she eyes me like I might have said the worst thing in the world.

I rapidly scramble onto my feet as well and back away from the table. "Please. I just want to know who my parents are, then I'll leave."

She shakes her head and juts out her arm toward me. "Too late."

An invisible punch pummels my chest, sending me reeling backward and onto my ass. I gasp for air, looking up as she saunters over to me. Who in the world is this woman? Her powers are crazy strong, and now I understand why she sent all the guards away. She doesn't need anyone's protection.

"It's opportune that you happened to turn up when I've been trying to find a way to bring you back to our court." She speaks with a smile as though everything is rosy. Except I know the truth—that I'm the one thing that stands in the way of Unseelie completing their curse on Shadow Court.

My skin crawls as she studies me. Shadows dance around her face, signaling that I need to tread carefully. We may both have Unseelie blood in our veins, but she is my enemy. I see it in the pleasure she takes out of bringing me pain, hear it in the unsaid promise of my death on her lips.

I push myself off the ground and stand tall, remembering that the power to open and close portals runs inside me.

Another invisible punch to my gut has me groaning and bending over to clutch my stomach. "Enough," I cry. "I never asked for this. Never asked to be your curse carrier so you could get revenge on your enemies."

She doesn't move for a moment until she sits back down on a seat and faces my way. "You're right. You never asked for it, but your very presence is an abomination, and we should have disposed of you when you were born. Then none of this would be necessary. This is why Seelie and Unseelie can never be together." She wrinkles her nose at me as though I am used gum stuck to her shoes.

My mouth drops open. "You are so vile. How can you speak like that about me?" I can't work out why this woman, who is clearly someone important, would take so much interest in someone like me. If she's telling the truth, not even the princes knew about my father, as they insisted my parents lived in Ash Court.

She shakes her head as if I'm inconsequential.

"At least tell me what happened to me if you're going to take my life away," I implore, stalling while concentrating on drawing out my power and working out how to open a portal with the ease the fairy showed me.

She cocks her head to the side. "Who's in charge of the magic in Shadow Courts these days? Is it still Jasion?"

My blood runs cold at her knowing his name and asking about him, like she's had dealings with him before. Except I won't give this woman any information that might harm the princes.

"You keep changing the topic." I push through the pain. "Tell me about my parents. Why was I sacrificed?"

"You know the sad thing?" she says, like I ought to

know. "It's that you most likely saw your father, maybe even spoke with him in Shadow Court, since he's an asshole who takes too much interest in every woman who crosses his path. But what's even sadder is that he never even knew of your existence. So it will be no real great loss to the world once you're dead."

Fury courses through me at the way she speaks, like I mean so little. But my attention bleeds over her mention of my father, who I may have spent time with. He must be someone important enough for her to assume I spoke with him; it would have to be a crucial figure to take the interest of this fae. The answer slides into my thoughts like it's been there all along, but I was blind to it.

Dread falls right through me.

"No. No... No! He can't be my father." I suck in a jagged breath and the room spins.

"It took you a while, but you got there eventually."

I want the world to crack open and swallow me whole.

My father is the King of Shadow Court. I am part royal.

She swivels her head upward at me, screwing her pouty lips into a grin. "Yes, I would be shocked to have Seelie blood in my veins too, let alone to be a child of that pathetic king. Now you see why you are a mistake. So I'm doing what should have been done long ago if they'd listened to me."

I can't speak, torn apart by the news. Shock runs like lightning through my body.

Silence drags between us, then I finally find my voice. "Who's my mother?"

She's on her feet. "Does it matter? Let's put you out of your misery and be done with this. It's dragged on for too many years as it is. I've wasted too much time on this nonsense."

"Nonsense?" I can't stop myself. "This is my life!"

In a heartbeat, she hurls her hands outward, and I fly across the room. My back slams into the wall, my head cracking. I cry out in pain and slide down to the floor. My feet crumble under me, and I sink to my knees as I taste blood at the back of my tongue.

"Death is imminent for you."

More attacks collide into me. I'm thrust into the air, screaming, but none of that matters. No one knows where I am. No one will save me.

She stares at me, unblinking, as I'm suspended in the air, her eyes darkening. The room turns icy cold like someone has opened a window. My heart is speeding, and a heaviness is swallowing me from the inside out.

Hatred bathes her face when she looks at me. I doubt this fae has ever felt any sympathy for me... Not when I was a baby, and definitely not now.

I've spent enough time with the fae in Shadow Court to see their hatred for the Unseelie, but what I'm witnessing now is on a very different level. This Unseelie fae will kill thousands and not care.

Not even the king would... I choke again on the realization that he is my father. There is so much I need to talk to him about.

Frantically, I fight against the invisible bonds

holding me in the air, but it makes no difference. My mind lurches in every direction. Focusing is impossible. I've forgotten words, forgotten everything but the trepidation claiming me.

"You have a shadow on your heart, Guendolyn. You always have. A curse. That's what you are."

"Because your mages cursed me!" I shout.

One corner of her mouth quirks upward, as if proud of her handiwork.

"It was you, wasn't it? You did this to me!" I cry out.

"I am rather proud of how well it worked out. Payment and revenge against the Seelie."

I'm seething, my insides burning up. "What did they do to you personally that you hate those that are no different than you?"

"You speak to me with such disrespect. But I guess I shouldn't expect anything less from someone brought up by humans." She tosses her hand outward.

I'm flung sideways, slamming into a pillar, then I fall to the marble floor. Every bone in my body screams with pain.

A shadow falls over me, and she snatches me by the hair, drawing me to my knees. "The two races of fae are nothing alike," she spits in my face. "The Unseelie bloodline comes directly from the fairy queen herself. The Seelie are the fae who tried to murder her. I will cut your tongue out for saying we are the same."

My scalp stings from where she tugs on my hair, wrenching my head back.

"I must thank you for coming in today, while the king and queen are away from the court. It's like the gods have blessed me to finally fix the horrific mess your birth caused."

"Fuck you!" I shove against her, fury radiating over my body.

She snarls and drags me by my hair across the room and toward the table. "I'll take your tongue first, so you can learn a lesson before your death. You see, I even try to teach you something when I shouldn't waste my time. And this is why I have to fight so hard, to remind my son he needs to do anything in his power to stay king and take over all of the Wandering Realm. And with your death, little girl, you will eliminate one of our biggest obstacles. Your father."

"Why do you hate me so much?" I urge, scrambling to my feet so I'm not hauled forward like an animal.

"Have you even been listening to me? You are a mistake, and I am giving your life purpose. You will make every Unseelie proud when you die. Take comfort in knowing that you will have songs written about your sacrifice."

"Sacrifice?" I'm terrified, and I sure as hell don't want to die.

With incredible strength, she slams the side of my head onto the wooden table. Plates and cutlery clatter to the floor as my mind spins.

I cry out, pain biting into me where her fingernails dig into the flesh at my neck to keep my head pinned down.

"Hold still. It will be easier."

Terror crashes into me like waves, one after the

other, dragging me deeper. She's going to murder me, right here.

Her grip tightens around my neck, and her other hand clutches a long, sharp knife.

I feel sick, darkness smothering me. "Please no," I whimper, and she laughs at me.

I can't reason with her. She's the devil, so foul she's manipulated the Wandering Realm into a war. So much hatred, so much fear, and all because of this woman's need for power… she needs her son to rule over the realm. Is he any different than the crazy dictators back on Earth? I guess greed and power may wear a different mask, but they're the same sadistic sonsofbitches. I realize then that fae like her will never understand peace or sympathy. I am a means to an end to her, and I clench my hands into fists.

I'm trembling and sucking in raspy breaths as I fight against her hold, but with it comes a power that scrapes over my flesh and balloons in my chest.

Digging my fingernails into her arm, I tear at her flesh. But she only laughs and lowers her blade closer to my face.

"Stop! Please don't do this." Panic swallows me.

A brush of energy comes at me fast.

The table beneath me shakes, walls groan, and I embrace the power. I unleash all of the energy I have with tremendous speed.

A thunderous sound booms around us.

The whole room quakes violently. Chandeliers swing, dust falls from overhead, cracks zig-zag down the walls.

She pauses, glancing up at the disturbance, and I shove her hand off me, scrambling away.

"Don't ever touch me again!" I yell bitterly.

She scrunches her nose up in a grimace, looking ready to skin me alive. She throws her power at me, but I scream involuntarily, and with it comes every thread of power inside me.

It booms outward, and the air shimmers. Windows burst open, shattered glass tossed like rain in every direction. I cover my head as the shards pebble down on me.

The vile fae is thrown backward. She grabs a chair but instead of finding a source of stability, she takes it down with her. Huge cracks open up the walls, the ground rupturing, and I'm teetering on my feet. The main doors explode off their hinges, and an army of guards bursts inside.

I heave for each breath, my body humming with power as though I'm alight. I force every inch of me to dance with the power I embrace. Anger punches through me. I want to bring this whole damn castle down around my feet.

"Guendolyn?" Luther yells out, and I rock on my feet as I turn to see him by the door, held captive by guards with Ahren at his side. More and more fae are pouring into the room as if it's a spectacle to uncover what the hell I've done in here.

Desperation twists with fear in my gut. I glance over my shoulder at the woman who wants me dead, dragging herself to her feet.

Except I'm not finished. Not even close.

She attacks me again, catapulting what looks like fireballs right at me. She snarls with pure hatred.

I hold my arms out, and power shoots from my body in waves. It collides into everyone in the room, shoving them off their feet. They groan and cry out, but I don't care anymore about playing nice.

The fireballs fizzle, but not quickly enough. One strikes me in the chest and drives me back against the wall. Heat engulfs me, and I frantically flick the flames off me, patting them from my coat.

The clang of metal resonates across the room where the princes are battling the guards, backing toward me. Except more guards pour into the room. How far will we get if we manage to escape?

"Kill them all!" she orders. "They don't leave this room alive."

Exhaustion floods me, and I exhale as my power flatlines. I suck in the cold air sharply as a grim reality swallows me. We're trapped, and I only have one possible option.

Through labored breaths, I stand tall.

Luther looks over at me, fear twisting his expression.

Open the portal, little wolf. Do it now!

Back in the throne room, it was as simple as a single thought, so maybe my problem has been over-concentrating. Lifting my hand to my mouth, I tip the fingers backward, then exhale.

Nothing.

I growl under my breath, fiery anger lashing at me at

my inability to get this to work. So I dig deep and draw on the electricity that lingers in my veins.

Glancing over at the princes battling the guards, I realize they aren't going to last much longer. I collect everything I have left within me and open myself so the energy just rushes out of me. A tremor tears through the room once more, and panic rises on the woman's face. She stares at me with an unbelievable expression that someone like me, an abomination, can hold such strength.

More cracks snake down the walls. Wind blows in through the shattered windows, whistling, tugging at my clothes. Energy laces around me, the hairs on my nape lifting. This isn't a battle of brawn, not for us, but one of abilities. I can't stop searching the masses, scared the mages will show any moment now and take me down.

Urgency swells within me, and I call to the portal, thinking of the Shadow Court castle. Of Deimos. Of survival. Of my power.

A storm of wind and quakes surges through the room, ripping it apart. It grows worse the more I attempt to draw on my power. Chunks of walls fall over, and guards darting in every direction to escape death. Before me rise shadows and fog, growing in size to loom over me. The center opens up to pure darkness.

I turn my head to Ahren and Luther, who are running toward me at full-tilt, guards on their heels.

"Go through!" Ahren yells.

With a quick look behind me, I meet the fae woman's startled gaze. She had no idea of my ability...

not until now. This is my power to master, and I'll find a way to strengthen it. There's no hiding now; I know that she'll tell the king and queen, and then they will come for me. But with so much happening, the terror of what's to come sits numb in my chest.

Luther reaches me first and shoves me to get going.

I whip around and lunge into the pitch blackness of the portal.

The emptiness engulfs me... and then I'm gone.

CHAPTER 23

I stumble out of the darkened portal. Bright light blinds me momentarily as I try to find my bearings. Cold droplets of snow land on my face and coat the woods around me, yet I don't recognize this place.

Ahren bursts out of the portal next, blinking against the light, stumbling to catch his footing. "Where are we?"

Luther darts out just as fast, grasping his sword, glancing around. "Where'd you bring us?"

"I don't know. But please tell me you have the cure for Deimos."

"We got it," Luther states.

Unease clings to my ribs as I see no sign of any castles nearby. Where exactly are we?

When another figure emerges from the portal, Luther pushes me away and raises his sword. He and Ahren wait on either side of me, weapons raised.

"You better be working on closing this portal fast."

Ahren growls as an Unseelie guard stumbles out. The prince grabs him by the neck, then plunges his sword into his chest. There's no hesitation or remorse. This is life or death, and the princes are trained to battle until the end.

I lift my hand just as I did back in the throne room and picture the gateway shutting.

Three more guards shove forward, bellowing their war cries, swords drawn.

I extend my hand and blow out a long breath. The hairs on my nape shift as I feel the magic rippling on the wind. Blue energy shimmers around the portal, but it doesn't vanish. It just sits there, quivering.

"Guendolyn!" Ahren roars.

"I can't get it to shut. I don't know what I'm supposed to do."

Guard after guard comes out, and panic strangles me. How am I meant to help when I can't even control my power? I groan and fist my hands, wanting to scream in anger. Snow falls quicker now, its touch icy on my skin.

I turn on the spot, my head whirling with how to fix this. Running won't help, and how long before a mage steps through and annihilates us? If Deimos were here, he'd be able to command the forest to attack the enemy. I feel so damn useless.

Turning back to the portal, I find the princes battling the guards, slaying them. Luther is bleeding across his cheek, and a large gash on his arm drips with blood.

My heart is racing as I lift my hand, trying once

again. Shadows rise on either side of me with frantic movements, and I whip around to the fluttering of wings.

Fairies. They're just fairies, and my heart beats with adrenaline, hoping that they're on our side.

A rainbow of colors surrounds us, and there are so many fairies, so many that I'm left intimidated. What if they belong to a different clan and have nothing to do with Hiss? I don't even know where I teleported us, and now fear creeps into my chest that we're in bigger shit than I thought. These fairies could be our enemies.

The swarm rises higher, looming over us like a shadow, baring their sharp fangs. They hiss and dart toward us but swoop back at the last minute.

I duck from one, and fear presses on my chest.

"What the fuck is going on?" Luther snarls as he plunges a blade into a guard's throat, then kicks him aside.

The only way I know to get the fairies on our side is to feed them. It seemed to work with the others back in the Shadow Court.

I rush over to a dead guard and frantically grab his knife. Without thought, I run the sharp end down my palm, the bite stinging like a bitch. I grit my teeth and stagger to my feet while sticking my cut hand out to the fairies.

"Taste!" I offer my blood to them, hoping they will understand and aid us.

But none of them approach me. They flutter about, staring at the dead bodies, at the princes fighting.

I dart up to them. "Take it, please. Just help us." They

part at my approach, and only then do I see that behind them lie beehive-type homes hanging from the trees nearby with fairies flying in and out. Then I glance around to really see the forest. Dozens upon dozens of these homes are suspended from the branches.

We're in the middle of a fairy village or nest. No wonder they seemed angry. We just crash-landed in their home.

For those few moments, I don't know what to do, how to get out of this mess.

So I return to the portal and try again. I raise my hand, blood dripping onto the soil, and push out the energy bubbling inside me.

Close. Fucking close.

Something small falls into my palm out of the air, sliding into the small puddle of blood from my cut.

I flinch at first, then carefully inspect it.

A red crystal sits there…a ruby, just like the one Hiss stole.

I jerk my head up, and above me, those beautiful blue wings beat frantically.

"Hiss!"

She glowers at me and points to the portal. Right!

I fold my hand around the stone, and a sharp prickle of power digs into my palm. It zips up my arm, racing through my body as though I've touched an electrical socket.

Bringing my fist to my mouth, I unfurl my fingers and blow over the stone.

A tremendous wind comes out of nowhere and buffets into me. It races past and collides into the guards and princes, sending them stumbling, and fairies flutter crazily around us.

But my eyes are only on the portal. It starts dissolving just as another guard steps out. But he's too late… The mouth of the portal vanishes with him in mid-transit, and all that's left of him is his chopped-off leg. It drops to the ground, his blood soaking into the soil.

My hair billows in my face, the wind's whistle deafening in my ears, and I curl in on myself.

But something feels different inside me. A burning erupts in my chest, deepening, hurting to the point where I can't stand still any longer. Energy rolls through me, the sky overhead snarling.

Something slithers over my flesh, and I scratch at my arms to find it's nothing. Everything inside me clenches tight, and I wrestle to see anything but the chaos of trees blowing, leaves rustling. Fairies are being flung in every direction, and I can no longer see the princes.

I lick my dry lips as the weather rages. "Luther, Ahren, where are you?" I cry out.

In a heartbeat, everything dies. The portal has vanished, the winds quiet down, fairies fly as far from me as possible.

And my princes are on the ground amid the dead guards.

My heart hits the back of my throat as I throw myself toward them, tears already pooling in my eyes.

"Ahren," I cry, snatching his coat to turn him on his back, coldness slicing right through my heart.

This isn't meant to happen. They aren't supposed to

be hurt. They, and Deimos, are the only ones who made me feel like I belonged, who captured my heart.

All this is my fault. If only I knew how to use my power correctly... I sink to the ground between the princes. My fingers shake as I check Luther for a pulse, but his skin is cold, and I choke back a sob. No, no—this can't be happening. I can't lose them. Not now, not after everything.

I grasp Ahren's shirt, fisting it, wanting to bring him and Luther back, no matter the cost. Tears flow fast and furiously down my face.

A groan comes from Luther, and I jerk around to face him.

He's pushing himself off the ground, groaning, his hair sticking upward and tangled with leaves.

I throw myself into Luther's arms, causing him to fall back down with me on top of him. I can't stop laughing and kissing him. His hands clasp the side of my face, and the way he kisses me back tells of someone who has been to death's door and back.

"Don't you ever die on me." I breathe the words into his mouth.

"I've no plans to go anywhere, little wolf."

Breaking away from him, I swing toward Ahren, who's kneeling beside me. I throw my arms around him, then tuck my face into the curve of his neck, hugging him tightly. "I thought I lost you for a moment there. Don't ever scare me like that again."

When I pull back, he kisses me, and I'm lost to his touch. It amazes me how much almost losing them reinforces what my heart wants.

I glance around to find the fairies have returned, but it's Hiss who hovers near to us, looking at me with a strange expression.

Eirian. Her voice trails over my thoughts, just as easily as Luther's does when he speaks in my mind.

Hiss points to my hand, and I open my fist where I'm still holding the stone.

Ahren gasps as he looks down at the ruby.

"Please tell me that's not the missing piece from our stepfather's throne?"

"It doesn't belong to him," I explain. "This is a fragment of the fairy queen's crown and should be with the fairies, not a showpiece in someone's chair."

I'm on my feet and step toward Hiss, my hand stretched out, handing her the ruby. "This is yours," I say.

She shakes her head. *Eirian,* she says again.

All the fairies suddenly flutter closer to me and land on the snowy ground to kneel before me, their heads low, their wings curled around them.

Hundreds of fairies fill the land.

"What did you do?" Luther asks.

"They won't take back their fairy stone. I don't understand. But Hiss keeps saying the word 'Eirian' in my head."

"You can hear it talk to you?" Ahren asks in disbelief.

I glance over my shoulder at him. "Well, I'm not sure I can count one word as speaking to me." I offer him a crooked smile, imploring him for any kind of help.

"Um, little wolf. Do you know what 'Eirian' means?" Luther asks.

"Of course not."

"It's the ancient word for fairy queen."

I burst out laughing at his implication. As if things aren't weird enough.

"It's not funny," he reprimands me. "There are legends that speak of the fairy queen's spirit living on through a few chosen. What if—?"

"Don't even say it. I can't take any more surprises." I can barely deal with knowing my real father is the King of Shadow Court, and somehow, I need to break the news to the princes.

"We need to go home," Ahren interjects. "Deimos doesn't have much time." I turn to the sea of fairies bowing before me, and I feel anything but prepared or worthy.

"Hiss," I murmur. "We need to go back to the kingdom." I don't know if she understands me, but she looks at me, confused.

I point at myself and the princes, then into the distance.

She nods, then flutters over to me. Her huge, dark eyes study me, then she speaks to me in my head...but the words make absolutely no sense to me. She then points to the stone and nods.

I think she might be telling me I can use the stone to contact her? I have no clue, to be honest, but I smile. "Thank you."

Once more, she studies the ruby and then her hand sweeps to where I indicated earlier about traveling in the distance. This I understand—use the ruby to get home. She leans over and lowers her head to the cut on my hand, licking the blood. I wait until she's had her fill, then she pulls away.

She sings, and her soft tune is like a maiden crying with loss. The other fairies raise their heads and spread their wings, then break into the same song. The sound grows louder, hypnotic and beautiful. As they all fly back into their homes, the area turns magical with gorgeous colors everywhere.

I turn toward my princes, and they're both staring at me with awe in their eyes.

"What?" I ask.

"I think you're so much more than any of us realize," Ahren admits.

Shrugging, I saunter toward them. "You don't know how true that is. I have lots to tell you both, but let's get to Deimos first."

I raise the hand that's holding the ruby, and I blow a lungful of air over the crystal, picturing Deimos in bed.

Before us, shadows rise and quickly form into a portal. "Are you ready to go home?" I ask, feeling more confident than I have in a very long time.

"Fuck, yeah." Luther takes my hand and leads me to the portal.

I step forward, and in that moment, I realize why that portal opened up in the throne room, across the grounds from where I was, on my first day at the Shadow Court castle. It was because of this ruby. It called to my power...

CHAPTER 24

GUENDOLYN

*I*n one heartbeat, we're in the snow-covered forest surrounded by fairies, and the next, we're in Deimos' bedroom back at the mansion. He's over in the palace, but who the hell cares if I got the room wrong? We're in Shadow Court. The portal brought us here and not somewhere across the Wandering Realm.

I turn back to the portal and close it with the simplicity of blowing my breath over the stone in my palm.

"Thank the Seven Hells we're back," Luther mutters.

My emotions are all over the place, so tangled and chaotic that I don't know what to feel. Fear from everything we've gone through, elation that I managed to control the portal for once, and an undulating surge of anxiety about meeting my father again. How will he react?

Ahren steps alongside me, his hand sliding into mine. "Are you all right?"

I nod, but my insides are jumping. "We need to go to Deimos now."

"Agreed." Luther opens the door and we rush into the hallway. It's silent with not a soul in sight, but all I can think about now is Deimos. About seeing him smile again.

Please let the cure work.

As we cross the bridge, we're battered by a snowstorm, the day darkened by bruised clouds. I push ahead, one step in front of the other. It isn't long before we enter the palace and race down the corridor, Luther taking the lead.

But something is wrong. Really wrong.

Why are there no guards around? Where is everyone?

Luther leads us to a set of grand marble stairs that sweeps upward in an arc.

When Luther pushes open a door to his right, we hurry in behind him. My breaths are raspy, my lungs aching from sprinting here so fast.

Across the room stands an elaborate poster bed made of black wood. Magic encases Deimos, just as it did the last time I saw him. I step forward eagerly and gasp at how far gone he looks. He's so much paler... almost gaunt in his face.

"Is he okay?" I squeak as I swallow past the boulder in my throat.

"He's deteriorated faster than I hoped. He should have had another day, but..." Ahren's fear goes unsaid, but we're all thinking the same thing. Deimos has run out of time. We do this now, or he will slip from us.

Invisible claws clench my heart at the thought of losing him. I can't live with that. I won't live with that.

Luther digs into his pocket and pulls out a small golden box, flipping open the lid. He stares down at the contents, and his brow furrows with worry.

"What's the problem?" Ahren asks, looking down at the box.

"Is that the cure?" I ask.

Luther licks his lips and glances over at us. "It's a powder. How do I get this into his system? I don't know the magic words. Fuck." He shuts the box with a snap and starts pacing. "I should have asked the mage for the words as well. I know better. Magic comes with words," he bellows, his voice echoing around the room.

"Luther." I walk up to him and take his hand into mine. "There's always a way."

"Jasion," Ahren says. "He'll know!"

My stomach drops at hearing his name, at remembering the Unseelie king's mother speaking of him.

"Ahren, no." I turn toward him, but he's darted through the doorway and left us alone. "Shit." I glance up at Luther. "We can't trust Jasion."

He doesn't seem to hear me, only staring at his brother. Blood drips from the wounds on Luther's arm and cheek, but there's no reaction, as though he can't feel the pain. I leave him with his thoughts as I move to the window and look outside. The view is of the kingdom city, the people wandering about, shutting down stalls.

I don't know how much time passes, but Ahren still

hasn't returned. I finally turn, finding Luther hasn't moved from his brother's bedside.

"Maybe I can try healing Deimos?" I suggest.

I open my hand that still holds the ruby, blood dried on my palm and the stone.

Luther shakes his head.

"Hear me out. What if some of my ability comes from fairies? You saw what happened back in the woods. So, what if I can use the stone to heal Deimos?"

He glances over at me, his eyes looking straight through me, and I can't even tell if he heard a word I said.

The door creaks open, and I jerk around just as Ahren marches inside. His cheeks are red from running, his brow streaked with blood from the earlier battle.

"I can't find Jasion or any of the mages." His words are panicked and aggressive.

"Guendolyn will do it." Luther finally speaks. "We have no other option. The sun is going down, and our brother's life ticks away."

Both princes look at me, and I squeeze the ruby tightly in my hand, suddenly doubting myself.

"I can try."

Luther steps toward me and opens the golden trinket box. I look inside to see a small amount of powder that smells like dried herbs and something acidic that burns my nostrils.

"Any recommendations on the best way to do this?" I ask the princes.

"When I've watched Jasion work, he dusts the

powder over the person he's spelling while speaking words of what he wants to happen."

"And the ruby?" I ask, studying their faces for some kind of indication that this will work, but they offer me nothing but worry.

I can't sit back and do nothing. "I'm going to try. We have enough powder for what looks like two tries."

"I don't think we should split the potion," Luther says. "Half might not be powerful enough."

Grimacing, I chew on my cheek.

"We get one go." Ahren breathes the words as though he can't bring himself to say them. He stares at the door, then at me. "I'll be right back. I have to try to find Jasion again."

"Ahren, no," Luther barks. "What if Guendolyn is right and Jasion can't help Deimos? What if it isn't in his best interest to heal Deimos?"

Ahren's brow tangles. "Not this again. I know you've always hated him, but—"

"The Unseelie king's mother asked me about Jasion," I say, butting in. "Why would she ask about him by name unless there's something going on?"

Both princes look at me with dread in their eyes, and I can tell what I revealed sits heavily with Ahren. He trusts Jasion, has all his life, but I don't.

"Are you ready to do this?" Luther asks.

"Yes." Not really, but I hide the fear and wear my bravery. This isn't a time to let trepidation into my mind.

We move closer to Deimos' bed, and I take my place alongside him. I have no idea what the right way to complete this is, so I follow my instinct. I offer Luther my free hand, and he pours the contents from the golden box into my palm.

If I do possess some trickle of fairy magic, then maybe that's where my healing ability comes from. Maybe the fairy queen's ruby will enhance my healing magic like it did with the portal magic, allowing me to treat Deimos' wounds once the powder has counteracted the curse. In theory, this should work.

I slide a hand through the magic bubble encasing Deimos and place the ruby over the bite mark on his shoulder, the stone sitting between him and me. Before I say a single word, a fiery heat erupts across my palm, unbearably hot. But I won't move. I don't dare. In my mind, I am healing him. It's all I can picture—the poison leaving his body.

I bring my other hand with the powder over his face.

Please let this work. Please.

I tip my hand, and the herbs sprinkle over him. "Heal the poison from his body."

Silence falls over us, only my heartbeat singing in my ears.

Heat curls over me like flames licking at my flesh. I try to find a memory to hold on to where Deimos is healthy and untainted. That's what I picture in my mind, coupled with my deepening emotions for him, and I drive all those feelings into him.

Heal.

Scorching heat engulfs my hand and slithers up my arm. I know that's the venom from his body. I feel the ache, the way it cuts into me like blades. The toxin fills me, swallows me. Still, I stand tall and don't back down.

Energy crashes over me, and I grit my teeth as I drive the poison out of me with thought and strong will. I embrace every inch of my power and pummel the full force of it into the infection.

Blue threads of light curl around my arm and over Deimos, binding us, driving the power of healing into him. I feel the river of electricity over my skin, and the stone beneath my palm pulses faster.

My breaths quicken, and the pain gathering inside me is becoming too much. It's a fire burning me from the inside out, leaving me barely standing, my whole body shuddering.

Deimos releases a loud exhale, his body arching upward. His brothers are by his side, and I hold on with all my strength as the thread that binds us throbs, thinning with each second it eliminates the poison.

My legs shake beneath me, my whole body weak. When the last thread vanishes, I let go, unable to hold on for a moment longer.

A scream tears past my lips, unleashing a heart-shattering sound. Black smoke curls out from my mouth into a wisp, fading away. My stomach churns and roils while my knees give out from under me.

I fall to the ground, gasping for air, every inch of me shaking with exhaustion. The ruby is still in my hand, and I grip it tight, refusing to let it go. All I can picture is Deimos' response to the healing, praying he's okay. My whole body buzzes, and each exhale rips from my lips.

"Guendolyn." Luther crouches next to me, his hand on my arm. His touch is like a spear through me. I push his hand away, but it's too late. His touch has done something to me.

I scream with pain again, and I'm swallowed by blackness.

Images pop into my mind like lightning, flashing in and out. They're of me at school, Luther speaking to me in my mind, teasing me, flirting. Then I'm carried in his arms into a dark world...the Wandering Realm. We're running, always running.

The snapshots come at me so fast, all I can catch are glimpses. But the memories spread over my thoughts like a web, filling in the missing gaps of the past few years.

Meeting the three princes. Luther keeping me hidden in the mansion from the king.

Luther showing me the Ferris Wheel he made for me, then our first kiss. I melt at the memory, at the intensity of our first connection.

The image vanishes, and in its place is the blonde Unseelie fae who tricked me into leaving Shadow Court and going with her to Ash Court. Me stepping into their kingdom and unleashing the curse.

Heartache shreds me to pieces. The emotions for the princes I haven't had access to all this time because I couldn't remember them come at me. Hitting me, ripping me, taking everything I held on to until there's nothing left. Nothing but me, the woman who lost her life the moment she was born. Who fell for a fae prince way before she ever met him. Who then lost him…and now those memories are a blade slicing into me.

I'm crying, agony and rage filling me at what I lost. I cry for the hunger in my heart that I was denied feeling until now. All those times I went to a therapist over the last two years about my confused feelings only to be told it was hallucinations or something. This explains why I felt this pull toward him, but I didn't really know why… not until now.

"Guendolyn," Luther calls.

My eyes spring open, but his face is blurry behind my tears. I can't stop crying, and I feel like my chest is splitting in half from the heartache I caused Luther, from getting Deimos bitten.

"Are you hurt?" Luther collects me into his arms, and I curl in against his hard chest. I fist his coat, holding him tightly against me.

"I'm sorry," I murmur. "For so long, I didn't remember us." I can't stop the tears.

He cups my face and looks down at me, his thumbs wiping my wet cheeks. "What's going on? Why are you apologizing?"

"I remember us. I remember our past, Luther. Everything, from you taking me from my home, to our first kiss, to you saving me from the Bloodcursed before I stepped into Ash Court." My voice trembles because it's not just the loss of the memories of the events themselves, but the emotions that accompany them, that has me hurting. For two years, Luther suffered while I vanished, and when I did return, I didn't recall our past.

I suck in hard breaths.

"Little wolf," Luther says with a smile, his eyes glistening.

He helps me to my feet, and Ahren is by my side, pushing the hair off my face, looking at me as if searching my face for some kind of answer. Except the truth lies in the ruby that opened up my memories after all this time.

"Why the fuck does it feel like I've just eaten a rat?" Deimos croaks.

We all turn toward him, and I choke on a laugh.

Deimos pushes himself to sit up in bed, shadows still caught under his eyes, but the glint in them has returned.

A cry falls from my mouth as I rush toward him and throw myself into his arms. "You're back." I hold on tightly, not planning on letting him or any of these princes ever leave my side again. I'm tired of death being around every corner in this realm. For once, I want calmness and peace. And I'll claw and scrape for every second I can get.

"How are you feeling?" I ask.

Ahren and Luther sit on the bed next to their brother. Deimos clears his throat and looks at us, bewildered, taking in our disheveled and bloody appearances. He has no clue what we all just went through, but I'd do it again in a heartbeat.

"Have I missed much?" Deimos mutters.

"Brother, you have no idea," Luther says. "Get better, and you'll hear all about it."

The thundering sound of the door thumping open has me jumping in my skin.

Mael, Ahren's advisor, bursts into the room, his gaze petrified and wild. "Your Highnesses," he begins, his voice trembling.

"What's wrong?" Ahren asks, standing up from the bed.

My heart does that thing where it knows something bad has happened and it's preparing to break out of my chest.

Mael's face grows three shades paler. "The King of Shadow Court is dead! He's been murdered!"

Thanks for reading To Tame A Fae.

Reviews are super important to authors as it helps other reader make better decisions on books they will read. So if you have a moment, please do leave a review here.

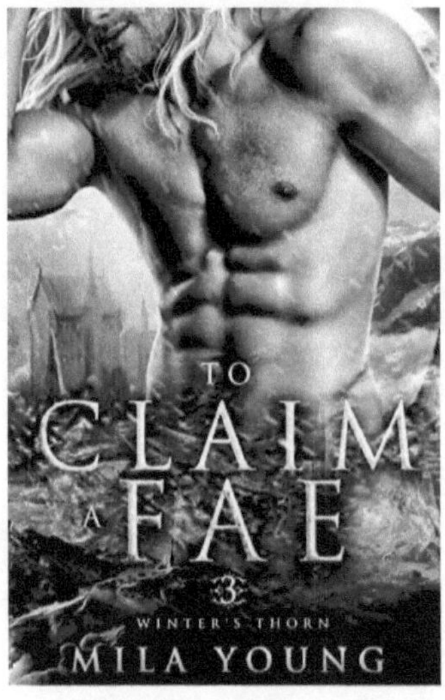

Discover more books from Mila Young and find your Happily Ever After!

www.milayoungbooks.com

ABOUT MILA YOUNG

Best-selling author, Mila Young tackles everything with the zeal and bravado of the fairytale heroes she grew up reading about. She slays monsters, real and imaginary, like there's no tomorrow. By day she rocks a keyboard as a marketing extraordinaire. At night she battles with her might pen-sword, creating fairytale retellings, and sexy ever after tales. In her spare time, she loves pretending she's a mighty warrior, walks on the beach with her dogs, cuddling up with her cats, and devouring every fantasy tale she can get her pinkies on.

Ready to read more and more from Mila Young?
Subscribe: www.subscribepage.com/milayoung

Join Mila's **Wicked Readers group** for exclusive content, latest news, and giveaway.
www.facebook.com/groups/milayoungwickedreaders

For more information...
milayoungauthor@gmail.com

www.ingramcontent.com/pod-product-compliance
Lightning Source LLC
Chambersburg PA
CBHW050804190726
48285CB00005B/1787

9 781922 689115